THE HEART OF A HELLION

THE DUKE'S BY-BLOWS BOOK 2

JESS MICHAELS

For Mackenzie Walton, the most amazing editor and terrific friend a girl could ask for. Thank you for always pushing me a little further.

For all the readers who told me what I do matters during this difficult time.

And for Michael. If I could write a hero who accepted the heroine for everything about who she was, it's only because you have always accepted me for everything I am. Thanks for being my quarantine buddy and best friend.

CHAPTER 1

1816

Selina Oliver sat on a chaise in the corner of her brother Robert's parlor, a drink clenched in her fingers as she watched the rest of the room from a distance. It was an elaborately embroidered seat, stitched with peacocks strutting across vistas. She was fairly certain some of the threads were real gold. No wonder it felt so uncomfortable beneath her bottom.

Not because it *wasn't* comfortable. No, her brother and his wife had never been one for show and not substance. But more because Selina knew she didn't belong on a chair that was possibly worth the wage some people made per annum. Most of the time when she encountered such luxury she was trying to figure out some way to…

Well, it didn't matter what she would normally be trying to do. She wasn't about to do that here.

She continued to watch the room. Her brother Robert and his wife, Katherine, were the Duke and Duchess of Roseford. He was the only legitimate son of the long-dead and never-mourned last duke. And Selina…well, she was one of many bastard children that terrible man had left in his wake. Ones who had been taken care of financially, but never welcomed into the fold.

Until now. Until Robert had opened his arms and his home to them with varying degrees of success.

Even now, Robert stood with her two older half-brothers, Morgan Banfield and Nicholas Gillingham. Although one could see the similarities, neither of them looked as like to Robert as she herself did. She shared his sleek, thick dark hair, the angles to the face. Only her eyes were her own, blue when her brothers shared Robert's dark brown ones.

She shook her head as Nicholas turned toward her and speared her with a smile. He moved across the room, slowly and with a pronounced limp that made her heart ache. He had entered the army and served admirably. Until he was nearly killed in battle nearly two years before. He was still recovering from the injuries.

She forced her reaction from her face as he reached her and settled in beside her on the settee with a grimace. "Is this where the outsiders sit?" he asked.

She shot him a side glance. "The only outsider here is me, Nicholas. You belong anywhere you go. You'll belong even more if they grant you that title for your bravery."

His lips thinned at the comment, but she thought she saw a flutter of emotion in his eyes. He shrugged. "That isn't certain."

"It should be," she said softly. "No one deserves recognition and land and a pile of money more than you do."

"Hmm," he murmured, and shifted as if uncomfortable, though she wasn't certain if the discomfort was more physical or emotional. "Well, I think we're *both* outsiders now, if only because the couples there are so exquisitely happy."

She followed his stare back to their brothers and their wives. Robert had been married to Katherine for years, but there remained a chemistry between them that one would have to be blind not to see, even if they didn't always seem to need to touch each other.

And their other brother, Morgan, had very recently married his wife, Lizzie. Less than six months before, actually. The newlyweds were clearly blissful and had been enjoying their time in London before they returned to the estate of Lizzie's brother, where Morgan now worked as his man of affairs.

Robert looked across the parlor at Nicholas and Selina with a smile, and his voice elevated to reach them. "I was just telling Morgan and Lizzie how sad Katherine and I are that they cannot join us for our fete in Roseford next week."

Morgan smiled, and Selina was happy for him in that moment. Her once-wild brother had always had a strained relationship with Robert. Now they were growing closer and he was obviously much...happier now that he was settled. She would have been jealous of that, perhaps, except she had no interest in being settled. It wasn't her nature, after all.

"We are disappointed as well, but I know my brother and Amelia require our help now that the baby is so soon to be born." Lizzie's face lit up with happiness for her own beloved brother. "And I do want to be there."

"Of course you do," Katherine said with a reassuring smile. "But unlike the two of you, who have a prior engagement, I think Nicholas and Selina might be able to join us. Won't you both?"

Selina stiffened and felt her brother do the same beside her. Though she guessed their reactions had very different origins. Nicholas cleared his throat as he slowly pushed to his feet.

"I-I'm afraid I am not in any shape to travel, at present," he said, motioning to his body. "It is...difficult still."

Katherine's cheeks paled. "Of course."

Robert's brow wrinkled. "Have you seen that doctor the Duchess of Willowby suggested? She's a great healer, Nicholas. She knows of what she speaks."

"I'm sure," Nicholas said, and it was clear the words were pushed past clenched teeth. "I'll be certain to look her up. But I cannot attend."

The eyes of the room moved to Selina and she got up to stand beside Nicholas. "I-I'm afraid I have things to do," she said, and forced herself not to think of those things so she would reveal nothing on her countenance. Robert was good at reading people. Morgan was even better. She didn't need either of them digging around in her affairs.

Katherine shifted. "It won't be a large party, Selina. Mostly friends."

Robert made a rude snort and speared his wife with a look. "The ridiculous Earl of Winford and his nasty wife are not our friends."

Selina stiffened at that name. "You're inviting Winford and his wife?"

"Yes," Katherine said, distracted before she pivoted to face Robert. "Of course they aren't. That woman is a nightmare and her husband has the personality of a trout. But you know *why* we're inviting them."

Robert's expression relaxed and he even looked chagrined. Selina watched the transformation in awe. He truly had been changed by love over the years. The Robert she knew once upon a time would have reacted quite differently. Not cruelly, of course, he'd never been like their father in that way. But he wouldn't have softened.

"For Baldwin and Helena, of course," he said. "I realize Baldwin needs to secure Winford's support for his latest venture with Grayson Danford. I just want to make it clear I do not like the man."

"No one likes the man, not even his own wife," Katherine said with a small laugh. "The things we do for love."

"Indeed," Robert said, playfully stern.

"Is that what you do now?" Nicholas said softly. "Help the unfortunate?"

Robert's playfulness vanished in a moment as he jerked his gaze to Nicholas. "Are you referring to Baldwin?"

Nicholas shrugged. "The Duke of Sheffield's financial fall and the slow rebuilding of his empire are not unknown, even in lowly circles such as my own."

Robert's eyes narrowed, and it was clear he felt defensive of his old friend. One of a group of dukes their brother had run with all his life. A club he was closer to than his own siblings, truth be told.

"If you know he is *rebuilding* his empire, then you know he *isn't* unfortunate. I help those I care about, Nicholas. Including you and our sister, if you two would not be so bullheaded at every turn." Robert pushed his shoulders back. "I think I'll take a turn on the terrace, if you don't mind excusing me. I'll be back momentarily."

Katherine sighed as Robert exited the room. She glanced at Nicholas briefly. "The way you hold yourself back from him, sometimes I fear you judge him for what he once was. I wish you could see him for what he's become."

Then she followed where her husband had gone, leaving the remaining siblings behind. For a moment there was an awkward silence, then Morgan crossed the room and he and Nicholas stepped away to talk quietly.

Selina found herself moving toward Lizzie. The younger woman lit up as she came near, and Selina couldn't help but smile. No wonder Morgan loved her. She was light and sweet and everything his previous life had not been.

"They'll work it out," Lizzie said as Selina reached her.

Selina looked back over her shoulder. Nicholas's jaw was set, but he was listening to whatever it was Morgan was saying to him. "I assume they will. I wasn't worried."

"Weren't you?" Lizzie asked softly. When Selina glanced back at her, she shook her head. "Of course, I would not presume to tell you how you feel. But I hope you'll at least consider Katherine's invitation to their fete."

Selina smiled at her, this woman who had lived such a sheltered life. Certainly she couldn't understand what Selina was, who she'd always been. How she was proud of both those things, despite what Society would say to the contrary. "Well, Nicholas refuses him. Are you going to speak to him, too?"

Lizzie laughed a little. "I think my husband is doing a fine job already. And he and Robert are very different. It might take some time for them to...find their way."

"Oh." Selina blinked. "You think that Robert and I must find our way, *that* is why you encourage me to take the invitation."

Lizzie looked off toward Morgan, her expression softening with love. "I know the understanding Morgan and Robert have come to over the last few months has been very important to him. I would only wish an increased closeness like that on all the children of the last Duke of Roseford. For their sake and for Robert's."

Selina considered the statement. She and Robert spoke, of course. The fact that she was invited to and had chosen to attend this gathering tonight proved their relationship wasn't outwardly strained. But she wouldn't disagree with the point Lizzie was gently making: that she and her brother were not close.

"Perhaps my problem with Robert is that he and I are too alike. I'm as wild now as he once was," Selina mused softly before she glanced at Lizzie again. "I'm surprised you want anything to do with me, *Lady* Elizabeth."

"Perhaps I just long to hear the stories you could tell."

Selina flinched. She could well imagine the censure she'd receive from this lovely woman if she told her stories. What would shock her more? Actions? Drives? Desires? Oh no, Lizzie could surely not be ready for any of that.

"My stories aren't as interesting as you might think," Selina lied.

Lizzie tilted her head, and for a moment Selina felt as though the younger woman could see through her. Then she smiled gently. "Well, then I suppose I will continue my pursuit of a relationship with you because you remind me of Morgan. And based on everything he tells me about you, I know your wild side is not your only side."

"Hmm," Selina mused, suddenly uncomfortable with that idea. Not many people saw any other side of her than the one she chose to present. And that wild side was the one that reminded her she wouldn't belong at her brother's house party any more than she'd belonged at this gathering tonight.

It was also the side that whispered she *should* go to Roseford. To have fun. To cause trouble. And to take care of something she'd been trying to do for weeks. The party offered an opportunity now. But should she take it and risk exactly the relationship Lizzie was speaking to her about?

"Just think about it," Lizzie said, and stepped away as Robert and Katherine returned to the room. Nicholas approached and the two men spoke softly before they shook hands. But Selina recognized the strain between them remained. It was a shame, really.

Perhaps Lizzie was right, after all. This party afforded her the chance to get a little closer to her once-wayward brother. And if she was careful, he'd never have to know her ulterior motives.

It couldn't hurt, in the end. She would make sure it didn't.

∽

"Have you seen Gillingham since the incident?"

Derrick Huntington lifted his gaze from his paperwork to his partner, Edward Barber. The carriage they were riding in rocked slightly as they turned a corner, and he steadied himself before he spoke.

"The *incident*," Derrick repeated with an arched brow for his friend and partner. "Is that what we're calling the moment where the man nearly died in battle for his comrades? For *us*?"

Barber's hand moved to touch the shoulder where he had been shot in the battle. Derrick's own arm tingled as they spoke of it. Minor injuries, enough to put them both out of service, but most of the men in the company had survived unscathed thanks to Gillingham's bravery. His injuries had not been minor.

"Since his return to London, then," Barber corrected himself. "Have you called on him?"

"Once," Derrick said. "At the beginning. He likely doesn't recall it, he was in such a bad way."

Barber's head bent and his lips pressed hard together. For a moment the carriage was quiet, and then Barber shifted the papers in his lap. "Well, if he is kind enough to help us, then it will make things easier."

Derrick nodded, but their conversation was cut off as the carriage arrived. He stepped out, stretching his back. Damned carriages were always hell on him because he was so tall. He preferred to ride a horse, but when it came to calls like this, the carriage was a necessity.

They walked up together to the door and were greeted by a redheaded butler with a scar that slashed from his forehead, down under the patch on his eye and across his cheek below. Derrick caught his breath at the same time Barber did.

"Evans?" they both said together.

The butler gave them a grin and motioned them into the foyer. Once the door was shut, he extended a hand and the men broke normal protocol with a servant by shaking.

"Aye, it's me," he said. "And a pleasure to see you both, it's like old times."

"You serve Gillingham?" Derrick asked. "You weren't the butler when I came to call right after his return."

"Still recovering myself," Evans said, and some of his joviality faded. "But you know Gillingham. He's too decent a lot not to help. He hired me...it will be a year on the fifteenth, actually. He doesn't seem to care that his butler has a bit of a cockney twist. Though I do try to..." He straightened his shoulders and stifled a grin as his accent went far more proper. "...intone with gravitas."

"That's wonderful, Evans," Derrick said. "He's expecting us, yes?"

Evans nodded and led them up a hall to a parlor. It was a fine room, elegantly appointed and neatly kept. Evans motioned to the tea that was already laid out on the sideboard and then disappeared to find their host.

"He's certainly bringing himself up in the world," Derrick mused as he stepped up to a painting that hung on the wall next to the fire. A beautiful piece that must have been expensive.

"But not forgetting those he left behind," Barber agreed. "It speaks highly of him."

The door behind them opened and Nicholas Gillingham appeared. He leaned heavily on a cane and seemed stiff as he stepped into the room. For a moment, his expression was cool, distant, but then his dark eyes twinkled and he extended the hand not on his cane as he came toward them.

"I cannot say how happy I am to see you both," Gillingham said as he shook their hands in turn and then motioned them to sit. For a while they spoke, catching up on their time in the army, the whereabouts of old friends and the state of current military politics.

At last Gillingham leaned back in his chair with a satisfied sigh. "That you were both to come to call today was a high point of my week, I assure you."

"We should have come sooner," Barber said. "It's been too long."

"Too long, indeed," Gillingham agreed. Then his dark gaze flitted between them. "But I'm wondering when you'll tell me the *official* business you've called about."

Both of Derrick's brows lifted. "You think we're here on military business?"

"No." Gillingham sipped his tea before he continued. "Both of you left all that after your injuries. The Bow Street Runners for you, Huntington, but not for long. And about six months ago, you and Barber started your own, more private investigative service."

Derrick stared at him for a long moment, keeping any reaction from his face. "You know a great deal."

"I kept up on my comrades," Gillingham said softly. "Especially those injured the same day I was. I didn't want to leave anyone behind."

"It's how you ended up hiring Evans," Barber said.

Gillingham nodded. "Yes. But you two were making your way

just fine without my interference. Still, I admire your ingenuity. Both of you are fine minds, and with the connections to your grandfather, Huntington, I assume you are getting cases from the upper class. People who need discretion."

"Yes," Derrick admitted, but added nothing else.

His silence seemed to amuse Gillingham, and he smiled slightly. "Then I have to assume that since you're both here, you are in the midst of a case already. I don't know how in the world I could help, but I'll try if that's what you need."

Derrick exchanged a quick glance with Barber and the other man gave a slight nod. The time had come to ask their favor, and given that Gillingham was, himself, an intelligent man with his own ability to investigate, there was no use dancing around the subject.

He drew a long, deep breath and said, "Have you heard of the Faceless Fox?"

Derrick watched as Gillingham flexed his hands in his lap as he said, "The jewel thief."

"The very one," Barber said with a smile. "Though some of what you read in the papers is exaggerated."

"A puff of smoke who curls into the best of Society and steals the finest jewels, all while never being seen? One that the ladies wax romantic about?" Gillingham tilted his head with a smile. "Some of that is exaggerated? You don't say."

Barber laughed, but Derrick didn't. It was important to stay focused now. "He's been wreaking havoc across London for a year, officially. Though I think he's likely been at it far longer, it's only now that the papers have linked the more recent robberies."

"He leaves a card behind, doesn't he?" Gillingham asked. "A drawing of a fox?"

"Taunting us," Derrick agreed with a frown.

"Taunting you, not the guard?"

"The guard is officially investigating, of course," Barber said. "But the matter is...sensitive, as you might well imagine. Some of the titled gentry are not interested in talking to someone who isn't of their rank." He arched a brow. "Or their skin color."

"Because they're spoiled dolts," Derrick interrupted with a frown toward his friend. "As if the fact that my grandfather is an earl is any indication of my intelligence or ability to solve a crime. You're far more quick-minded than I am."

"Well, you trade in what they want regardless," Gillingham shrugged. "No harm in that. So you were contacted by one of the victims?"

"Two, actually," Derrick admitted. "They want their jewels back and they're willing to work together to find them. Barber and I have been investigating."

"I hate to break it to you, gentlemen, but I am not the Faceless Fox," Gillingham said with a chuckle.

"That's a relief, or the question I'm about to ask you would have been awkward, indeed," Derrick said. He leaned forward, draping his elbows over his knees and holding his old friend's gaze evenly. "The Duke of Roseford is your brother, isn't he?"

"Half-brother," Gillingham said, and his smile faded.

"And he's having a fete at his country home in about a week?" Derrick pressed. When Gillingham nodded, he continued, "Barber has found some evidence that the Fox might be trying to make his way into that party. There will be several important people in attendance. Several tempting jewels being worn by a handful of potential victims."

"You want me to try to get Robert to...to stop the party?" Gillingham asked.

"No," Derrick said. "I was hoping you could obtain an invitation for us."

Gillingham blinked, and for a moment Derrick felt the sting of his position. Grandson of an earl or no, he had been out of that world for years, and had never fully belonged there to begin with. If his friend was trying to find a nice way to tell him there was no possibility he'd be invited to a duke's soiree, this was going to be uncomfortable, indeed.

But instead, Gillingham pushed to his feet and made his way slowly to the window. He stared out over the garden, stretching his back and then turned back. "I have no doubt that my brother would gladly extend an invitation to you if I ask. But he'll have questions. He'll want to know why I'm asking this favor because we are not...close."

"Will he believe a lie?" Barber asked.

Gillingham gave a small smile. "My brother? No. He has a disconcerting ability to suss out lies. Probably because he once told so many himself. He'll know if you're untrue."

Derrick set his jaw. It was always better the fewer people knew about an investigation. He thought of what he knew about the Duke of Roseford. Once considered a wild child of the Upper Ten Thousand, he had certainly never been considered a villain. And he associated with several men who Derrick respected enormously. Since his marriage to the duchess, Roseford had been changed. Everyone commented on it.

"Very well," he said softly. "Tell him the truth and see if he'll extend an invitation. If he does, I'm happy to fill him in on the particulars once we reach Roseford."

"I'll do my best."

Derrick moved forward and extended a hand, signaling that the meeting was at its end. But Gillingham still looked friendly as he shook Barber's hand and then moved to Derrick. "The role suits you. Savior of the world."

Derrick shrugged to push away his discomfort. "That's you, friend. I'm just a man who recovers the jewels of fops who might not deserve them. I hope we'll talk again soon."

"After you return from London, I'd love to see you both more regularly." They moved toward the foyer together and said their goodbyes.

Derrick got into the carriage, and as Barber tapped on the wall for them to go, he arched a brow. "You think he'll manage it?"

Derrick looked out the window at the image of their friend, damaged by war and sacrifice, disappearing in the distance. "We both know Nicholas Gillingham doesn't fail. He gets the job done if it needs doing." He sighed. "So we must make it worthwhile. You and I have been hunting this thief for months. We need to catch him."

"So you're saying more focus," Barber said with a nod. "No distractions."

"No distractions," Derrick repeated. "I'm going to end this one way or another, Barber. By whatever means necessary."

CHAPTER 2

K atherine linked her arm through Selina's and smiled at her.
It was impossible not to smile back, no matter how Selina's
stomach churned.

"I'm so glad you changed your mind and came down to Roseford
with us after all," Katherine said. "I love spending time with you."

Selina blushed as her sister-in-law gave her a squeeze, then
pulled away to greet the next set of guests who were riding up the
drive at present. It was a funny thing. Selina had trained herself over
the years not to have too strong a reaction to almost anything. She
didn't blush when it came to sex or language or behavior. She didn't
mince or preen, unless it suited whatever game she was playing.

But one kind word from Katherine and her cheeks heated.
Because she wasn't accustomed to such full-throated acceptance in
Katherine's world, she supposed. Nor to be part of a welcoming
party to her brother's guests, as if she were his full sister, not
bastard half-blood.

She'd watched Robert welcome his friends. Watched closer when
he greeted his dearest ones, the dukes who were in attendance for
the ten days they would share at Roseford. The Dukes of Sheffield
and Crestwood, Baldwin and Simon, and their wives, Helena and

Meg. There was no denying how close Robert was to them. How warm their bond was, as if *they* were the siblings.

She'd been a little jealous to see it. She could admit that. Worse, she'd felt even more on the outside looking in at their little tableau.

She smoothed her skirt and tried to find some focus. This wasn't why she was here. She had to remember why she was here.

Clearing her throat, she managed to force her attention onto the drive. Two men, one black, one white, had arrived on fine stallions, which the footmen were leading away toward the stables as their riders smoothed themselves and looked up at their hosts.

She straightened up a bit. They'd both served in the military. She'd long ago learned to recognize the stance of a man who'd once worn a red coat. Each had ramrod straight shoulders, perfect posture that spoke of discipline. Her brother extended a hand to the black man. They spoke together for a moment before they motioned the second man forward.

Her gaze lingered on him longer. Good lord, but he was handsome. Tall, so very tall, with an angled face and a hard jawline. His hair was thick and brown, not too long, not too short. Every piece of it laid perfectly, probably placed there with the same discipline that every other line of his body showed. He and the other man were talking to her brother now, talking to Katherine. They all looked serious.

They didn't look like they belonged at a fun little garden party meant to distract bored friends with money.

Her brother motioned toward her and she stepped forward. "Miss Selina Oliver, may I present Mr. Edward Barber," he motioned to the first gentleman he had greeted.

"Mr. Barber," she said, shaking his hand. He was a handsome man, as well, with a friendly face and bright brown eyes that took in everything around him.

"And Mr. Derrick Huntington," her brother added. "Gentlemen, my sister, Selina Oliver."

As Mr. Barber stepped back, Derrick Huntington moved to take his place before her. Yet again, she was struck by how tall he was. How he moved like a tiger in a cage, all lean muscle and dangerous intent. *His* face was not kind. It was hard and angled and focused and intensely beautiful. As were his brown eyes that swept over her in one long glance.

He extended a hand, and she found herself looking at those long fingers, incased in fawn leather riding gloves. Delicious.

"How do you do, Mr. Huntington," she said, and heard how husky her voice was.

"Miss Oliver," he said, and his brow furrowed as he speared her with a stern glance.

She removed her hand from his, mostly because her body was reacting to this man in wild, wanton ways. Ways she'd never avoided in the past. Ways she'd celebrated, for what was wrong with pleasure?

But once again, this was not why she was here.

"Mr. Barber and Mr. Huntington served with Nicholas in the war," Robert said, apparently oblivious to the explosive energy Selina felt pulsing through her entire body.

Energy that ceased the moment her brother said those words. Her lips parted and she looked at them differently. "You did?"

"Yes, Miss Oliver," Mr. Barber said with a nod of his head. "Your brother is a fine man. We were both honored to fight at his side."

She blinked. She'd never met anyone who had served with Nicholas. "Were you with him when..." She trailed off. She couldn't finish the sentence.

"Yes, miss." Huntington answered this time. His voice was lower now, rougher. "We were. He saved both our lives. Neither of us will ever forget it. He was kind enough to suggest we join the party."

Robert nodded. "And I could not refuse, even if I had wished to. Please go inside, gentlemen. You'll be shown to your rooms and I look forward to..." Robert's jaw set. "...to continuing our discussion after you settle in."

Barber inclined his head at him. "Thank you, Your Grace. Though there is no hurry if you have other guests to welcome."

Katherine smiled at him. "You're too kind, but you are the last. Our final guests, the Earl and Countess of Winford, have sent word they are waylaid in joining us. They'll not be with us for a few more days, it seems."

That drew Selina from her musings on the handsome Derrick Huntington and his relationship with her brother. She looked at Katherine. "I did not realize."

Katherine shrugged. "Something about a pressing business matter in London. It matters little, they will come later and we shall be a happy party, though smaller, until their arrival. Come, let's go inside."

They all did together and the two gentlemen were escorted away by Robert's butler, Jenner. Robert kissed Katherine's cheek, whispered something to her and then smiled at Selina before he headed up the hallway away from them. Selina couldn't help but notice Katherine's troubled expression as she marked his departure.

Yes, there was something going on.

"I didn't know we would be welcoming some of Nicholas's friends," Selina said, working on a way to press without pushing too hard and overplaying her hand.

Katherine shook out of her distracted state. "Yes, they were... er...late additions, made at Nicholas's request. They seem like very decent gentlemen, though. I'm sure they will only add to our party."

"I wonder why Nicholas would make the request, though. To have them come to a party where he was not even in attendance?" Selina pushed.

"I could not say. Perhaps they were simply in the area and Nicholas thought to match our party to theirs." Katherine's cheeks turned slightly pink and her smile was forced. "You know, Meg and Helena and I were going to have a bit of tea and catch up apart from the other attendees. You could join us."

Selina arched a brow. Katherine looked truly uncomfortable. Her sister-in-law was not good at lying, it seemed. Something that could be used against her if need be. But not now. Selina could easily find out what she wanted to know without forcing a confidence.

She caught Katherine's hand and squeezed gently. "You go and catch up with your friends privately. I'm sure I'll have plenty of chances to get to know them as our party progresses. I think I'll just take a turn around the garden and get some air."

Katherine appeared relieved that the subject had been changed. "Very good. I'll see you later for drinks before supper, if not sooner."

"Good afternoon," Selina said as Katherine moved off to join her friends. But as soon as she was gone, Selina walked not toward the exit that would take her to the garden, but toward her brother's study. Because she had some investigating to do. And she had to find a proper place to do it.

~

Derrick clutched the snifter of brandy the Duke of Roseford had insisted upon pouring for him and Barber, and watched as his host paced the room. Roseford had a grim expression and a focused air about him. Derrick still wasn't certain what to make of the man, what with all the rumors that had once swirled around him. He'd been wild, but love had tamed him, they said.

He did not look tamed at present.

"So, now that we are in private," Roseford said. "Tell me more about your situation, gentlemen."

Barber glanced at Derrick again and then cleared his throat. "What did Gillingham tell you, Your Grace? Perhaps if we know that then we can fill you in on the rest."

Roseford shook his head. "He told me very little, in truth. Just that you two are investigating the Faceless Fox and you think coming here might help you find him."

Derrick nodded. "Those are essentially the facts of the matter, Your Grace."

Roseford's eyes narrowed. "I understand not wanting to give out too much information, but if you are using my hospitality to find a criminal, I think I must have more of it. Why do you think this Faceless Fox is somehow associated with my party?"

Derrick observed him for another moment, reading every tiny expression, every flicker of Roseford's gaze and movement of his hands. Then he said, "Because of Lady Winford."

"Lady Winford?" Roseford repeated before he grinned. The expression took five years from his face and made him look far more likely to be the rake. "You think that wretched woman is the Faceless Fox?"

Derrick recoiled. "No, indeed not. I think Lady Winford is the next victim of our intrepid thief."

"Intrepid," Roseford repeated, both eyebrows lifting. "You admire him even though you hunt him?"

Barber tossed Derrick a quick glare. The matter of the Fox's admirability was one they debated regularly. Barber was on the side of criminals being criminals. For Derrick, it was more complicated.

How could one not respect a man who could put himself in the middle of the most important parlors and bedrooms and ballrooms in London, take what he wanted without violence and then disappear like smoke on the wind?

"The Fox has skills," Barber admitted, almost begrudgingly. "And certain tastes. Lady Winford very famously just inherited the Breston Necklace from her late mother."

Roseford's expression changed. "Yes, I recall hearing about it. What is it, diamonds and a sapphire?"

"Three hundred diamonds," Barber corrected softly.

"And the sapphire is huge," Derrick added. "At least thirty carats, perhaps more. Her mother's mother was the Duchess of Stanford."

"And they own mines," Barber said, his voice becoming strained.

Roseford held Barber's gaze a moment and then inclined his head. "I understand. So it is of great value, then."

"And since it has been under lock and key for about twenty years, it also has interest. It would be a prize of unlimited worth to the Fox, both monetarily and as a way to cement his legacy as a master thief."

"Would Lady Winford be so foolish as to wear it here?" Roseford asked, then stopped himself and shook his head. "Never mind. I'm thinking of the woman now. Of course she would wear it, no matter the danger, because she is the sort who wants everyone to see her worth."

"Or whatever she counts that worth to be."

Roseford nodded. "Still, she must have had the jewel available to the Fox in the months since her mother's death. Why do you think he'll move here, specifically?"

Derrick shifted and glanced toward the window. There was a flash of a shadow outside and he got up, moving toward the curtains. He parted them and saw...nothing, except that the window was slightly cracked.

He frowned. The shadow was likely just a gardener or servant passing by. The window was probably cracked to let in the air so the room didn't become overheated.

He turned back and looked at Roseford. There was some information Derrick didn't regularly share with people outside of Barber. But since they were using Roseford's home and the man had not shown himself to be a complete bastard yet, he offered a little more than usual.

"We did receive an anonymous tip that the Fox had intentions here," Derrick said.

Barber jerked his face toward him, but then shrugged. "It's credible."

Roseford steepled his fingers and considered the matter for a moment. "I do not think I invited the Faceless Fox to my soiree."

Derrick smiled. "You would not have meant to, I'm certain, but the kind of access this man has had in your world says to me that he is one of a few things: he could be a man of title."

He waited for Roseford to bluster or refuse to believe a person of his rank could do such a thing. He didn't. He simply shrugged. "I know a few men who could be living double lives as you describe."

Derrick continued, ticking off a second finger. "He might be a family member or friend of someone titled. Again, access to their rooms and areas without suspicion." He sighed. "Finally, he might be a servant of some kind. One who can slip in and out, almost invisible because he is expected to be there."

He and Barber were silent. Often when this matter was discussed, men of Roseford's ranks clung to the idea of a servant thief. One of his employers, a marquess whose signet ring had been taken by the Fox months ago, had tried to force Derrick and Barber to drag his servants out one by one. He'd threatened to sack the lot of them.

But Roseford seemed a different man. "It leaves a great deal of options out there, it seems."

"I'd like to assure you, Your Grace, that we will do everything in our power not to disrupt your guests if we can."

Roseford waved his hand. "That isn't my concern. They could all do with a bit of disrupting. It will be the most excitement some have had in years. I've also taken the liberty of having a workspace set up for you in a quiet, little-used wing of the house. One where you will not be disturbed. I'll have Jenner show you there after you're settled into your chambers."

Barber exchanged a surprised look with Derrick before he said, "That is incredibly generous of you. It will be very helpful to us."

"Excellent. If there is anything I or my staff can do to assist, please don't hesitate to ask, either of you."

Derrick stared at him. He couldn't help but be impressed. Roseford was clearly far more than the wild rake Society had labeled him to be all those years. Likely he always had been.

After Barber shook Roseford's hand, Derrick did the same.

Roseford smiled. "My brother is a decent man and he says you two are the same. I can see the importance of what you are doing and in the secrecy. Katherine knows what you're about, of course. We don't lie to each other. But my friends and my staff are all in the dark about your true motives. I'll leave it to you two to decide when, or if, anyone else should be told."

"Thank you, Your Grace," Derrick said, and then he and Barber made their exit.

As the door shut behind them, Barber leaned in. "Seems a decent fellow," he murmured.

Derrick was going to respond, but before he could he caught a glimpse of a scrap of blue fabric disappearing into the parlor next door. Blue fabric that looked suspiciously like the gown worn by Roseford's sister, Selina Oliver. He'd marked it, just as he'd marked almost everything about the woman during their brief introduction.

He thought about the shadow at the window in the study. Certainly it could not have been her. He was just on high alert with this case, and with the fact that when he'd met the lady he'd felt...

Well, attraction was natural, of course. He felt it often. Not always as strongly as he had when the lady had taken his hand and looked up at him with bright blue eyes that seemed to sparkle with a bit of wickedness.

"Derrick?" Barber said.

He blinked. His partner must have been trying to get his attention for some time, for Barber rarely used Derrick's first name.

"Yes, sorry. Just...distracted," Derrick said, following his friend up the hallway back toward the guest quarters where they could speak more privately and make their plans.

"The duke was unexpected," he said, and glanced behind him at the parlor beside the study. The door was closed now. "I think we may find a great many things to be not as they seem now that we're here."

THE HEART OF A HELLION

S elina was able to keep the serene smile on her face until she crossed the threshold into her chamber. Once she shut the door, she pivoted toward her companion, Vale Williams. Vale was a petite woman with pale blonde hair, freckles across her nose and dark brown eyes. Selina had always thought her to look a bit like a fairy in stories. Only she was the kind who didn't use magic for sweetness or light.

At present, Vale was seated by the fire and didn't bother to get up, though she did set her book aside. "Why the look?" she asked.

Selina shook her head. "Well, we are rightly fucked, my dear. Over a barrel, with hardly more than an 'as you please'."

That forced Vale from her seat and she moved toward Selina. "Why? How?"

Selina paced the room, mind racing with what she'd overheard at the window of Robert's study. "My brother has invited some unexpected guests."

Vale wrinkled her brow. "Not on the original guest list you pilfered from his home before we left London?"

"No," Selina said. "They arrived this morning. Former army, I think. I knew that man was trouble. I knew it the moment I looked up into his handsome face. A chin dimple is never to be trusted, Vale. Isn't that what we always say?"

Vale blinked at her ramblings. "I'm sorry, who are these men?"

"Investigators," she said, drawing out each syllable. "Looking for the Faceless Fox."

Vale's hands dropped to her side and her mouth gaped. "They're here hunting you!"

"Indeed." Selina sat down hard and scowled.

The Faceless Fox, her second name for years, the identity she'd hidden behind and lived through. So many had screamed that name into the night after she slipped their jewels from their pockets and danced away to the fence. What a life it had been. One she hadn't regretted...or at least not regretted often.

And now these two men had come to finish what so many others had started at and failed. To catch her in a trap and unveil her to the world.

CHAPTER 3

Selena sighed heavily. At least with Vale she didn't have to wear the cloak. The mask. Her friend had never betrayed her, and perhaps she was the only one who hadn't. Which meant she could trust her, at least more than she did anyone else.

"At present, they still think the Fox is a man," she said. "At least according to everything I overheard."

"Everything you heard? You were eavesdropping?"

"Of course." Selina made a face. "I told you I suspected the men of something."

"Tell me everything," Vale said, retaking her seat across from Selina. "Don't leave anything out."

So she did, telling what she'd overheard before that dratted Derrick Huntington had sensed her at the window. She'd sensed him, too, and barely made her escape before he pushed back the curtain and looked for her.

She told Vale about what they knew regarding Lady Winford's necklace and the intent of the Fox to seek it out. And as her friend and partner sat and considered all she'd said, Selina did her own pondering about how she'd come here.

At first stealing had been a lark. She'd been on her own, for all intents and purposes, for so long. Being untamed and wild and unfettered was easy. It was fun. Most of the time it was fun, at any rate. But it didn't come cheap, that was for certain. Sometimes her father's allowance just wasn't enough, especially if a game of cards didn't go well.

The first time she'd slipped coins from a lady's gown pocket at the Donville Masquerade it had been out of necessity. But oh, the thrill of it. Especially since she'd seen the lady being nasty to a courtesan just a short time before. Talking down to her as if she, herself, weren't at an underground sex club taking her pleasure.

Taking that coin had led to taking other things. Playing the game, for fun and sport and profit. Selina had gotten very good at it. Good enough that she'd once slipped the ring off of Lady Tinman's finger and the woman hadn't been the wiser for hours.

And the Fox? That alter ego all of Society now whispered about? *That* had been born almost by accident. She'd always loved to sketch. It had been her one of her few acceptable pastimes as a girl. She'd been hiding in a gentleman's bedchamber behind the curtain one night, waiting for the household to settle so she could steal the beloved signet ring of an arse who had assaulted a friend of hers from the theatre, and she'd sketched herself a little fox while she waited. When she'd taken the ring, she hadn't realized the tiny drawing had fallen behind.

When it was found after he discovered the missing ring...well, the accident had been believed to be a calling card. So it had become one. She loved to sketch her little foxes, a way to tell those in power that someone was in the midst, destroying them from within.

That everyone thought the Faceless Fox had to be a man was sometimes irritating. But oh, what one could get away with when others underestimated one!

"You should have come to me first," Vale was saying, and it drew Selina back to her present position. "Why bring me as your pretend companion if you don't intend to use me for at least advice and support?"

Selina frowned. She hadn't meant to keep Vale out of her plans. The woman had been her friend and a partner to the Fox for years. She'd even saved Selina's life. That moment had bonded them and inspired Selina to bring her into the fold.

"It was a spur-of-the-moment decision," she explained. "I had to make my move before the gentlemen met with my brother in his study. I barely had time to crack his window and take a hidden position to hear."

Vale seemed comforted by that explanation and smiled at her, the expression softening her pretty face. "It sounds as though it went well, at least. They don't suspect you. But then, *they* never do. There have been investigators before. The guard, even Bow Street Runners. None have come close to you."

Selina worried her lip as she thought of Derrick Huntington and Edward Barber. "I don't know. There's something more...competent in them both. And when Huntington looked at me on the drive when we met..."

She trailed off as she relived that stern expression as he looked into her eyes. It had done things to her body, that smoldering expression. Things she more than understood the consequences of. But she'd retained enough common sense to also realize this was a man who could read others. A man truly dedicated to his duty, whatever he felt that to be.

A man who wouldn't stop until he got what he wanted. She shivered.

"This time just feels different," Selina said. She worried her hands before her. "I wonder if we should walk away. I could probably find some excuse for us to go back to London so that Huntington and Barber's interest isn't heightened. There will be other opportunities to get the Breston necklace. God knows Lady Winford flaunts her receipt of it to all who will listen."

Vale tilted her head. "Is the great Faceless Fox actually *scared* of a man?" she said with a laugh.

"No!" Selina said, and then shifted in discomfort as her friend pierced her with a stare. Vale was too long an acquaintance not to know some of the truth of her. "Yes," she corrected. "Perhaps. He and his partner just feel...unique. Dangerous."

Vale leaned back in her seat and folded her arms. "Well, you've never backed down from a challenge, my dear. And that's what this is. A challenge, nothing more."

Selina wasn't certain and it must have shown on her face, for Vale let out a long sigh. "At the very least, you should determine whether or not these men are even as competent as you've told yourself. Plenty look to be and turn out to be worthless."

"How do you expect me to do that?"

Vale shrugged. "I see you get all fluttery when you talk about the one, Huntington. You've mentioned more than once that he is handsome."

"Yes," Selina admitted through gritted teeth.

"Well, then you find out his worth...by *any* means necessary," Vale teased.

Selina tensed. Sex. Vale was talking about sex, or something close to it. And she wasn't wrong. Seduction in a case like this would certainly allow Selina to find out things about Derrick Huntington that would be harder to determine by other means. Unlike many women of her day, Selina had never believed it when she was taught sex was inherently sinful for a woman to participate or revel in. She did both. There were lovers in her past and there would be lovers in her future. She felt no shame in either fact.

So if she decided to test the limits of the spark she'd felt flare between herself and Huntington, she was certainly equipped to handle the experience. Anyway, it would be fun to tease a man like that. A man with such control pulsing through every single inch of him.

Breaking that control would certainly be a game worth playing. And if it got her what she wanted? What she needed? All the better.

"Well," she said at last. "There is that." She settled back and folded her hands behind her head as she stared up at the ceiling. "At any rate, I have a few days to decide. Lord and Lady Winford are coming late to the party now. So I won't have to think about my mark while I play with the hound who is trying to tree this fox."

Only Huntington didn't put her to mind of a hound. A wolf, maybe.

Vale seemed more relaxed now that Selina had accepted her advice. She picked her book back up from the side table and flipped it open to begin reading again. "Excellent. There is no one more capable than you, my dear. And I can't wait to see this man who you find so interesting."

Interesting. Derrick Huntington was definitely that. Now Selina just had to figure out how to play her interest...and his...to her advantage.

~

D errick stood in the middle of the Duke of Roseford's vast library, looking up around him at the beautiful bookcases that vaulted high into the room above his head. Hundreds of books, all waiting to be read.

He'd always appreciated a library. When he was taken to visit his grandfather as a lad, he'd loved nothing more than to go to his library. First to escape, for there had always been yelling during those visits. But escape had transformed to pleasure as he lost himself in stories and history and learning.

Now he rested his fingers against the woven spines of the books, dragging the tips across their uneven rows and breathing in the scent of pages and words and adventures yet to be had. Before he could choose one of these future friends to pluck from the shelf, he felt a frisson of awareness up his spine. He was being watched.

He turned, guarded but trying to keep that from being obvious before he knew who was staring at his back. What he found made his heart thud.

Selina Oliver was standing in the doorway. She wore a red dress with a deep v-neckline, one that only skirted the limits of modesty because of a silk rose that rested between what appeared to be lovely breasts. Her hair had been curled and piled artfully on the crown of her head, with a silk ribbon laced within that matched the scarlet gown to perfection.

She was stunning, just as she had been on the drive. With her bright blue eyes that flitted over him and dusky pink lips curled into a cocksure smile, the kind most women were forced by Society to hide.

But this woman hid nothing. And that artless seduction in her every look and move woke something...dark in him. Stirred his interest and his cock in equal measure.

"Mr. Huntington," she said, her rough, breathless voice breaking the silence that had stretched between them since he saw her in the doorway.

"Miss Oliver," he managed to choke out. His throat was suddenly very dry. "I have your brother's permission to explore the library."

Her brow wrinkled and then her smile widened. "Why wouldn't you? You're a guest, after all."

He frowned. He'd been so taken aback by her appearance he'd almost forgotten his role of invited guest and friend, rather than outsider. Strange that she could so easily sweep his duties out of the way. Dangerous.

"Of course. I suppose I'm just not accustomed to roaming freely through a duke's home," he said. "Friend of his brother or not."

Her stare wavered at that and she stepped into the room. Now that they were closer, he could scent the faint hint of vanilla from her hair. He suddenly wanted to pull that ribbon from her locks and let the cascade of her sleek, dark hair fall around her like a waterfall.

What the hell was wrong with him? This was a distraction he could not afford. And if she knew his thoughts, she surely wouldn't welcome them, knowing smile or not.

"Are you a great reader, Mr. Huntington?" she asked, gliding past him close enough that the air between them stirred with warmth.

He cleared his throat and resisted the urge to loosen his suddenly tight cravat. "I don't know if I would say a great reader, but a passionate one."

She pivoted at that word. "A passionate reader. Is reading the passion in itself, or do you specifically seek out passionate subjects?"

He shifted. "Perhaps both, depending on the mood."

A smile twitched at the corners of her lips again. "Hmmm, yes, a great deal depends on the mood."

She held his gaze a moment and then pivoted away again. She lifted up on her tiptoes to see a shelf just above her sightline and her dress shifted against her backside. A very shapely backside at that.

He glanced at the fire. Why was it so blasted hot in here? That could not be good for the books. It certainly wasn't good for his constitution.

"And what about you?" he asked, hearing how low and rough his voice was in the quiet of the room.

She shrugged one shoulder. "Reading is a favorite pastime for me, as well. Perhaps that means we'll encounter each other here often during the party. We can...compare books."

He drew in a long breath and tried to find a modicum of decorum and calm in the face of the hurricane that was this woman. He was an investigator, sent here to do just that. He couldn't forget it just because a wildly attractive woman batted her exquisitely long eyelashes at him and gave him a come-hither look.

So what could he deduce about Selina Oliver? Beyond her beauty, beyond her intoxicating charm. She was bold, that was one thing. Brash, he supposed some would say, and they wouldn't be wrong. It was a playful boldness, at least on its surface. But as he gazed deeper into those lovely eyes, he also saw something...else. Something more purposeful.

As if this dance she was dancing had meaning beyond flirtation. And suddenly his interest became not just about her scent or the warmth of her or the directness of her attraction, but about what it was exactly she was trying to achieve by approaching him.

He thought of the disappearing blue gown earlier in the parlor. Hers, he was more and more certain. And that made him wonder about those motives all the more.

He cleared his throat and straightened up. "Any time you'd like to compare books, Miss Oliver, I am at your service."

She arched a brow. "Then I look forward to it."

Oh yes, this conversation and its deeper meanings were far too risky. He needed to draw her toward some other topic. Perhaps one that would let him see more of the real woman beneath this flirtatious façade he didn't fully understand.

"I was sorry your brother couldn't join our party," he said, and it wasn't a lie.

Just as he suspected, her expression shifted. The playful minx faded away and a second side to her emerged. A little anxious, much softer, just as intriguing.

"Nicholas?" she said, and nodded. "Yes, I wish he had come, as well. But his injuries..."

Derrick frowned as he recalled Gillingham's heavy limp when they'd seen each other in London. The expression of pain on his face. "Yes, they were grave. We thought we'd lose him that day."

She flinched. "We've thought that a few times since his return, to be honest. Though he does seem to be healing, at last. He is much better than he was even six months ago."

Derrick saw her concern. The one he shared. And he stepped closer without thinking. "He is as strong a man as I've ever known. I believe he will continue to recover."

She gazed up at him and nodded slowly. "Thank you for that. It helps to hear it."

Her voice and expression were genuine. He could see her deep fear for her brother's future, her pain for what he'd suffered in the past and even now. And for a moment, he longed to take her hand. He flexed his fingers at his sides so he wouldn't do something so foolish.

He needed to stay on task.

"Well, it's been a pleasure to see you, Miss Oliver," he said. "But I should—"

She raised a hand. "Do not run away on my account, Mr. Huntington. I promised Katherine and the other ladies that I would join them for drinks before we all gather for supper, and I am already fashionably late. I will see you tonight, I hope."

He nodded. "Indeed. Until then, Miss Oliver."

"Until then," she repeated, and turned away. He watched her as she went and at the door she turned and sent another saucy smile toward him before she glided from the room.

He sank into the closest chair after she did so and dragged in a breath of the air she'd stolen when she entered the room. The woman was...fascinating. He could very easily read most people. It was why he'd taken so well to this profession. And though he caught a glimpse now and then of the realness beneath her façade, most of the time Selina Oliver was utterly unreadable.

That should have warned him off. Should have done a great many things. But instead it made him throb for her all the more. Made him want to peel off all that pretense, along with her gown and her underthings, and mount an exploration of all that was beneath.

"Bloody hell," he muttered. "Find a lightskirt if you need relief. Get yourself together."

With those words said, he pushed back to his feet and returned his attention to the books on the shelves. Only he could no longer seem to find focus for the titles.

And he had the strangest feeling that stealing his focus was exactly what Miss Oliver wanted.

CHAPTER 4

The ladies had all gathered in the large parlor near Katherine's study, and it was a jolly group, on the whole. Everyone was beautiful in their finery, friendly in their conversation, and there were jewels galore for Selina to admire. And covet, though she refused to allow her attention to be drawn away from the necklace she was here to steal.

Apart from everything else? Well, that was harder. Her encounter with Derrick Huntington in the library replayed over and over in her mind. She'd intended to play a little with him, flirt with him and set him on his heels. She thought she had succeeded in that.

And yet she didn't feel fully satisfied by the meeting. There had been moments when he'd almost effortlessly pulled away the mask she wore. Moments where she thought he could...see her.

If he could do that, he was a dangerous investigator, indeed. And she'd have to work hard to keep him off her scent if she decided to follow through on her plans for Lady Winford's jewels.

"Miss Oliver?"

Selina pivoted and found that Katherine's friend, the Duchess of Sheffield, had approached her. Selina smiled in welcome, both because the duchess seemed so kind and also because Selina had a keen interest in the lady. After all, her quarry had been invited to this party for the sole purpose of her husband's potential assistance to the Duke of Sheffield.

"Your Grace," Selina said. "Oh, and please, just Selina. *Miss Oliver* sounds so strange to my ears."

"Helena," the duchess said with another of those pretty smiles. "I also struggle with the formality."

It didn't surprise Selina. After all, Helena was rather famously *American*. That was how it was said, too, in good circles when she wasn't around. *American*, like it was a disease the lovely woman carried. She'd also been rumored to have once been hardly more than a servant.

It seemed Katherine, Robert and their group were fond of collecting outsiders. Which made them very likeable to Selina, even if she could never truly be part of their special circle. She was a bastard, after all. And a wild one, at that. She could never be *fully* accepted.

"It's so lovely to finally meet you," Helena said with a truly welcoming smile. "Katherine always speaks so highly of you."

"Does she?" Selina said, arching her brow as she gazed across the room to where her sister-in-law stood with the Duchess of Crestwood and a few other ladies. "I suppose I'm surprised she speaks of me at all."

Helena tilted her head. "Of course she does."

"Well, she is a wonderful woman," Selina replied, and meant every word. "I've become very fond of her."

"I know she was thrilled to have you join the party," Helena continued.

Selina glanced at Helena. This was a perfect opening to discuss Lady Winford. After all, the countess was their shared quarry. For Helena, the woman represented a hope for the future for her husband. For Selina...well, the necklace...and a little bit of comeuppance for bad behavior.

"Of course, it's not yet a complete party," Selina said, and watched Helena's gaze flicker to the door, almost as if she were anticipating the arrival of Lady Winford even now.

"Yes, the Earl and Countess of Winford, our latecomers," Helena said, and her hands clenched at her sides.

Before Selina could respond, Katherine and the Duchess of Crestwood approached together. "What are you two discussing so seriously?" the Duchess of Crestwood asked as she slid an arm through Helena's and squeezed.

Helena smiled up at her. "The party, Meg. And how wonderful it is already, with such friends to be met. I'm so glad we could do this, Katherine. We love seeing you and need to do it more often."

"Actually, we were discussing the friends yet to come, Your Grace," Selina said.

"Meg," the duchess corrected her. "To my friends and family, I'm just Meg. Robert and my Simon are practically brothers, so you follow the line of that, my dear."

Selina felt heat flooding her cheeks at the kindness of both duchesses. They were so easy and kind, so welcoming without any hint of ulterior motive. She had not expected it, but it was...nice.

"Meg." She arched a brow. "I was just about to tell Helena that I am not particularly sad that Lady Winford and her husband have not yet joined us."

Meg let out a little sound of surprise, laced with just a touch of admiration at Selina's candor. Katherine dipped her head, barely smothering a smile, and Helena blushed.

"So direct!" Meg said with a laugh.

Selina lifted a hand to her chest. "Too far?" she asked with feigned innocence.

Meg shook her head. "Not at all. I find the candor refreshing. And I happen to agree with it. I've always found Lady Winford to be...cold."

"Cruel," Selina whispered softly.

Katherine jerked her gaze to her. "Lady Winford was cruel to you?" she asked.

"Not to me directly...at least not yet," Selina admitted. "But I've seen her do it to others, especially those she deems too unimportant to be able to fight back."

Helena shifted. "I admit, I have also experienced some of her bad ways. I'm so sorry that you felt compelled to invite her because of Baldwin and me, Katherine."

Katherine took her hand, and the warmth between the women was almost palpable. "No, dearest. I'm happy to help. Certainly, we all interact regularly with people who aren't our favorite to spend time with. It is part of the world, unfortunately. And at least in this case, it could lead to some good."

That seemed to ease Helena's worries a little, and she smiled. "By the time they arrive, it will only be a week left. And perhaps she won't be so terrible this time."

Meg snorted. "You keep that faith, my dear, because you are too good."

Selina couldn't help but smile at their sisterly camaraderie. She'd been alone most of her life. She'd grown close to three of her brothers to varying degrees, but she hadn't met any of her half-sisters. She hadn't truly experienced this kind of bond.

"Now I must ask," she pressed, pushing aside whatever longing she felt at that thought. "What do you think of our other new friends?"

"New friends?" Katherine repeated. "Are you speaking about Mr. Huntington and Mr. Barber?"

Selina nodded. "Yes."

"I met Mr. Barber briefly in the garden a short time ago," Helena said. "He seems a very friendly man. We shared our common interest in roses. He gave me good advice on a problem I've been having with mites in my own little garden on our London estate."

Katherine shifted and Selina felt her slight discomfort. Selina hadn't been able to eavesdrop long enough at the study window to find out if Katherine was aware of the men's investigation, but now she had to believe the duchess was. But Robert and she were obviously keeping the truth quiet.

"They are friends of Robert and Selina's brother Nicholas. They served with him in the war. I believe Nicholas discovered they were spending time near Roseford, and asked Robert to include them. They both seem very decent men."

Selina nodded slowly. She wanted to get closer to the efficacy of Huntington and Barber's investigation, which meant getting closer to them. Or at least one of them. Huntington, since the attraction between them was patently obvious.

So it was time to throw a lure into the conversation and see if Katherine would jump for it.

"Very decent, given the brief interaction we shared on the drive. And very attractive, as you'll all see at supper. Mr. Huntington is uncommonly handsome, I would say."

Katherine's gaze slowly shifted to Selina, and she pretended not to notice the interest in her sister-in-law's stare. The calculations she was making. But Selina felt them being made, felt the desire to matchmake rising up in the duchess. She just hoped it was an itch Katherine wouldn't resist scratching.

But judging from all the duchesses' faces as they changed the subject to something else, she would wager a farthing she would be seated next to Derrick Huntington that very night. Now she just had to figure out the best way to read him, and which way to play the game that had begun hours before.

As Derrick entered the dining hall with Barber at his side, he drew in a long breath. It was a lavish room, beautifully appointed, with fine bone china and sterling silver utensils at each place. Other guests were already settling in at their seats, which were labeled by a sophisticated, swirling hand.

"Here I am," Barber said, pointing to a seat. "Mr. E. Barber. Ah, and I'm next to the Duke and Duchess of Sheffield. I met her earlier in the garden. She is a lovely woman."

Derrick nodded. "Wonderful," he murmured. "Then you'll be happy. God knows who I'll be placed by. Excuse me as I continue to look."

He left Barber to settle in, pleased as could be about his seatmates. Derrick looked along the seats, passing each name by until he came to the opposite side of the table. And there he was, Mr. D. Huntington. He glanced at the surrounding names. One was Mr. Grimes, a third son of an earl. A very good thing, as Derrick wanted to get to know the man a bit better. Grimes had access to Society due to his father and brother. There were some small rumors about a financial issue. He fit the bill for the Fox.

But before he could formulate a plan to deal with the man, he noticed the name on the other side: Miss S. Oliver.

He blinked and looked up just in time to see the lady approaching, a wide, almost triumphant smile curving those luscious lips.

"Mr. Huntington," she declared as she reached him. She gave him a pointed look, then glanced at her chair. He blinked and then pulled it back to allow her to sit. "Fancy meeting you here," she finished.

He eased into his place and reached for his napkin. As he placed it in his lap, he made note of that wicked twinkle in her eyes. The one that seemed to tug directly on his cock. He cleared his throat. "Yes. Of all the table placements in all the country…"

She laughed, then glanced up in thanks at the footman who was pouring her a glass of madeira. Once Derrick had his own, she tilted hers toward him. "Then let us toast to the seating chart."

He had no choice but to do so. Their glasses clinked and they both sipped their wine.

She set her glass back on the table. "Perhaps it wasn't accidental, though."

"No?" he said, nodding to Mr. Grimes as he took his place. "Good evening."

Grimes sniffed toward him and grunted, "Good evening." He immediately put his attention to the lady on his right.

Derrick frowned before he let his attention drift back to Selina. "Why would we be placed together?"

She leaned in and whispered, "Don't you know? I don't belong here either."

"You don't think I belong here?" he said, watching her carefully. Although her expression wasn't closed off, it didn't reveal anything either.

"I *know* you don't," she whispered, and winked at him.

He pondered pressing her, trying to determine if her statement was pure snobbery or something she thought she knew for certain, but this was not the place. If their conversation were overheard, it could damage the cover provided to him by Roseford's invitation and the explanation behind it. Later, perhaps, if they were alone…

Although, looking at Selina Oliver, he did not think that being alone with her was a good idea. He generally avoided temptation. Losing control never led to anything good, at least not beyond a moment or two of pleasure. She was the kind of woman who snapped a man out of control with hardly a bat of her eyelashes.

"Very well, so you think me out of place," he said softly. "But how can you be? You're the sister of the duke, after all."

That smile faltered just a fraction. Not enough that most people would have even noticed it. But he did. "Bastard sister," she murmured.

He raised both eyebrows. "So direct."

"You have no idea." She sipped her wine, then arched her brow at him again. "But you aren't, I don't think."

"Direct?" he asked. She nodded. "You don't think so?"

He leaned closer despite the danger of it. He couldn't help himself but to draw in a deep breath of her scent. Vanilla and cinnamon and sin. And goddamn but he wanted to…do things to her in that moment. He blinked at the inappropriate thoughts and forced himself to focus on his plate.

"I know so," she whispered, that low, husky voice taunting him.

He gripped a hand on the tabletop and then gave her a tight smile. "If I have offended in some unknown way, Miss Oliver, I do apologize."

He didn't wait for her to respond, but pivoted his attention to Mr. Grimes instead. Better for it, too. Men like Grimes were the reason he was at this party, after all. Not to flirt with Selina Oliver. Not to think about all the ways he could remove that gown, including with his teeth. Not to ponder all the swirling desires he normally kept controlled.

The rest of the supper passed without incident. Mr. Grimes did not provide any valuable information. In fact, he seemed determined to avoid direct conversation with Derrick as often as possible. Selina Oliver also avoided any further scandal with him. She spoke mostly to the woman on her opposite side, the Duchess of Crestwood.

But Derrick was not entirely iced out. The Duke of Crestwood was seated across from him and seemed a decent fellow. They'd had a fine enough conversation, though not exactly enlightening about any details Derrick could use in his pursuit of the Fox.

Eventually the meal came to its end and the parties rose, talking and laughing as they moved off to their post-supper enjoyments. The men would go take port and play a round of billiards. The ladies were meant for sherry and cards. Selina linked arms with the Duchess of Crestwood and they walked together, while Derrick found Barber and fell in beside his friend and partner.

"Find out anything of interest?" Barber asked.

Derrick pursed his lips, trying not to be distracted by the twitch of Selina's hips beneath that gown. "Not really. I tried to make some headway with Grimes, but he didn't seem in the mood to talk. Apparently my serving in the army with the duke's bastard brother doesn't elevate me to the status of one worthy of polite conversation."

Barber let out his breath slowly. "Well, some will judge us. We knew that when we came."

"Aye," Derrick muttered.

"It seemed you were getting on well with Miss Oliver," Barber suggested, dropping his voice.

Derrick stared straight ahead for a moment, then allowed himself to look at Barber as they entered the billiards room. Roseford was pouring the port for his friends, his face bright with pleasure as he moved like a honeybee from flower to flower.

Somehow Derrick didn't think he'd have the same expression if his host knew Derrick's inappropriate thoughts about Selina.

He cleared his throat. "She is a friendly enough woman."

"Hmmm," Barber murmured, and Derrick knew the tone. The men had been friends long enough to call each other on their nonsense. He waited for Barber to do so, but they were interrupted as Roseford reached them with his port.

"This is a thirty-year port," Roseford said as he handed over a glass of the rich liquid to each man. "My father would hate that we've opened it and so I do it with glee. Enjoy, gentlemen."

As Roseford flitted off to his next guest, Barber sipped the wine. "Oh, that is good. A fine flavor." Then he turned to Derrick and held his gaze for a moment. "Be careful, mate."

Derrick gripped his glass a fraction tighter. He knew what Barber was referring to, who he meant when he made that admonishment. But he shrugged. "I'm always careful. The job is to be careful, isn't it?"

"Except when it isn't," Barber said with a smile at the quip they liked to make to each other. "Only I'm not talking about the job. You don't often show your thoughts on your face, Huntington. It makes you excellent at what we do. But tonight, for a moment, I saw those thoughts when you were talking to Miss Oliver. Who can blame you? She's a great beauty and seems to have an...interesting set of beliefs when it comes to life, if the rumors are to be believed."

"Well, I'm not here for whatever you think you saw," Derrick said through gritted teeth. "So it doesn't really matter in the end, does it?" Before Barber could respond, Derrick leaned forward and tapped his glass against his friend's. "To the case."

Barber held his gaze for a moment, then nodded. "To the case. May we find our Fox swiftly and collect our blunt with pride."

Derrick laughed, and then they were approached by some of Roseford's friends, so they were not able to speak on the subject of that case, or of Selina, any longer. A good thing, perhaps, because Barber's advice was still ringing in Derrick's ears.

Be careful.

Yes, that was exactly what he should do. Only he wasn't feeling careful, not when it came to Selina. He was feeling something else entirely.

And he needed to push past that and forget about it before it disrupted not only his case, but his life and the control he had cultivated in every corner of it.

CHAPTER 5

Because the weather was divine, the next day Selina found herself out on the expansive lawn watching her brother's friends play what she assumed they believed was a rousing game of bowls. At present Robert's ball was closest to the jack and he was crowing about it rather mercilessly, to the great amusement of his friends.

She had never been a fan of bowls. In truth, she never felt fully comfortable with these sorts of games. Her life had not required she learn about them until she was much older and trying to pretend to fit in, rather like she was doing now. So none came naturally. Give her a deck of cards and she could dazzle anyone, and probably end up with their money in her reticule, too.

But roll a ball down a green with any skill? *That* felt foreign.

Vale stepped up beside her, the perfect image of a companion if ever there had been. Only Vale had slept long into the morning and certainly hadn't helped with hair or clothing. The act of companion was just that...an act. Not that Selina expected more. She'd learned to take care of herself long ago and preferred it, truth be told. If one depended on someone else, they would surely be let down.

"Well, you did not lie," Vale said. "Derrick Huntington is, indeed, a very handsome man."

Selina jerked at the statement, for it forced her attention back to the man she'd been trying to avoid for the past day: Huntington. God, even when she just thought his name in her head, it was a drawn out purr of every syllable. He stood on the opposite side of the lawn, observing the game just as she was, not participating. Unlike his partner. Mr. Barber seemed to be enjoying himself very much, as he stood watching the game, speaking to the Dukes of Crestwood and Sheffield intently.

"I'm afraid he is, indeed, intolerably good looking," Selina said with a theatrically sad shake of her head. "It's almost unfair. I mean, that jawline. It's practically poetry."

Vale chuckled. "I won't argue that point. He's very well favored. But...is he competent? *That* is the real question."

Selina sighed. She had spoken to Huntington twice and neither time had she been able to fully question him, drill into his mind. To have done so either in the library or in the dining room would have only sparked his suspicions. However, there was still a clear answer to the query. One the man carried as easily as his broad shoulders or his dark, annoyingly soulful eyes.

"I fear he is quite competent. It is evident the moment one speaks to him." She shook her head. It would have been so much easier if he were just pretty to look at and nothing to fear.

"Damn," Vale said, her shoulders rolling forward in a small display of defeat. "Well, that complicates things. But the next question is one I cannot help but think I already know the answer to, though I'll ask it anyway. Is he distractible?"

Selina flashed to those same dark eyes holding hers for far more than a beat too long. She'd trained herself long ago to instantly recognize a man's attention. It kept her fed as often as it kept her safe. "Possibly," she said. "He is...*interested.*"

"As are you," Vale said. Said, not asked.

Selina looked at her friend. Despite their long acquaintance, she still wasn't accustomed to allowing herself to be read so easily. She didn't like it. If Vale could see, someone else could see. Including Huntington. His job, after all, was to read those around him. She saw him doing it all the time. Even now, his gaze flitted from player to player, and she could all but see him making notes in his head about every person at the party.

"You think?" she asked, forcing herself to be breezy.

"I know you do," Vale insisted. "It isn't very often that a man truly lights you, so when it happens it is something of note. You are lit. Like a candle. Like a fire. Like an inferno."

Selina shifted. She'd been trying to avoid that realization in herself, truth be told. She didn't want to be lit, and certainly not by a man who was dedicated to hunting her. Not that he would catch her, but it was playing so close to the edge. She didn't want to fall. Not now when it felt like things were coming together. Where she was almost...safe.

She waved her hand in the hopes she would appear unconcerned. "I wouldn't go so far."

Vale shrugged. "Fine, keep your counsel. But what are you going to do?"

Selina dared to look at him again. His attention had shifted away from the field of players and now locked slowly but firmly on her. They held gazes across the grass, his stare never wavering. She forced her own to remain just as still and firm.

And in that moment, it became clear what to do to regain the upper hand on a man who threatened her world in more ways than one.

"I'm going to tell him what I know," she said with a little smile for her friend.

"What?" Vale gasped, her eyes widening.

Selina laughed at the reaction and reached out to pat Vale's arm. "Trust me, dearest. I know exactly what I'm doing."

With that she sauntered off across the field toward her quarry, leaving Vale behind to whatever her reaction was. But even though

Selina pretended all the confidence and faith in the world in her new plan, the nerves she wasn't showing were tearing her apart. She had to tread very carefully with Derrick Huntington. And careful had never been her strong suit.

~

D errick watched as Selina strolled her way across the playing field toward him, her bright blue eyes locked on his. She was such a purposeful creature, one who obviously knew the value of every swish of her backside, every lick of her lips. He didn't judge her for that, of course. He just knew to be wary of the game.

Or he should have been wary. That wasn't his true reaction. No, in truth his stomach clenched and his cock stirred and he shook his head at the physical reaction that betrayed him. He was always in control. He'd fought very hard to get that way.

And this woman he didn't even know knocked him right off his axis with hardly more than a puff of breath.

"Mr. Huntington," she all but purred as she slipped up to him.

"Miss Oliver," he managed to say past a suddenly bone-dry throat.

She stepped to his side and for a moment made a great show out of watching the games on the field. At present the Duke of Roseford had been knocked from his perch as champion by his own wife. And he seemed all the happier for it, though he teased the duchess mightily. Their chemistry was on display for all to see.

Derrick had to make sure he didn't reveal himself so obviously. Difficult when he could feel the warmth of Selina beside him, smell that unique vanilla muskiness of her skin and hair.

She leaned her head closer to his and without taking her eyes off the field, she whispered, "I know what you're doing, Mr. Huntington."

He drew in a long breath and let it out slowly before he answered, hoping to find prudence in the midst of the chaos this woman caused in his chest. "Do you? Are you in the mood to tell me what you think that is?"

She pivoted slightly and lifted her chin. How he longed to drag his thumb along the line of it, let his fingers rest against her throat, then take his mouth along the same path.

"I know you aren't here as some mere favor from my brother," she said. *"You're* here investigating the famous Faceless Fox."

His eyes went wide and panic washed away attraction as he stared at her. She was not guessing. She knew the truth. It was plain she knew, from her cocksure expression to her even stare. And since he had no idea what she would do next—if she would expose him to the party at large—he had to move and he had to do it now.

He darted his gaze around the yard and found the shadow of the orangery on the side of the house behind them. Close enough that he could get her there quickly, secluded enough to have a conversation, not something that would draw too much attention if he did this right.

He caught her elbow in one swift motion, trying to ignore the frisson of awareness that shot up his arm when he touched her in even this benign way. She sucked in a breath and that didn't help, because it almost was a sound of pleasure.

He ignored it all and guided her away from the yard and the others. They were all so engrossed in the game of bowls that no one seemed to notice their hasty escape. He hoped it would stay that way as he all but dragged her across the grass toward the orangery.

Selina's heart throbbed as Huntington hauled her into the orangery. His fingers trailed along her elbow as he released her, then he leaned back against the door. It was an almost casual posture, but the tension that lined his face told her differently.

"What do you *think* you know?" he asked, his voice rough.

She ignored the question for a moment. Partly to regain some of her authority, and partly because if she spoke right now he'd hear the husky break in her voice and her desire would be too obvious. He could turn the tables.

And as fun as that might be, it wasn't the plan.

She looked around the room as she gathered herself. It was a small conservatory, glass-encased and filled with flowers, small trees and even a small pond in the center with water lilies floating on its surface. The glass had streaked over time, fogged from the steamy heat on the room. No one on the outside would have a completely clear view until they were all but pressed against the windows.

Which made this a private place, indeed.

"Answer me," he said, an order that sent another thrill through her body.

She pivoted and faced him. He was watching her intently, his gaze focused on her face, but when she took a step toward him, those eyes skittered lower, looking over her from head to toe. He wanted her, that was clear. He was fighting the want. He was just on the edge of control of it.

Which meant he could be pushed back or pulled forward until he fell.

"I don't *think* I know anything," she said softly. "I know I know. And I want to help you."

His brow wrinkled and her smile widened. Oh, he hadn't been expecting that. He was trying to formulate some response. Trying to find some way to grapple back on top.

He cleared his throat. "If I were doing what you think I'm doing," he began, a weak denial if ever there were one. "Why would you want to help?"

"The thrill," she lied, clasping her hands together to better affect a bored little miss who knew little of the world. "I've read all about the Faceless Fox in the papers and I know it would be so exciting to have a part in catching him."

His brow lowered further and he speared her with a questioning stare. She might have laid it on a bit too thick there. He didn't seem certain of her. She ducked her head so he wouldn't read her too closely.

"I can't let you do that," he said, his voice rougher in the quiet of the orangery.

She smiled as she looked at him once more. "So I *was* right! What I overheard is true!"

He shook his head slowly, but she could see the twitch of a smile on his lips. Those extremely nice lips. "What you eavesdropped on, you mean," he said, giving her a stern glance.

Her stomach fluttered, but she ignored it as she lifted a hand to her chest and pretended to be affronted. "Eavesdropped? Whatever do you mean, Mr. Huntington?"

Now she knew she'd gone too far. He chuckled, low and dangerous. "Come now, you needn't play with me. I saw you. I saw your shadow at the window when I was talking to your brother in his study yesterday afternoon. And then I saw you darting away from me into the adjoining parlor later."

She blinked. She'd known he suspected someone was at the window, but she hadn't realized he'd caught her slipping into the parlor later. Now she blushed and it wasn't a game.

His gaze flitted over her face once more. She saw desire in him again and it called to her own. At some point, she could see there would be an explosive end to that. She was looking forward to it.

He cleared his throat. "You are too clever to deny what you already know, so I won't sport with your intelligence. Yes, I'm an investigator, Miss Oliver. Yes, I'm looking into a certain jewel thief who has made quite the name for himself, and with good reason. I haven't encountered so talented a criminal in a long time."

She almost preened at the compliment, but managed to keep herself in check.

"But as I said a moment ago," he continued. "I can't let you help me."

She pursed her lips. *Let her.* Yes, that was the way of the world.

Men had the power. Or so they thought. Only she refused to let that stand. She refused to live her life that way.

"And why can't you *let* me?" she asked, just barely keeping the disdain from her voice.

"You spoke to me of the thrill of the situation. That comes from danger, Selina." The color left his cheeks. "Forgive me, Miss Oliver."

She smiled at the slip. Oh yes, she was already getting under this man's skin and hardly even trying. So maybe it was time to try. "I don't mind if you call me Selina," she said softly. "*Derrick.*"

His cheek actually twitched, but he took a step away. The way he shifted his weight, clenched his hands in and out of fists at his sides, it all revealed him. Revealed control that was so tightly coiled in him at present. Great God, what fun it would be to just…snap it. What would happen then? What kind of man would Derrick Huntington be if he just…lost his grip on control?

She shivered at the thought.

"Miss Oliver," he continued, his voice firmer now. "You must listen. I understand that the idea of pursuing a criminal might seem exciting to you. But I assure you that it is a world you don't want to pursue. This man could very well be dangerous, especially if he ends up cornered. So I must, again, insist that you cannot be a part of my investigation."

She pretended disappointment, bending her head with a long sigh. "I suppose I understand. Is there anything I could say or do that would change your mind?"

He shifted again, and his voice was even huskier when he said, "I'm afraid not. Though I do have a request."

She arched a brow and took a step toward him, closing the distance he had created when she called him by his first name. "What is it?"

"I hope you won't reveal what you know to anyone else at the party, even your companion or your friends. Only Roseford and the duchess are aware of what Barber and I are doing, and secrecy is, as you might imagine, paramount in this situation."

She edged a little closer, until she was just in front of him. God's teeth, he was tall. Like a tree...and she'd always been a good climber. She reached out, surprised her hand was trembling a fraction, and rested her palm on his chest. There seemed to be a ripple that moved through him when she touched him, though he managed to keep his face impassive.

"Secrets," she whispered. "I'm very good at keeping those, *Derrick*. You needn't worry about me."

His fists clenched tight at his sides and his jaw flexed. She could see him fighting, all that control trying to stay in place, all those lovely edges fraying, fraying, fraying. Oh, how easy it would be to just...

She lifted up on her tiptoes, sliding her hand up his chest, resting it on his shoulder as she brushed her lips against his jawline. The beginnings of stubble abraded her mouth and she longed to nip there, to feel that chin rub her breasts, along her inner thigh. She'd had every intention of stopping just there but now, well, now she wanted just a little more.

She lifted higher and let her mouth take his. For a fraction of a moment, he was still. But then his arms came around her as control wavered. He pulled her tight against his hard chest and his lips parted to welcome her seeking tongue inside.

Selina was not a virginal young lady afraid of a kiss. She'd done this very thing many times and with many men. She liked kissing, with all its angles and emotions and connections. She especially liked the thrill in the blood that always accompanied a first kiss.

But despite all her experience, despite the game she was playing, the moment Derrick's rough tongue pressed into her mouth, she recognized something shocking.

This was unlike any kiss she'd ever shared before.

This was...*animal*, passionate, a claiming unlike anything she'd ever experienced. It was out of control and that was frightening. She, like the man before her, was always in control, especially when it came to something physical.

Despite that, she didn't want him to stop. Now that their mouths were crushing together, innate hunger yearning to be sated, she never wanted to stop.

He wasn't gentle, though he had a great deal of finesse as he tangled his tongue with hers with an urgency that spoke to desire and skill mixed in one. He sucked her tongue as he molded her closer, a flash of pain that made her fingertips dig hard into his back through his jacket. She sank into the sensations his mouth created. Pleasure that arced through her body, tingling through her limbs, into her core, throbbing between her legs as she lifted into him and tried to find the friction that would ease this wild ache.

The moment she did so, his mouth stilled on hers, and then he pulled away, taking a step back. His breath was short, his lips wet. She could still taste him on her tongue, still feel his overwhelming energy surrounding her like a cloak that only the two of them had ever worn.

She had won this battle in the war he didn't even realize they were fighting. And yet she felt no triumph in that.

No, she felt something far more dangerous. She felt a longing she hadn't experienced in a lifetime. A need for more. And that was dangerous, because it required depending upon another person for her pleasure, for her happiness, for her satisfaction. That was one thing she did not do. Not ever.

"I-I won't tell a soul," she promised, shocked at the stammer and the shaking of her voice. He would read it as a missish response to the kiss rather than what it was, but she knew better. She knew she'd been moved when she hadn't wanted to be.

And she turned on her heel and bolted from the orangery to escape that truth and the man who had revealed it with his expert kiss.

CHAPTER 6

D errick sat before the hearth in his chamber, his fingers steepled before him, his chin resting against them as he stared into the dying fire. In less than an hour the gathering before supper would begin in the parlor. And he would have to see Selina again.

Considering he hadn't stopped thinking about kissing her since she slipped from the orangery, that was a dangerous truth, indeed.

She was playing a game with him, of course. He would be a fool not to see it. She was toying with the idea of being sweet and innocent, playing a role, but it didn't fully…suit her. She wasn't sweet. She was saucy and seductive and sharp as a blade. All equally attractive, but none of them *sweet*.

And innocent? Well, that he didn't know about. It was none of his business, really. She was the sister of a duke, bastard or not. She had likely been raised in a sheltered environment. He might simply be the toy of a bored aristocrat, stretching the bounds of her world because she knew his secret and it titillated her. Or she might be… something else. He couldn't tell. He couldn't fully read her. That was both troubling and intoxicating.

She was intoxicating, from the softness of her body molding to his to the flavor of her lips, to the little sound she'd made deep in her throat when he'd driven his tongue into her mouth and staked the tiniest of claims.

Wrong, all of it. But it had happened, and now he was going to have to live with whatever consequences came, including the heated memories that kept making his cock rock-hard and his mind too foggy to think.

Tonight he needed to think. The Earl and Countess of Winford would arrive tomorrow with her blasted Breston necklace and he wouldn't be able to spend hours pondering the fullness of Selina Oliver's lower lip, how much he'd wanted to tug on it with his teeth until she ground her hips against his.

"Fucking hell," he cursed, and dragged a shaking hand down to the placard of his trousers. He was to meet Barber before the gathering so they could strategize, but there was going to be none of that until he took care of this pulsing desire the only way he could, or should.

He unfastened himself with a flick of his wrist and his cock pushed free of the confines of the fabric. He was already hard, at attention, and he let out a breath of relief at no longer being constricted. He stroked a thumb over his head, wetting himself a little with precome. The sensation of skin on skin forced a hissing breath from his throat, and he scooted lower in his chair so that he was slouched. He spit on his hand and reached for himself again.

He began to stroke, trying to focus on the pleasure, not let his mind wander. He didn't want to think about Selina and her warm body rubbing against his, seeking release. Seeking exactly what was hard in his hand right now. He didn't want to think about dragging her down onto the floor of the orangery and shoving her skirts around her waist. He didn't want to think about holding her down with one hand while he licked her until she screamed and twitched.

He didn't want to think about gliding his hard cock deep inside her body, grinding deep inside of her until she spasmed around him and milked him dry.

"Fuck," he muttered, because of course he was already thinking all those things. Pleasure grew, spreading up his cock, through his balls, making him weightless and effortless as he jerked harder, harder, imagining Selina Oliver in the most depraved positions. Imagining her pleasure as he took her, claimed her, made her say his name before she could come.

And then the pleasure peaked, swift and powerful, and he groaned out *her* name as he came, covering the tip of himself so that he didn't stain his trousers.

He sat there for what felt like a lifetime, too sluggish from pleasure to get up and put himself back together. At least that was done. It would mute whatever desire still burned in his veins for this unexpected woman he could not want. Should not pursue. Certainly shouldn't kiss.

He would be focused now. And that would be the end of it.

He pushed to his feet at last and tucked himself back in. He washed his hands in the small basin and then smoothed his hair and straightened his jacket. With a sigh, he headed out of the chamber and downstairs to the parlor where the party would gather shortly. He found Barber waiting for him, and he turned as Derrick entered.

"You are never late," Barber said with a laugh. "I was going to send out a search party."

"It was five minutes," Derrick muttered, perhaps with less good nature than his friend's teasing required. He hadn't told Barber about the kiss. He had no intention of doing so.

Barber wrinkled his brow at the sharp response, then shrugged. "The others will be here soon. Should we discuss our strategy?"

Derrick shook off his ill humor and nodded. "Yes. But one moment." He moved back to the door and checked the hallway. As Barber watched him, he crossed to the window and checked it, as well. Once burned, twice shy, after all.

"You can never be too careful," Barber said.

Derrick shrugged. "Apparently not. But we seem to be in the clear." He did not add *this time*, though those words rang in his head and reminded him, once again, of Selina. He cleared his throat and returned to business. "With Lord and Lady Winford's arrival tomorrow, the investigation will take on a more urgent tenor. We need to be organized. What are your thoughts on the party so far? Do you have any suspicions?"

"Based on our guidelines that the thief must have some level of access to Society, some way to move within their circles without being suspected and someone who is also here..." Barber pulled a notebook from his pocket. "I still think Mr. Grimes is a potential."

"I agree," Derrick said, pleased to be back in the game. "When I sat beside him at supper last night, he was...well, he wasn't my favorite person. Now he might have been rude because of my station in comparison to his own..."

"You're both grandsons of earls," Barber said with a shrug. "He has little room to judge."

"Perhaps, but that never stops them," Derrick said. "You know that more than most."

Barber gave a wry smile. "I'll give you that. We'll keep a closer look on Mr. Grimes, and perhaps we can have Roseford give a little nudge to make him friendlier."

Derrick shifted. "The next name on my list is going to be more complicated, especially when it comes to our host." He lowered his voice a little and whispered, "I wonder if we must look closer at the Duke of Sheffield."

"I thought the same thing, though I hate it," Barber said with a shake of his head. "I sat near the duke and duchess at supper last night, as you know, and they are charming companions. They're kind and clearly in love with each other."

"But Sheffield's financial problems are at least somewhat well-known. I've heard whispers that Lord and Lady Winford were invited here because Sheffield wanted to discuss an investment with the earl."

"That is the saving grace," Barber said. "Sheffield was very open about how he's working with Grayson Danford on a number of projects. Danford's canals made a good deal of money in the last few years, Sheffield was in with him from the start."

Derrick nodded slowly. "So he's rebuilding his fortune by what appears to be legitimate means."

"That seems to be the case," Barber agreed. "So while I wouldn't remove him from our list of suspects, he has exactly the access the Fox would need and a motive for taking jewels of value. But I'd move him lower on the list."

"I spoke to some of the staff, as well," Derrick said. "With a little persuasion..."

"Payment?" Barber teased.

Derrick laughed. "It's the client's money, not mine. But yes, greasing a few palms never hurt anyone. A few seemed uncertain about the footman of Squire Barton Filligrew. I had the impression, without pushing so hard that I aroused suspicion of my own, that he has some odd habits and movements."

Barber wrinkled his brow. "A squire could very well have been invited to the events where items were stolen. And his footman would certainly be able to sneak in without much notice. I have the guest lists we compiled from the previous events where items were taken. I'll cross check, though you know it isn't perfect."

"I know." Derrick sighed. "Uninvited guests seem to come to every party. It is the way of Society. But it makes our job so much harder."

Barber tilted his head. "And who is the uninvited guest here?"

Derrick's eyes went wide. "A very good question. One I'll raise with our friend the Duke of Roseford when I next get a moment of his attention. We should also examine those who come with Winford."

Barber nodded. "It would make sense. If the thief resides with Lady Winford herself, they would want to wait until a larger party to make their move rather than steal the necklace at home. I'll make inquiries as soon as they arrive. Is that everyone?"

"I don't know." Derrick paced the room, restless energy unable to let him be still. "It feels incomplete somehow. Like we're missing something."

Barber checked his notes. "If we are, I can't see it. But I trust your instincts, so we'll keep digging. We're going to catch the Fox, Huntington. I feel it in my bones."

Derrick nodded, buoyed by his friend's certainty, but before he could respond, the door to the parlor opened and Selina stepped into the room. And when she sent a knowing, playful smile his way...well, it was more than his heart that throbbed. She didn't make her way toward them, a fact for which he was both grateful and disappointed. She moved to the sideboard to peruse the liquor lined up for the guests and the door opened again as others began to trickle into the room for the pre-supper gathering.

"You still with me?" Barber asked.

Derrick blinked and forced his attention back to his friend. "Yes, yes, of course. I'm fine. I'm here. I'm listening," he stammered out.

Barber's eyebrows lifted and he stared at him a moment. Then he nodded slowly. "Yes, you seem very present. What is our game plan, then, for tonight?"

Derrick edged to the side, putting his back to Selina, who was now perched on the edge of the settee, engaged in close conversation with none other than Mr. Grimes. If the gentleman had been standoffish with Derrick, he was certainly not with Selina. Before Derrick cut off his sightline to the pair, Grimes was leaning forward, engrossed by her...or her breasts, for that was where the gentleman kept looking. Derrick fisted his hands at his sides in frustration.

"We..." He shook his head. "We should see who we're seated next to at supper tonight. That will help guide who we garner information from without arousing suspicion. Then we regroup after the meal and see if we need to dig a little deeper with any one person or persons."

Barber nodded. "If you don't mind, I think I will start with Mr.

Grimes. It seems Miss Oliver has left his side and he is temporarily alone."

Derrick pivoted and found, indeed, Selina had left Grimes's side. She had moved to her brother and sister-in-law and was smiling brightly as she chatted with them. A real smile. Not as playful or cheeky as the one she always gifted him. That smile that was a test... and she probably designed it that way.

Barber continued, oblivious to Derrick's thoughts. "Perhaps he'll be more amenable to speaking to me than he was to you."

"Excellent," Derrick said, and scanned the room to see if he could find a target as far away from Selina as possible. He found Squire Barton Filligrew at the fire. "I'll talk to Squire Filligrew. I believe he knows my grandfather, so it's as good a time as ever to trade on the earl's good name."

"He'd love that," Barber chuckled as the two men parted ways. Derrick crossed the room slowly, trying to maintain a casual air, when in reality, he was massively aware of everything in the room around him. Including the woman across it, the one whose lips he could still taste, even though it had been half a day since he'd claimed them.

Selina traced her fingertip along the edge of her wine glass as she surveyed the room around her. Supper had been uneventful, unlike the previous night. She had not been seated near Derrick this time, so that gave her a little breathing room.

Of course, it also had given her a chance to observe him talk to those around him. She couldn't hear him, but his body language was fascinating. The way he leaned in when he was curious. The way his cheek twitched just before he smiled. The way it didn't when the smile was false.

She also got to observe him as he watched the room at large. He was a collector, that much was obvious. Gathering up little bits of information, cataloguing them in his mind. Hunting the Fox.

Hunting *her*.

And that idea should have terrified her, but when his gaze flitted to her from time to time, when his pupils dilated with what was obviously desire, she didn't mind being hunted. Captured by a man like that? Oh, the possibilities were endless. An intelligent mind like his would surely find a thousand ways to…punish her. Her body ached even now thinking about it.

She shook her head. Supper was long over now, the men and women of the group had separated and now regathered. There was talk of games and shadow puppets as an entertainment. No one's attention was on her, even his. A good thing, probably. The space allowed her to collect herself.

And to make a move that had nothing to do with Derrick Huntington. Since Lord and Lady Winford were to arrive tomorrow, she had sent Vale out to speak to the servants and find out which chamber was to be theirs. Her "companion" had come back just before supper with the answer. Tonight, Selina meant to do reconnaissance. This was the time to do it, when the room was distracted by boisterous laughter and the servants moving tables and setting up games.

She stepped into the hall and her shoulders pushed back. She was the Faceless Fox now, and she felt the costume of that persona fall over her. Her footfalls came lighter, her awareness was higher, she focused, forgetting all the things that had been distracting her since her arrival. What mattered now was the chamber. What mattered now was discovering entries and exits, hiding places, all the details that would make her final attack all the more successful.

She reached the guest quarters quickly. Of course it was quiet. Right now the household and its staff were distracted, so it was the perfect time. She stepped up to the door of the chamber and tested it. Not locked, not yet, as no one was staying there. She smiled.

"Selina?"

She froze at the deep voice behind her, saying her name for only the second time. How it moved her, those three syllables in that voice. And terrified her, for she had been right and truly caught.

She pivoted and Derrick stood there, arms folded across his broad chest, staring at her. Her breath caught and she forced a smile.

"D-Derrick." The missish stammer and heated blush which flooded her cheeks came easily, for the man unnerved her. Luckily they also served as a mask to protect her.

He arched a brow. "What are you doing here?"

CHAPTER 7

S elina swallowed and drew a long breath to calm her racing
mind. She'd been in difficult situations before, almost caught,
and had always found a way out. She needed to do the same now.
She just had to find an excuse. Except when Derrick speared her
with those dark brown eyes, thoughts and plans and strategies were
much harder to find.

"I was just about to go into my room," she blurted out, and
immediately regretted it because his jaw set.

"That isn't your room," he said softly, arching a brow as if daring
her to press on her lie.

She glanced at the door and back at him. She needed to get
herself back together, and quickly. She took a breath to calm her
throbbing heart and come back to herself. She was the Fox, after all.
She knew how to do this.

She smiled. "How silly of me. These big houses, you know, I get
so turned around. Of course it's that way." She motioned behind
him toward her actual chamber and then stepped forward, determined to pass him by and play this farce out.

He wouldn't allow it. As she brushed past him, his hand snaked
out and he caught her elbow, gently but firmly. She was captured,

caught, far too close to him, far too aware as she tilted her face up toward his. He was leaning down, and it felt like there was only a breath between them. Her heart began to pound again, wild in her chest, fear and need combined and it was...intoxicating. He was intoxicating, and in that moment she wanted to just drink him down and let herself be changed for a little while.

"Selina," he whispered, his voice rough in the quiet, but demanding. Firm.

She shifted, but didn't try to escape his grip. She didn't want to. But she did need a better explanation. She dipped her chin and batted her eyelashes. "I'm *sorry*. I know you told me not to, but I wanted so much to help you."

He let out his breath in a long sigh and his grip loosened slightly. He believed her. She didn't feel particularly good about that. About the lie. Even if it was necessary to stay alive, stay protected.

"Don't make that sound," she continued. "I just thought I might look at Lady Winford's chamber and see if I could garner any information about it to share with you."

"I don't need help," he said. Then his lips pursed. "Though it is a good idea. It was mine, too, actually, to check out the chamber before the earl and countess arrived tomorrow."

"You see! I am well-suited to help you!" she insisted.

The corner of his lip twitched like he wanted to smile, though he didn't. She reached up and covered his hand with hers, feeling the lean strength of those long fingers as she brushed them.

"Please," she whispered. "It isn't truly dangerous, is it? Lord and Lady Winford aren't here yet—no one will be in the room. I can help. Two heads and two pairs of eyes are better than one."

His breath exited his lips again in another sigh, but this one she thought might be of acquiescence. He glared down at her, an unyielding look that curled her toes in her slippers, even as she tried to remain unmoved by it. By him. By...*this*. Whatever this was.

"It's not a...*bad* idea," he said with a shake of his head. "And since you are here and I am here, then yes. We can search the room together."

She grinned up at him. "Excellent! I'm so pleased."

His fingers tightened on her arm and his thumb moved slightly, stroking the underside of her bicep and sending a shiver up her spine. "But Selina, you must understand, this is the end of your grand adventure. After this, you must remove yourself from any idea that you'll help me investigate."

She found her breath. "Yes, Derrick," she whispered.

His pupils dilated at those two words and he released her, stepping back. "Is the door locked?"

"No," she said, facing the barrier again so that she wouldn't have to look at him. "It's unlocked."

"Then let's go," he said. "Before more *helpful* guests arrive and we have to move the entire party into the chamber."

∼

Derrick tried to find his focus, but it was almost impossible to do as Selina opened the chamber door and stepped into the darkness. It obscured her figure, making her nothing more than alluring curves and edges. Things he so wanted to explore, even though he shouldn't. Just as he shouldn't have let her come search the room with him.

But it was happening, so he had to make the best of it.

The room was unlit, of course. No servant would light a fire here until tomorrow when the earl and countess were closer to arrival. As a result, Selina was just a shadow as his eyes adjusted. A shadow who seemed very comfortable in the dark, for she moved forward and found a candle. He heard flint rasp and then she turned, the light haloing around her face.

"There's another one here, take this one." She held out the candle and he took it. Their fingers brushed and the same awareness that had shot through him when he took her arm in the hall rocketed through him now. More intense because they were alone. In a bedchamber. And no one was going to come looking for them here.

He cleared his throat and watched her light a second candle off the flame of his.

"Very good," he muttered, wishing he could think of something better to say. He backed away and turned to begin pacing the perimeter of the room. He wanted a sense of its scale, the edges of it. While he did so, he occasionally glanced over his shoulder.

Selina wasn't asking him about his actions, but was deliberately acting on her own. She opened empty drawers, feeling into them. She felt floorboards, and sometimes the candlelight caught her gaze and he saw her looking at the door to the hallway and to the dressing room attached to the main chamber.

Exits and entrances. She was clever to naturally understand the importance of those things.

"Lady Winford is..." She paused and then laughed. "Have you ever met her?"

He darted his gaze up. "I haven't," he admitted. "Not exactly my circles, not anymore."

Her eyes flitted over his face. "Not anymore? Were you once of my brother's world? The Upper Ten Thousand, as they love to be called? I suppose that makes the rest of us the Lower Million."

He smiled but didn't argue the point. "I, er, had some attachment to this world once, yes. My grandfather is the Earl of Brillshire. My father is his third son."

Her eyes went a bit wide and she tilted her head. "You almost sound embarrassed by that fact."

"My grandfather is embarrassed by me. I suppose I return the favor when I can," he said, and then wished he could take those words back. Although many people in the ton knew of his relationship to the earl and that allowed him access to their problems for his work, he didn't speak of the man often.

Nor to him.

Selina turned her back on him and moved to a writing table. She opened each drawer carefully, then shut them before she said, "I don't know why he should be."

"He doesn't like that I didn't follow the path he laid out for me," Derrick said, trying not to let the pain he'd once felt at that rejection pass through his blood. "He wanted me to be someone *important*. He wanted to pay my way into the service as an officer. When I refused that...well, our relationship soured."

She glanced at him from the corner of her eye. "You had an honorable military career, escaped with your life, but only barely, and now you help people with their problems. How could all those wonderful things be considered unimportant?"

"You ought to know," he said. "You grew up the same way I did."

She froze and slowly turned. He could see her struggle on her face in that moment, the mask gone to reveal a real flash of pain. And of battle. Like she was waging war with herself about what she would say next.

He leaned closer as he waited, holding his breath.

"No, I didn't," she said at last. "I may be the daughter of a duke as a point of order, but as a truth, I was just a bastard. I didn't grow up in this world. I didn't have any link to it. My life couldn't be more removed from it until..."

Derrick moved a step closer, drawn in by this little tidbit about the woman who was taking up all the air in the room at present. All the air in his lungs, at least. "Until?"

She pursed her lips. "It's a boring story. I'm sorry I started it. The fact is that I'm not of this world, and my brother, for some reason, is not embarrassed of me. He is currently parading all his bastard siblings out, helping us all make a future for ourselves."

"You sound bitter about it," Derrick said softly.

She shrugged. "I shouldn't be. He means well. He wants...he wants to be something more than our father was. And he is that. Robert is far and away a better man. I'm lucky, I know. But I'm not of this world. And I never will be."

She took a short breath, like she was gathering herself, then smiled at him. There was the mask again. Flirtatious, outrageous, wicked to the core, but in the very best way.

"But I *have* met Lady Winford," she continued, and stepped up to him, now just a few inches away. He could reach out a hand and touch her without even fully extending his arm. But he wouldn't, even if his palm itched to do so.

"And you think your interior knowledge of the lady will help me?" he asked.

She giggled. "Oh no. All I can tell you is that she is a raving bitch. One of the worst people I've ever had the displeasure of meeting. Picture the nastiest, most petty person of power you've ever met. Not evil, mind you. Not criminal. Just...*mean*. Mean to those she wields power over, mean to those she ought to protect. *That* is Lady Winford."

He arched a brow. "That sounds personal."

"Everything is personal, Derrick," she said with a little shrug. "When it's happening to people. So when I'm walking around this room I'm trying to put myself in her wicked, nasty, tiny little mind. Trying to ask myself where I'd hide the Breston necklace if I were Lady Winford."

He stared at her a moment, eyes widening at what she'd just said. His hackles and his suspicions rising with every passing second. "How do you know that what the Fox is after is the Breston necklace?"

She arched a brow at him as if that was a foolish question. "I don't," she said. "But what else would it possibly be? Lady Winford inherited the piece recently. Everyone knows it is of great value—she makes certain we all know that. Exactly the sort of thing this Faceless Fox man seems to take regularly...under everyone's nose. I assumed."

"Clever," he said softly.

"Thank you," she said, and he picked up the pink of her blush even in the dimness of the room. "I try."

"You might do better at this investigation thing than I gave you credit for. You seem to be able to enter the mind of the person you are looking into."

She shrugged. "Oh, only sometimes. Perhaps because I've had negative interactions with Lady Winford, that makes it easier. Should we look at the dressing room?"

He nodded and stepped toward the adjoining door. She was at his elbow as he did, the warm vanilla scent of her teasing his nostrils and heating his blood. He needed to get himself back under control, but it was becoming increasingly difficult the longer he stood at this woman's side. It was torture.

They entered the dressing room and repeated their search as they had in the main chamber. Only this time, Selina stayed with him, watching what he watched, noting what he noted. She was a quick study and occasionally made observations that even he had missed about the room or its contents.

"I think that's all we—*I* need," he said as he turned to go back into the main chamber. He stepped left as he said it, but she moved right and collided with his chest.

He reached out to steady her, his fingers closing around her bare arms for the second time that night. And he was just as moved this time by her soft skin and the feel of her so close.

He cleared his throat as he released her and stepped around her and into the other room. "As you can see, it isn't that exciting," he said, wishing his voice wasn't so rough with desire he shouldn't feel.

"I wouldn't agree with that," she said, following him into the chamber and shutting the door. "It was quite...titillating."

He frowned as he faced her. There was that flirtatious, playful expression again. The one that challenged him and taunted him and tormented him and made him want to pull her against his chest. The one that made her so irresistible.

"I should apologize for what happened in the orangery this afternoon."

Her eyebrows lifted. "Why?"

He pursed his lips. "Is that a real question, Selina?"

JESS MICHAELS

The teasing faded from her face and she folded her arms, a sudden flare of armor to protect herself. "Well, we both know each other's background, don't we? Do you not think me good enough to kiss now?"

"You know that isn't it. And it isn't for a lack of wanting, which I have a sense you know equally well." He let out a sigh and ran his fingers through his hair. "You are a lady, whatever your past may have been, and—"

She waved her hand and cut him off with a snort of derision. "Please, don't start reading to me from the book of good behavior for ladies," she snapped, her voice elevating. "I am *not* some innocent made of glass who doesn't know what she wants."

The passion of those words, the intensity of their tone, the meaning of them hit him in the chest like a shot. He rocked back a fraction. "And what do you want, Selina?"

He heard himself say those words, laced with innuendo, going against every promise he'd been trying to make to himself about propriety and decency and boundaries in the home of this duke who allowed him to investigate within his party. He wanted to take them back. He also wanted to know the answer.

She smiled. "I liked kissing you," she said, her tone soft and breathless in the dimness of the room. She set her candle down on the table by the door. "And you liked kissing me. I felt it. Are you going to lie and tell me you didn't?"

He shifted as she eased up in front of him, her breasts just barely brushing his chest, her fingers tracing the top of his hand. "I don't lie," he whispered.

She smiled again, this time softer, and lifted up on her tiptoes. Closer and closer, almost to heaven. He should have pulled away, but he didn't. He should have refused, but he couldn't. Only just before she could brush her lips to his, there was the sound of a door closing in the dressing room behind them. Likely the servants coming in through their entrance to finish readying the room.

He expected Selina to gasp and blush and duck away, but instead

70

she caught his hand with a soft giggle and pulled him toward the door. Like this was a game. Like it was fun. He followed, letting her drag him into the hallway.

The bright light of the lamps there hit him, and it was like reality smashing him in the face with a frying pan. He wanted to kiss this woman. He wanted to do far more than just kiss her. But that didn't mean he should. That didn't mean he *could*.

She pivoted back and grinned at him. "Just barely escaped. But that's what makes it exciting, isn't it?"

He caught his breath and clenched his fists at his sides so he wouldn't touch her. Then he said, "Selina, I did enjoy kissing you. And I won't lie, everything in me wants to it again and again and again."

"Good," she whispered.

"But," he said, catching her hands as she tried to lift them to his lapels. "*But* I'm not here for pleasure. And if I go too far, there won't be any going back. So we can't do it again."

Her gaze flitted to his mouth and held there for a moment. Then she sighed as she looked back up at him. He readied himself for arguments or even tears. But she didn't do either. She just extracted her hand from his and placed it on his chest.

"Not even once?" she whispered.

The control he'd worked so hard on practicing frayed to the point of breaking as he looked down into those stunning blue eyes. His body leaned in toward her without him wanting it to, his hands unclenched so he could reach one out and skim it along her side.

"Once," he acquiesced. Then he dropped his mouth to hers.

She lifted into him, gripping his lapels with both hands and pulling him harder into her. Her mouth opened, welcoming him, her tongue greeting him and tangling with his own in a passionate display of desire and need. He drowned in it for a moment, that voice telling him he shouldn't fading deep into the background as he took and took and took what she offered. As his body edged him toward taking even more.

But it was she who broke the kiss this time. She nipped his lower lip just a fraction, scraping the tender flesh with her teeth, and then backed away, smoothing her skirts with both hands.

"Good evening, Mr. Huntington," she said, arching a brow, as if daring him to break his control even more.

He drew in a few rough breaths and then forced himself to say, "Good evening, Miss Oliver."

He turned on his heel and marched away, back toward the party they had each abandoned for their own purposes. Away from the temptation he could not surrender to again. Even if it meant every night he was here would be one he dreamed of her and took his pleasure in his hand in frustration.

CHAPTER 8

"I keep thinking about that servants' entrance into the dressing room," Barber said, sifting through his notes without looking up at Derrick.

A good thing, too, or he likely would have commented on the far-off expression Derrick knew was plastered on his face. How could it not be? All he could think about were those two kisses from the previous day.

"Yes, the servants' entrance," he repeated, dragging himself back to the present with difficulty. He shifted papers around on the desk that Roseford had provided in a private chamber where he and Barber could work. "It's the perfect opportunity to access Lord and Lady Winford's chamber, even when they're in it. And we...*I* found a few places where the countess might hide her jewels, as well."

"We?" Barber repeated. "Are you royalty now, Huntington?"

"Something like that," Derrick said with a chuckle he hoped would put his far-too-clever friend off the scent. How else could he explain taking Selina Oliver into the room, investigating with her? Barber would tear into him. Derrick would deserve it.

"Are you certain you're...well?" Barber asked, pushing his papers aside and leaned forward. His dark eyes were filled with worry, and guilt tugged in Derrick's chest.

"I'm fine," Derrick lied. "Right as rain."

Barber tilted his head. "Seeing Gillingham before we left London brought back memories for me—I assume it is the same for you. Not all of them good. And being here, amongst these toffs, it must be odd after being out of that life for so long."

Derrick shifted, thinking of what he'd told Selina about his grandfather. About his past. And what she'd said in return. That unexpected confidence had stirred up some old feelings. Ones he'd thought he'd buried.

"Gillingham nearly lost his life for us," he said softly. "You and me and all the others. So I suppose I do feel a sense of responsibility when it comes to this case because we've involved him. As for my family, certainly being back in halls like this, Your-Gracing and my-lording all these...toffs is the best word...well, it's odd. Perhaps I'm not on my top game, just as you suggest."

Barber shook his head. "You're always on your top game, mate. You don't have any other option, it seems. Run, run, run. Go, go, go. It's what makes you the best. But if there's something I can do to help—"

Derrick lifted a hand to stop him. He couldn't let Barber go on offering him assistance when the problem was Derrick's cock and what it so inappropriately wanted.

"Don't worry about me, friend," he assured him. "When the Winford party arrives today, I will be more than ready to play the game."

Barber looked as though he might say more, but before he could, there was a knock on the chamber door. Derrick turned toward it. "Yes?"

The door opened and the Duke of Roseford stood in the entry-way. "Gentlemen," he said. "I'm sorry to disturb your work. May I come in?"

Derrick and Barber both pushed to their feet and Derrick nodded. "Of course, Your Grace. What can we do for you?"

Roseford stepped into the chamber and softly shut the door behind him. His face was lined with worry as he paced around the room. "Ah, good. It seems you've been set up well here. I assume your private accommodations are comfortable, as well?"

"Very much so, Your Grace," Barber said with a brief, questioning look at Derrick. "Your home is beautifully appointed and both of us have been made to feel most welcome."

"And you are," Roseford said, facing them. "Genuinely. You are both a wonderful addition to the party. All my brother's kind words about you have proven to be true. But I have...concerns."

His gaze flitted to Derrick as he said those words, and Derrick's stomach clenched. Did Roseford know? Did he know about what had happened with Selina? Had she told him in a fit of conscience? Had someone seen them imprudently kissing in the hallway? That was a recipe for being called out or kicked out. And Barber would be furious, rightly so, as would Nicholas Gillingham.

"Of course, Your Grace," Derrick said cautiously. "What is on your mind?"

He braced himself for the answer as Roseford took a long step toward them, his gaze still locked on Derrick. "The Winfords will arrive today. I've had word it will be some time after luncheon."

Barber nodded slowly. "Very good. Then we can really begin our investigation."

Roseford shifted, his discomfort evident on every line of his face, every restless movement of his body. He drew in a deep breath, and Derrick braced himself, but instead of confronting him about Selina, Roseford asked, "Will you two discuss the danger to them when they arrive?"

Derrick blinked, shocked that he had misread the situation so entirely. When he didn't answer immediately, Barber stepped forward, shooting him a pointed look as he said, "Well, Your Grace, that is a consideration we must make on many of these cases. To reveal or not to reveal."

"And why would you...not, if you don't mind my asking," Roseford pressed.

Derrick shook off his reactions, his bad assumptions, and focused. If he didn't, it was only going to cause more trouble. "The Winfords were not the ones who hired us, Your Grace. We are simply using the threat against them in order to find the Faceless Fox."

Roseford nodded. "I understand that and it makes sense on one hand. But on the other, these people are my guests, even if they are not my friends. They are coming to my home with a certain expectation of security and safety. I'm a bit uncomfortable with knowing there is a threat against them, but not telling them the truth. The danger is real, is it not?"

"The Fox has never been violent. In fact, just the opposite. Even in tricky situations, he uses his cunning, not weaponry or his fists. Not a single victim has ever been in physical threat of any kind, even the smallest."

Barber sniffed behind him. His partner always complained that Derrick was too quick to defend the Fox. Where Derrick respected some of the man's clever methods, Barber only saw a criminal.

He ignored the sound of derision and continued, "I understand your concerns. They speak very highly of your respectability."

Roseford laughed at that. "Perish that thought. Certainly never spread it around, I have a reputation to uphold, you know."

Derrick and Barber both laughed at the quip, and it was genuine. It was impossible not to like the man.

"For now," Derrick continued, "I'd like to leave what we're doing a secret. If only so that Lord and Lady Winford act naturally and don't alert the Fox to the truth about our presence here. The fewer people who know the truth, the less likely it is that he'll realize we're right on his tail."

Roseford seemed to ponder that for a moment, then nodded.

"Very well, that makes sense. I assume if anything changes, we'll reevaluate at that point."

"Indeed," Barber said. "And keep you apprised about anything that requires your assistance."

"Thank you. I'm not trying to be troublesome or interfere in something I know nothing about. I just feel a certain obligation to my guests and my family."

"Understandably," Derrick said, his mind flashing to one of Roseford's family members in particular. The man would be furious if he knew Derrick was allowing Selina to flit around in this investigation. And kissing her. And wanting to do far more than kiss her.

"I'll leave you to your work," Roseford said. "I need to see my wife, and then we'll ready for the arrival of our final guests. Until later, gentlemen." He inclined his head, then left the room.

When he was gone and they were alone, Barber speared Derrick with a sharp gaze. "What were you concerned about when he came in?"

"Concerned?" Derrick said with a scoffing laugh he hoped covered the truth. "What could I be concerned about?"

"I saw your face," Barber pushed. "I know you."

"Damn but you do, it's annoying as hell," Derrick said with a chuckle. "I like Roseford, I do. He seems a decent fellow. I just don't want him interfering, even with the best of intentions."

Barber narrowed his gaze, and Derrick could tell he didn't completely trust the lie. But he sighed as he retook his place and pulled his paperwork back toward him.

"You're not wrong," Barber said. "And that's why we don't generally involve outsiders in investigations. It only ever leads to trouble." He glanced up. "Also, you're a bloody awful liar, at least to me. But you can keep your counsel on your troubles if that's what you like. I just hope it won't endanger our case."

Derrick forced himself to meet Barber's eyes. "It won't," he promised. "I'll be sure of it."

That seemed to appease Barber, for he went back to organizing his notes. But Derrick's own words did nothing to appease himself. He knew the trouble he was in. He knew the cause of it. And he knew he had to get back into total control now or risk more than this case.

～

Selina stood on the drive beside her brother, watching as a carriage came up the long road from the gate toward the estate house. Her heart jumped as she watched it, because she knew her quarry was inside. The necklace she had been longing for since she heard of its existence, the woman who deserved the loss of such a beautiful thing—everything was coming together at last, and she could barely keep from bouncing with excitement.

As the carriage pulled onto the drive, she hesitated, for she felt a prickle up the back of her neck. Like she was being watched. She turned and looked up at the house. The front parlor window had its shades pulled open and there, standing at the glass, was Derrick Huntington.

Not a huge surprise considering her quarry was tied to his own investigation. Of course he would come to watch the arrival, read the situation as he so frustratingly could. Except he wasn't. He wasn't looking at the hustle and bustle on the drive.

He was watching her. His gaze burned into her from behind the glass, and she felt her body react even if it shouldn't. Even if she didn't want it to. When he looked at her with that stern, focused stare, she wanted things that went beyond a seduction to gain control. She wanted more than sex for fun or to make her true motives invisible to him. She wanted pleasure. She wanted burning, powerful sensation. She wanted all the promises she saw in those eyes, the ones he tried to fight. And it had nothing to fucking do with a necklace or the Faceless Fox.

Just like the previous night in the Winfords' chamber hadn't been about the jewels or his investigation. She had...told him things.

About her life, about her past. Things she didn't speak about to anyone. Why? *How* had he drawn that from her without effort?

Was it the darkness of the room, where confession felt safe? Was it the strange, powerful energy that seemed to course through them? Was it the thrill of the hunt, one she rarely shared with another person? Vale might be her associate, but she only did research, distraction when necessary. The Fox worked alone. Until last night when Selina had searched the room alongside a man bound to hunt her down.

In the end, perhaps it didn't matter *why* she'd whispered about her past, her father, to Derrick. She'd done it, and now she was... vulnerable. She couldn't be vulnerable. Not with what was to come.

"Selina?"

She jolted as she realized Katherine had laid a hand on her arm and drawn her back to the situation right in front of her. She pivoted around and found Lady Winford standing before her. The woman was lovely, no one would deny her that. She had thick, rich auburn hair that was done just so, bright green eyes and a wicked sneer on her lips as she glanced up and down Selina's form.

"May I present our sister, Selina Oliver," Katherine said, squeezing Selina's elbow gently in a movement of solidarity.

She needed it, for though the countess gave a polite greeting, it was clear she thought nothing of Selina. Because everyone in Society knew exactly what Selina was. Or at least most of what she was.

The nasty expression on the countess's face was almost the same as if she had whispered the words *they* loved to say behind Selina's back. *Bastard. By-blow. Illegitimate. Not our kind.*

"Lady Winford," Selina forced herself to say. "I've heard so much about you. What a pleasure to finally meet you."

She could risk that lie because she doubted this woman remembered the real first time they'd met. In passing at some other party. When Selina had watched her berate a servant until the girl was weeping hysterically. The servant had been sacked, out on the street before the next morning. And Lady Winford had flounced off with a smirk on her face, ready to go back to her damned party and dance the rest of the night away.

She wouldn't remember Selina. She probably wouldn't remember the servant. People like her never did.

"Indeed," Lady Winford said with a sniff.

"And this is Lord Winford," Katherine said, motioning to the man coming up to stand beside his wife.

The earl was an older man, far older than his wife, with a perpetual scowl and temples that had gone further gray every year of his marriage. The whispers around Town were that the man was miserable, despised his wife and hated that she crowed about inheriting her mother's necklace. All of which could potentially be used against the couple. Selina would just have to watch how their interactions played out, how they moved together.

"My lord," she said, smiling at the man. Of course his gaze moved to her breasts. God, these fools were easy to manipulate.

"Come into the house, why don't you?" Robert said, his voice strained as he motioned the party inside. "I'm sure you're tired after your long journey. My man Jenner will show you to your chamber and see to any needs you have before tea this afternoon."

Lady Winford was complaining about something as she followed Robert into the house, all but dragging her husband behind her. As they went in, Selina and Katherine exchanged a look, and Katherine smothered a giggle.

"She is just as pleasant as I recalled," she whispered conspiratorially. "Perhaps even more so."

"Yes, she's…something," Selina said, forcing herself not to go too far. Temperance was best in these situations, and she had to find it even though she knew her own personality. Restraint had never been one of her virtues. She linked her arm through Katherine's as they slowly made their way up the stairs to the house. "You and Robert are good to invite her to help your friend."

"We take care of those we love," Katherine said, with almost a faraway tone. Then she pivoted and looked Selina full in the face. "*All* of them. It's the best thing we can do, isn't it?"

Selina was torn by two different emotions. First was a strong pull at the idea that her brother and his remarkable wife...loved her. She'd believed they tolerated her, yes. Felt responsible for her, of course. Even liked her from time to time when she was particularly clever or reminded them of the good parts of Robert's wild past.

But Katherine was obviously trying to say that it was more than all those things. And that touched Selina's heart far deeper than perhaps it should have.

The other feeling that clenched in her chest at those words was colder. Sharper. If Katherine was saying that she and Robert loved Selina, that meant the love could be lost. If they knew the truth about her...if they found out she was the Faceless Fox, would they love her anymore? Could they?

Or would they abandon her like the rest of her family had all those years ago?

"Selina?" Katherine said, squeezing her hand gently as they stood in the doorway between the outside and the foyer. "You've gone pale. I hope I haven't upset you."

"Not at all," Selina choked as she forced a smile. She refused to lose her new family's love, for she wasn't going to get caught. She was the Fox, damn it.

"Oh, it looks like Jenner is glancing my way, with a look of help all over his countenance. I ought to intervene before Lady Winford causes my staff to go on strike."

Selina released her with a more real smile and watched as she hustled away, that easy expression of calm on her face. Katherine had been through a great deal. Scandal had once followed her. But now she seemed so comfortable in herself. She'd once told Selina that love had helped do that. Robert had allowed her to have faith where once she'd only questioned.

Selina turned away with a wince and found herself facing the parlor where she'd seen Derrick standing a short time ago. Was he still there? She ought not to go find out. Right now she was a bit discombobulated, off her game thanks to the emotional connection Katherine had implied. Selina shouldn't face an...well, she supposed she had to call Derrick an enemy since he was hunting her.

And yet she couldn't resist doing just that. She slipped away from the chaos of the foyer and into the room.

He wasn't standing by the window anymore, but he was in front of the fire. Just standing there, arms folded, gaze focused on the door...as if he were waiting for her. He was not wearing a jacket. She could see it draped across the back of a chair behind him. Just a plain black waistcoat and the sleeves of his linen shirt rolled up to his elbows, revealing muscular forearms. One of them had a scar across it.

Behind her, the voices in the foyer faded as Jenner and Katherine finally convinced Lord and Lady Winford to go and see their accommodations. In that moment, Selina and Derrick were alone.

"Mr. Huntington," she said at last, her voice far softer than it should be. The tremor there was something he would surely mark.

He cleared his throat, but his voice was still low and rough when he said, "Miss Oliver."

Her breath felt very short as she stared at him. She'd never met a man who caused that cliché loss of breath, but here he was, standing in her brother's parlor. She had to regain some control of herself, for God's sake.

So she arched a brow and retook control. "Whatever did you determine, Mr. Huntington, when you were watching me so intently on the drive?"

She saw the flutter of frustration on his face, but also interest. Her smile grew more real at both of those. She liked testing him. It was fun, as well as functional.

He shifted a fraction and then took a long step in her direction. He seemed to loom up in front of her, too tall and too present and just...too. She edged a bit nearer, as well, and now they were less than an arm's length apart.

"I was watching Lady Winford," he said.

She smiled at the lie and tilted her head toward him. "If you say so."

His jaw clenched a little. There was that control, balanced on a knife's blade. And she still wanted to know what would happen if she ever...snapped it.

"Did she say anything of interest to you?" he asked.

She lifted her hands to her hips as she glared at him. "Oh, so now you want my help again."

"No, I only—" he began, but she didn't let him finish. She stopped him by lifting a hand and placing it flat against his chest. Through the fabric, she felt his heart rate elevate, saw his pupils dilate. Felt the coiled strength of him tighten all the more.

"*You* need to figure out what you *want*, Derrick Huntington." She drew out every syllable of his name.

His breath hitched, and the room seemed to shrink as he stared down at her. And even though this was exactly the position she'd been trying to create, exactly the game she'd come here to play, now that she was standing here, touching him, feeling the pulse of the instant, heated connection between them, she found herself backing away. Her hand dropped to her side and blood filled her cheeks.

"Good afternoon," she stammered, then turned and hustled from the room before he could catch her arm and draw her back. Before he could draw her in. Before he could draw her out and win the game that Derrick didn't even know they were playing.

CHAPTER 9

As much as she willed them not to, Selina's hands were still shaking as she burst into her chamber. She wanted a moment alone, perhaps to flop on her bed and relieve herself of some of the pesky desire that still pulsed through her. But it wasn't to be. Vale was perched on her bed, lazing against the pillows, and she sat up as Selina closed the door behind her.

"The bitch is here," Selina said without preamble.

She didn't need it, for those words brightened Vale's expression and she clapped her hands together. "Excellent! That means the necklace is too. All these plans, they're about to come to fruition at last!"

Vale was right, of course, but Selina was having a hard time finding pleasure in that fact. All she could think about was Katherine and her welcoming Selina into the family.

All she could think about was Derrick and the way those dark eyes just bored their way all the way to whatever was left of her soul.

"You seem out of sorts," Vale said, and her tone yanked Selina back into reality. "Why?"

Selina blinked and Vale's face fell. "How many years have we been friends?"

"Vale-"

"How many?" Vale repeated.

Selina sighed. "Seven. Since the night you saved my life."

"I've known your secret. Have I ever even come close to telling it?"

Selina shifted, for Vale was right. But the reason she felt out of sorts felt...different somehow. Personal. Emotional. It could be seen as a weakness. And weaknesses could always be used as ammunition.

Vale folded her arms. "Is it Huntington?"

"No!" Selina heard how loud that denial was. How falsely quick and forceful. "No," she repeated, with a bit more control this time.

But the damage was done. Vale pushed from the bed, and Selina could see how troubled her friend looked. "I'm *worried* about you. You had better get whatever this is under control, Selina. Or else it might end the Fox."

Without another word, Vale left the chamber. And Selina collapsed onto the bed she had abandoned with a shuddering sigh. Vale wasn't wrong. And that wasn't even the worst of it.

Whatever was happening might not just end her as the Fox. She feared that this unexpected attraction to a man who was so very dangerous might actually end her completely. Because she already felt turned inside out. And she feared Derrick could do far worse the closer he got.

"You just have to find a way to control *him*," Selina muttered. Only she feared that doing so would expose her. And she'd have to be on the top of her game to avoid just that.

Derrick stood toward the back of the large ballroom, leaning against the wall as he watched the festivities around him. Glittering gowns, perfectly polished boots, overly loud laughter, all of it grated on him. All of it made him patently aware of how far he'd moved away from this world, to the point where he didn't belong.

But this was where the case took him, so what could he do?

The Duke of Roseford had moved to an elevated platform where the orchestra had been playing, and he held up a hand. Immediately the room went silent, directed by a man who wielded power casually.

"Good evening," Roseford said with a smile over the room. "This first ball was slightly delayed, but now that all our friends have joined us at last, I am so pleased to welcome you to our home. Now go dance and make a scandal."

The party laughed for the most part, though a few of the more straight-laced attendees pulled faces at the order. As Roseford came down and the music began to play, those on the ballroom floor peeled back to make room for the dancing, and that was when Derrick saw her.

Selina was moving slowly in the middle of the room, no longer surrounded by the milling crowd. And she was...exquisite. Her gown was a robin's egg blue, designed to match those outrageous eyes to perfection. It was edged in gold, including a swath of sash that lifted her breasts right to the edge of the low neckline of the gown. She turned as if she sensed him and her gaze caught his across the room.

Bloody hell, but he wanted her.

Then the couples began to swarm the floor and she was hidden in their wake. He blinked as he realized Roseford had somehow approached while Derrick was distracted.

"Good evening, Your Grace," Derrick managed to choke out.

"Bit of a dry throat, eh?" Roseford said with a smile. "I can solve that problem." He waved for a footman, who came over with a tray of drinks. Roseford plucked two of them and handed one over.

Derrick slugged back half of it before he realized Roseford was staring at him with wide eyes. "Forgive me. The heat of the crowd, you know," he lied.

Roseford's eyebrows remained high, but he didn't question the lie. "I thought perhaps you'd like an introduction to Lord and Lady Winford, if you aren't already acquainted."

Derrick blinked. Yes, the Winfords. The duty he kept forgetting whenever Selina Oliver sashayed near him. The duty he had to remember now or risk losing the opportunity this man was giving him.

"Yes, thank you. That would be helpful."

Roseford motioned him to follow and weaved through the crowd. Derrick was a step behind him and noted how everyone he passed greeted Roseford. He was obviously well liked by all who knew him.

At last they reached the Winfords, who were standing to the side of the dancefloor. Derrick focused on them as they approached, taking in whatever facts he could glean before they noticed him and began to hide things. Lady Winford was very pretty, no one could deny that. Her gown was too tight around the bust, causing her breasts to nearly pop out like overstuffed sausages from the top. An effect he assumed she was trying to create.

But not for her husband, it seemed. Though they stood together, they were each turned slightly away from the other, not talking. Not interacting at all. There was no warmth there. No interest. Perhaps they'd had a row. Perhaps this was their usual state.

Derrick would have to find out. One never knew which information would be important in the future.

"Ah, Lord and Lady Winford," Roseford said as they reached their guests.

Both the earl and the countess perked up at his arrival. And why not? Roseford was important. To be invited to one of his soirees was an honor to many.

"Your Grace," Lady Winford purred, leaning forward to give a better look at those breasts she had on display. "What a pleasure to see you again."

Roseford didn't even take a downward glance at the lady's offering. "I'm glad you were able to recover from what sounded like a truly terrible travel experience and join us," he said. There was a little tension to his voice, a twitch to his cheek. He didn't like the pair, though he hid it well.

"We wouldn't miss it, Roseford," Lord Winford said with a sniff toward his wife.

"Have you met our good friend, Mr. Huntington?" Roseford said, motioning to Derrick with what appeared to be a genuine smile. "He served with my brother in the war."

Lord Winford's gaze flitted to him, over him, and immediately Derrick saw the dismissal. He'd be passably polite, of course, but he didn't see the value in a mere soldier.

Lady Winford, on the other hand, let her gaze linger as she swept it over him. There was interest there, but not of a friendly kind. Derrick shifted.

"Ah, I see my wife motioning me," Roseford said with an apologetic nod. "The life of a host is never slow. I hope to speak to you soon. Good evening."

He slipped into the crowd as the Winfords said their good evenings, and that left Derrick alone with them. Here was the open door. He just needed to find a way through it.

"You're not just some common soldier," Lady Winford said, tilting her head. "Why do I know your name? Huntington..."

Derrick stiffened at the way she said *common soldier*. Dismissive, but that was a familiar experience when it came to people of this sphere. They couldn't see value in anything that was different from themselves. As if the luck of birth made anyone better than anyone else.

"The Earl of Brillshire, isn't it?" Winford said, his interest returning to Derrick in an instant. "Your father?"

Derrick fought the urge to be snide and remembered his case.

"My grandfather, actually. My father is his third son, the Honorable Roger Huntington."

"Really," Lady Winford said, the interest in her gaze jumping higher. "That must be it. I believe we've met your father before, at soirees in London."

"I'm certain you have," Derrick said softly. "He and my mother are happy to join the fray."

"But you are not," Lord Winford said, the dismissive sound back to his voice. "Happier to go slumming in the army, eh?"

Derrick set his jaw and was trying not to make a crude rejoinder when suddenly Selina stepped into the circle of their group. "Lord and Lady Winford, how lovely to see you again. Are you enjoying the party?"

The Winfords looked at her in what appeared to be surprise at her intrusion, but if she felt that, she didn't show it. Selina's expression was just one of pure innocence. A mask if he'd ever seen one, because he knew what wicked things lurked beneath it.

"Good evening, Miss Oliver." It was Lord Winford who answered first. And if he had looked dismissive of Derrick, now he had much more interest in his stare as he looked down at Selina. Derrick's stomach clenched at the leer the man didn't even try to hide.

Selina seemed oblivious to it. She merely pivoted toward Lady Winford with another of those dazzling smiles. "I admit, Lady Winford, I came over with the desire to see the famous Breston necklace!"

Derrick caught his breath at her boldness. What the hell was she doing? He fought an urge to catch her arm, drag her away and cause what would surely be a scene.

"That isn't it, is it?" she continued, apparently unaware to his discomfort as she pointed to a ring of diamonds around the lady's neck.

Lady Winford glanced down at herself and then shook her head. "These? Good gracious, no. This is just some silly thing Winford bought me a few years ago." Derrick noted the slight flinch and the deeper frown that comment elicited from Winford. "No, the Breston is far finer, I assure you. I wouldn't wear it to just *any* event, though I do have it here, of course. With that Faceless Fox character flitting around, one cannot be too careful."

"No," Selina said with a smile. "One can most definitely not. Wicked creature, that one. But will you wear it here? I do *long* to see it."

Lady Winford sniffed at her. "I'm sure you do. The little thrills one's betters can give must be what you live on. Perhaps I'll wear it at the end of the event." She turned then and speared her husband with a glare. "Come, Winford, I see the Duke and Duchess of Sheffield. They aren't the most important here, but they're friends of Roseford, so it will behoove us to do a good deed. Good evening, Mr. Huntington."

The couple didn't even say a proper farewell to Selina. Winford leered a bit, Lady Winford sniffed again, and then they were off, winding their way through the crowd toward the Sheffields.

Derrick pivoted on Selina, ready to launch into a tirade over her interference. He was stopped by the smile on her face, wicked and pointed and aimed directly at him.

"Well, Mr. Huntington," she said, reaching to take his arm. Her fingers snaked around his elbow, warm and firm and oh-so-tantalizing. "Aren't you going to ask me to dance?"

He blinked. "Dance?" he repeated, thrown from his game for a moment by the question.

"Yes," she said with a laugh that turned more than a few heads in her direction. "It's when you hold a lady in your arms and move in time to the music."

He fought a smile that threatened to twitch at his lips. "I'm aware of the particulars of the exercise, Miss Oliver. Do you want to dance with me?"

"That's why I asked you," she said with another of those flirtatious smiles. She caught his hand. "Come on, forget everything else and let's go."

She dragged him forward and suddenly they were in the middle of the dancefloor, the strains of the waltz rising up around them. He positioned his hand, one holding hers, the other resting on the swell of her hip. God, but he felt that curve in every fiber of his being.

As they began to move, she smiled at him again, that little wicked, knowing tease of a smile. "Derrick, no one else knows your true purpose here. In all their minds, you're a guest. So you better start acting like one."

Derrick let out his breath in a long sigh and then threw himself into the steps just like he'd been taught years ago when he was another man with another life.

Derrick's fingers were on her hip. Certainly, Selina had danced with many a man in her life. Waltzes and cotillions and everything in between. But never had she been so aware of the pressure of a man's long, lean fingers against her hip, almost like she wasn't wearing anything at all and those fingers were pressed there for another purpose.

She swallowed and tried to pull herself together. She was supposed to be in control in this situation, even if she turned it into a seduction. She needed to get to that control right now.

She held his stare for a moment. He moved gracefully, but she could see the effort it required. His jaw was clenched, his eyes focused, sometimes on her, sometimes on his own feet, and she could swear he was counting in his head.

She smiled, slow and flirtatious, and his eyes widened just a touch, his steps faltering a fraction before he recovered.

"Are you going to thank me?" she asked.

"For what?" The words were ground through those clenched teeth.

"For helping you," she said, batting her eyelashes slightly, like the sweetest little innocent in the whole country. "I was able to make Lady Winford speak of the necklace."

"I didn't ask you to come over and make anyone talk to me about anything," he said. "I was doing fine on my own."

"Were you?" she teased.

He gave her another of those severe, toe-curling scowls, but she thought the corner of his mouth twitched. She almost crowed in triumph. He was just as much a part of this game as she was. He liked how she toyed with him, even if he tried not to. And that made it all the more fun.

"You really shouldn't interfere, you know," he said.

She let him spin her through the crowd before she answered, "You keep saying that, but you keep needing to be rescued."

"I have a partner for rescue."

They both looked across the ballroom. Barber was standing with the Duke and Duchess of Crestwood. They were laughing together, though Selina was aware that the other man's gaze focused on the two of them often. And just like Derrick, Barber seemed well equipped to read a situation.

"Well, it wouldn't make as much sense for a man to ask about jewelry without rousing suspicion."

"Lady Winford wasn't very kind about it," he said with a slight frown. "She was very rude to you."

Selina shrugged as best she could when she was in his arms. "It doesn't matter. That's just who she is. I didn't expect a warm welcome. You know people like that, I'd wager. She's terrible."

"You said something similar about her last night in her chamber," he said. "What was your bad experience with her, exactly?"

She let out her breath. "I was at a gathering once where I watched her berate her ladies companion until the poor girl was almost hysterical. She sacked the woman without reference. She knew there would be consequences and she did it anyway."

"What happened to her? The servant, that is?" Derrick asked.

Selina pursed her lips. "I helped her. She was able to get another position when I...forged a letter of recommendation from Lady Winford."

His eyes went wide. "You forged—" he began, but she interrupted because if he started picking apart all the criminal things she'd done in her life, he would likely figure out the heart of her.

"You know, if you want to uncover something about Lady Winford, there's one way you could find out," she said.

His brow lowered and he looked at her in confusion. "And what's that?" he asked.

"You're joking, aren't you?" she said with a giggle. "You saw the way she looked at you. Like you're a sweet treat she wants to...lick." She darted her own tongue out with that last word and saw his pupils dilate as he watched her sweep her lower lip with the tip.

He cleared his throat. "I don't know what you're talking about."

She pushed aside the little flare of jealousy Lady Winford's attentions had caused. "You had to see it, feel it. And if you pursued it—"

His fingers tightened against her hip, cutting off her breath and her words. Great God, but she wanted him to do that without so many layers of silk in between the flesh.

"I don't play like that," he said, slowly and with a calm fortitude.

"No?" she asked, her voice dropping to a whisper as the song slowed and ended. "Then what is this with us?"

He stared at her without breaking contact, without gathering her to leave the dancefloor like everyone else was starting to do. "It's not that," he said at last.

Suddenly the room felt very close, not just with the desire that coursed through her body at those words. But also with the guilt. He was not playing a game with her. He said it and it was clear by the look in his warm brown eyes that he meant it. Whatever had sparked between them was genuine. And it was for her, too.

But she was willing to use it against him. No matter how wrong that was, no matter how little he deserved it. She was using his desire against him, stoking it and playing it. And in that moment, she hated herself for it.

She stepped away from him, heat burning her cheeks.

"Thank you for the dance, Mr. Huntington," she choked out softly. She didn't wait for him to reply, but turned and scurried away. She needed air, that was all. To regain her composure on the terrace away from this man who inspired feelings in her she had long ago put away. If that was possible.

She burst onto the terrace, gasping for air as she crossed to the low wall and gripped her fingers around the edge. The stone dug into her flesh, and she welcomed the pain because it forced her to be present, not relive every moment of her dance with Derrick.

"Please, won't you finally tell me what is going on with you?"

She startled and pivoted to find Vale slipping from a darkened corner of the terrace. She was wearing a plain ball gown, but she was so lovely that it could have been a sackcloth and she would have belonged in the ballroom behind them.

"I didn't know you were out here," Selina gasped, lifting a hand to her chest. "What are you doing?"

Vale arched a brow. "I'm your companion in this farce we're playing out, not your servant. It makes sense that I might join you for the ball to be of assistance and as your chaperone."

"I suppose," Selina said, fanning herself with her hand.

"I was watching you," Vale said, stepping up beside her to look out over the garden with her. "Through the window with Huntington."

Selina worried her lip. "There wasn't much to see," she said, lying and hoping to keep things light. "We danced. It was...boring."

"Bollocks," Vale whispered with a glance around to make certain the terrace was as empty as they both believed. "How long has it been since you had a lover?"

Selina tilted her head. "Getting a bit personal, are we?"

Vale smiled slightly. "We both know you aren't a shrinking violet. It's one of the things I admire most about you."

Selina shrugged. "I don't know, a month or two?"

"Then perhaps you're just lonely. Being lonely can lead a person to make mistakes, so I have to ask you, Selina—are you getting confused when it comes to Huntington?"

"No!" Selina responded immediately, but Vale pierced her with a withering stare. She folded her arms. "Fine. Maybe. He is just...so... honorable." She let out her breath in a huff. "Truly honorable. How can I—"

Vale snorted. "No one is truly honorable, Selina. And no one will take care of you but you, no matter how tightly he holds you on a dancefloor or how handsome he is." Her voice gentled. "You *know* that."

Selina let out a sigh. Her whole life she had known that. Depending on others had never ended well—she'd long ago stopped doing it. Selina held Vale closer than anyone else in the world. But even so, if Selina needed rescue, she still assumed she'd be rescuing herself. Old habits died very hard.

But now, watching her brother with his friends, watching Derrick and seeing how seriously he took his duty...

"I see kind people all around me," she said softly. "Loving people, Vale. Caring people who help others without a thought of what they could get in return."

Vale shook her head. "Don't get soft on me, Selina. That's the shortest route to an early death in our world."

Selina clenched her teeth, but before she could respond, the door to the ballroom opened and Derrick himself stepped out. Selina's breath caught, just as it always did when he stepped into her presence.

Vale arched a brow at the reaction and leaned in. "I'll go see what I can find out about Lady Winford's servants. Just be careful. Please."

Vale nodded to Derrick as she slipped off into the dark again, off to do the wicked things Selina had rarely thought twice about. Until the man who stepped up to stand before her made her think twice about...*everything.*

"Who was that?" he asked.

"My companion, Vale Williams."

"Ah." He said nothing more, but held her stare evenly, keeping her in place as much as if he'd nailed her to the terrace floor.

She fought to find her feisty self again. The one that challenged him. But her mind was spinning and her heart was racing and she was reacting the way she shouldn't, couldn't. Had always told herself she wouldn't.

Why did he do this? How?

He cleared his throat. "We were playing in there, I know, but I want to make clear that you can't be involving yourself in my work."

She folded her arms as a spark of annoyance flared in her. "You keep saying that. But perhaps *I* should make it clear that you shouldn't underestimate people, especially those you don't know. You have no idea what I'm capable of."

His eyes narrowed and she wished she could take those pointed words back. Especially when he said, "And what are you capable of?"

Panic flooded her, but she breathed into it. This man was no threat. No matter what he made her feel, she had the upper hand. And if she remembered that, she'd get out of this with her hide intact.

She forced calm and then stepped a little closer. She lifted her hand, watching him track the motion, and settled it on his hard chest. She clenched her fingers a touch, smoothing them along his jacket front. Watching his pupils dilate.

"Wouldn't you like to know," she whispered. Then she smiled and turned away, walking back into the house without another word. She could feel him watching her. She knew she had won this round in the game.

But she couldn't feel good about it. It was becoming increasingly clear that this was the most dangerous game she'd ever played. And she feared the bitter consequences if she didn't win.

CHAPTER 10

Two days after the ball, Derrick stood on the same terrace where Selina had whispered not to underestimate her, frustration pumping through his veins like a poison. Two days and he felt no closer to the identity of the Fox. Two days of watching and waiting and quietly questioning and all he had was a headache. The Fox seemed to leave no trace, no whisper in his wake.

Whoever he was, he was good.

And so was Selina. Derrick looked across the wide expanse of the parapet and found her instantly. Although there was a small party taking place around them, a tea with laughter and friends, she was alone by the terrace wall. Very near where he'd come out of the ballroom to find her two nights ago, actually. She looked off into the garden, the perfect image of repose and gentility.

Only that was a bloody lie. Over the past two days she had danced around him, smiling and winking and playing. Always near him, although she'd made what felt like a concerted effort not to directly speak to him. She was always off chatting with some other guest, enchanting them in a cloud of her boldness. Just like she did with him.

And what did she talk about? The same damned thing he was

asking around about. How many times had he tried to ask a casual question about the necklace or the Fox and had his companion say, "Funny, Miss Oliver asked me the same thing."

His jaw clenched just thinking about it. And looking at her in that pretty salmon-pink dress with the warm yellow highlights that seemed to draw his eye to every curve in her body. She just stood there being beautiful and he was going mad with it.

Madder still when she was approached by another guest. And not just any guest, but Lord Winford. Oh, he'd seen how the man looked at her over the past two days. Seen the ever-increasing leer. If Selina thought Lady Winford would give over secrets to him through seduction, certainly she would have equal luck with the earl.

And he hated it. Especially when she straightened, laughing at something the odious man had said to her. Seemingly oblivious to the way his gaze focused on a spot a foot below her eyes.

Lord Winford was dangerous. Derrick had gleaned that from the first interaction he had with the man. He had a cruel bent to him, a wickedness that radiated as much as the meanness of his wife. Derrick didn't want Selina near him, let alone laughing at his blasted jokes.

He forced his fists to his sides, trying not to involve himself where he didn't belong and cause a scene that could hurt his investigation. And he almost had himself under control when Selina looked past Winford in Derrick's direction. She met his gaze, held there and then...she winked.

She bloody winked, and it was enough.

He crossed the terrace in a few long paces, fighting to retain some semblance of calm on his face, knowing he wasn't by the way her eyes widened. Feeling it in the way Barber tracked him from the opposite side of the terrace where he stood with other guests. But it didn't matter. Derrick was drawn to Selina like a magnet to metal.

He reached the pair, breathless with incandescent rage at her recklessness.

"Miss Oliver, Lord Winford," he forced himself to say with what he hoped was a little politeness. "I hate to intrude, but I wonder if I may speak to you about that matter we were discussing earlier, Miss Oliver."

She stared at him, her eyes wide for a moment, then glanced at Lord Winford, who looked mightily annoyed that his seduction attempt had been thwarted.

"Ah, yes," she said slowly. "I suppose now is as good a time as any."

"The library might be a good place to talk about it, since it's in regards to that...that book," he stammered, wishing he could manage himself a bit better.

"We'll have to continue this conversation later, Lord Winford," she said with an apologetic nod. "Lead the way, Mr.—"

She didn't get to finish. He caught her elbow and guided her away, weaving through the crowd, hoping it didn't look like he was dragging her when that was exactly what he was doing.

He pushed through the terrace doors from the parlor and took her through the room and down the hall. The library was a few paces away and he pulled her inside, shutting the door behind them. He stared at the ornate knob with its little key in the shape of a feather sticking from the lock. And slowly, he turned the key, even though he knew he shouldn't. Then again, when it came to this woman, it seemed everything was what he knew he shouldn't do. And it didn't matter one fucking bit.

"Derrick, what are you thinking—" she said, apparently oblivious to the fact he'd locked the door.

"Lord Winford is not a safe person," he snapped as he pivoted to face her. "You are being foolhardy."

She arched a brow, the teasing back on her face. "Am I now? By speaking to a man in public view on my brother's terrace? You think that is more foolhardy than dragging me into the library and locking the door?"

He flinched. So, she *had* noticed he'd locked them in. But she hadn't protested. "I cannot have this conversation where we might be interrupted, Selina," he said, but his voice was shaky. "It is too important."

She was quiet a moment, then stepped a little closer. "Is a conversation what you want to have? Or is there some other reason you dragged me in here?"

"Selina," he groaned, running a hand through his hair. "God, but you test me."

"Are you passing or failing?"

He glared at her, but she winked again in return, and the frayed rope of his control, the one he had managed and controlled all his life...snapped. He barreled across the room and caught both her arms, pulling her against him hard. He looked down at her, expecting her to find fear in her eyes or some kind of regret at pushing him so far.

But instead, she looked up at him...and she *smiled*. And in that moment he knew he wouldn't be able to stop himself from taking what he wanted, no matter what a mistake it was going to turn out to be. He leaned down and his mouth crushed to hers, hard and hungry, and he claimed, at last, what he had been denying himself for days.

Selina had known that when Derrick's control finally broke it would be spectacular, but this was explosive. His mouth crushed against hers, devouring as their tongues tangled. His fingertips dug into her arms, holding her hostage against his hard, hot body. She didn't want to escape him, and she also didn't want him to loosen his grip. She nipped his lower lip and he growled from deep in his chest, backing her across the room.

They hit the wall with a thud, and his hands dragged away from her arms and found her hips. His mouth still hard on hers, he ground against her, his hard cock pressing into her belly as she lifted up against him with a muffled moan of pleasure. Yes, that's what she wanted, what she needed. And not just as a means to control this man.

As a means to everything.

He glided one hand to the back of her thigh, his fingers burning through her gown as he hitched her leg up. She locked it around his own leg and lifted as he thrust so that he hit her sex with every grinding movement. Pleasure arced, muted by the clothing between them, but already hot and powerful regardless.

She whimpered as she tugged at his jacket, shoving it down, dragging her lips away from his to lick along his jawline, bite his chin. He slammed against her again and her vision blurred. Christ, but he'd make her come before he had her skirts lifted.

She slid her hands down his sides, clenching against hard muscle, over his hips that churned against hers. Somehow she managed to wedge a hand between them, and he froze as she rubbed his cock through the rough fabric of his trousers. They held gazes, panting in time as she stroked him over and over. His eyes fluttered shut and he let out a low groan.

She smiled as she unfastened his fall front and tugged the loose fabric away. His cock bobbed free, pressing to her palm in heated insistence. She swallowed hard as she stroked him again, this time without impediment. Oh yes, this was going to be fun, because it was a fine cock. Thick and hard and perfect in every way.

He opened his eyes again as she stroked him, his pupils so dilated there was hardly any brown left in the circles. He tugged at her skirts, pushing them up, past her knee, over her thigh. His hands moved beneath, tracing the line of her legs, his fingernails abrading gently and making her twitch with pleasure. He shoved her drawers open at the slit and stroked his fingers across her, coating them with her wetness.

"Fuck," he muttered, she thought more to himself than to her. He peeled her open, thumb finding her clitoris, and for a moment they

JESS MICHAELS

just rubbed each other, eyes locked, challenging and surrendering all at once.

She was drowning in him. She felt herself going under with every expert flick of his fingers against her. Pleasure pulsed, harder, faster. She was going to come, that was a certainty. But she didn't want it to be against his fingers, nor him into her palm. She lifted slightly, and he nodded at the unspoken request and moved his hand.

She guided him to her and he helped by lifting her, pressing her hard against the wall as he slid into her in one long thrust. She cried out at the pleasure of him stretching her, then buried her head in his shoulder so the rest of her cries wouldn't bring the servants running to her aid.

And as she had hoped he would, Derrick fucked her. Hard and heavy and fast, he pinioned his hips against hers. Their mouths met again, and she lost herself in all the sensations of mouth and tongue and teeth and cock. He wasn't gentle and she didn't want that. She wanted his passion and he gave that gift freely.

His pelvis swirled against hers, she clenched in time and the pleasure that had been mounting between her legs since the moment he crossed the room like a bull to a matador finally exploded. She thrust out of control, digging her fingers into his back for purchase as an orgasm more powerful than anything she'd ever felt before ripped through her body.

He gave her no respite, taking and taking and taking until her head lolled back against the wall and her breath was nothing but short gasps. Only then did he withdraw, and with a long, heavy groan, he came against his hand.

He didn't part their bodies for a moment, but kept her helplessly pinned to the wall as he gasped for breath. She stared at him, the thin sheen of sweat on his brow, the utterly sated look on his face. She couldn't help herself. Pressing his control was too fun. She glided her hand back between them and caught his cock once more, stroking him, using his own essence as lubricant. He jerked against her with a cry as he glared at her and made her pussy flutter once more with need.

He set her down slowly, sliding her down the length of his body as he did so. When her feet were on the ground, she stared up at him. It was a funny thing. When he took her, that was such an intimate act. But right now when he was just standing there, staring into her eyes, she felt much more vulnerable.

So she slipped away to push her skirts back into place around her hips. She kept her eyes from him as she stepped up to the mirror above the fireplace and checked herself. She looked flushed, well-pleasured, but it wasn't something that anyone else might notice when she went back to the party on the terrace.

"I'm sorry," he said so softly from behind her that she almost didn't hear him. She pivoted and found he had also refastened and straightened himself. He was gathering up his jacket from the ground, shaking it out, brushing it off. But his head was bent.

She moved toward him. "For what?" she asked as she dared to reach out and touch his face. She lifted his chin so that he looked at her. "*I'm* not sorry."

"You're a lady and—"

She tilted her head back with a laugh. "Oh, not this again. Derrick, we have established more than once that I am not some trembling flower. I also wasn't a virgin—surely you must have noticed that. So you stole nothing."

His jaw set and she could all but see the wheels turning in his mind. He caught her fingers that were still resting on his jaw and tangled them with his own. "What happened to you?" he asked.

She flinched. There he was, seeing through her again. Ignoring the laughter she used to mask whatever pain she felt. She cleared her throat. "Nothing," she said. "I've been on my own since I was eleven. Out of my house since I was eighteen. I managed myself with only a little intervention from my father's estate. I surrendered my virginity to a man I *wanted* to give it to, a good many years ago. And I liked it, so I've had a handful of lovers since."

"I see," he said softly.

She arched a brow, defensiveness rising in her. "Do you want to call me a wanton, then, Derrick? Accuse me of being a whore because I treat my pleasure like a man treats his?"

"No," he said, quickly and with feeling. "I don't judge you. Why shouldn't you have pleasure? Why shouldn't you treat your body as if it were your own? It is, after all."

She hesitated. *That* was not the reaction she had expected. If she told the men on the terrace what she'd just confessed to Derrick, she would wager more than ninety percent of them would call her whore either behind her back or to her face. She would be shunned by the women, ladies all and born and bred to be delicate and chaste and fucking boring. It was, unfortunately, the way of their world. Women were chattel, their virginity a commodity. Their pleasure an afterthought, if a thought at all.

"Oh," she said softly.

"I was actually reacting to your statement that you've been on your own for so long," he said. "*That* seems a sadder statement than that you've had..." He cleared his throat. "...lovers."

He was pressing for information about her in this. Looking through her like he always did and finding things she had always chosen to hide. She didn't want that. If he dug too far, he would find the Fox there, too.

So she forced a smile. "Is that jealousy in your voice?" she asked. He lifted his gaze to hers and she saw that very emotion faintly flickering there. "You needn't be. That was...amazing. Different from anything I've ever felt before."

His lips parted. "Yes," he said, and nothing more. But the yes was enough. The yes was a triumph. She wanted to move him just as he moved her. She wanted it to mean something...

Even if in the end, it couldn't mean anything. There was no way for it, no path that could lead them to each other for more than the remaining days they would share here.

"Selina," he whispered, his voice no longer rough with desire, but soft with something else. She wanted to turn away from that, but he cupped her cheek and it froze her in place, staring up at him. His lips lowered and he kissed her once more.

Only this time, he didn't devour. He didn't claim. He wasn't rough. He tilted her head, deepening the kiss, and for a moment she sank against him, holding tight to the firm reliability of him. She hadn't had that in her life for a very long time.

Because it was always an illusion.

That reminder yanked her back, and she stepped from his arms and away from the vulnerability he made her feel all the way down to the tips of her toes.

"Don't worry yourself," she whispered. "I wanted this. I wanted it exactly as we had it."

He nodded slowly, tracking her as she backed toward the door.

"And..." She held her breath before she continued. Could she say what was on her lips? Should she? After all, she had leverage now. She didn't need more.

Except she did.

"And I hope we can do it again," she whispered.

He arched a brow, and she waited for the inevitable words that would fall from his lips. Admonishment, denial, refusal. Instead, he let out a low chuckle that seemed to cross its way into her blood stream. He smiled at her, possessive and hot and...real. Her heart stuttered even though she knew she shouldn't let it.

"You are trouble, Selina Oliver," he said on a laugh.

She couldn't help the smile that tilted her own lips. "Proudly," she said, then winked at him as she slipped out the door and left him to think on what they'd done.

And she could have crowed that she had the upper hand, except her hands were shaking as she re-entered the party and circulated back into the crowd.

CHAPTER 11

"What do you think about Lord Winford?" Derrick asked, keeping his eyes pointedly on the papers in front of him and praying his tone sounded casual.

He heard Barber shuffling papers, and there was a long pause before he answered, "What about him?"

That was a good question. What *about* Winford? Derrick had been watching the man ever closer since his approach to Selina at the garden party the day before. He was a bastard, that was for sure. But could he be a Fox?

"Huntington?" Barber said, his tone sharp. Derrick jerked his gaze up then and found his friend standing now, his arms folded across his chest, a pointed glare focused squarely on Derrick. "You have not been yourself since yesterday afternoon when you snuck away with Miss Oliver."

Derrick flinched. Yes, his friend was correct on that assessment. He hadn't been himself. How could one ever be oneself again after such a powerful encounter with a woman like Selina? The passion of their joining, both given and received, was all he'd thought about since. Both to reprimand himself, and to relive those moments over and over and savor every squeeze of her body, every scent of her desire, every sound of her orgasm.

Even now he could picture each second down to its finest detail.

"Will you ever tell me why you dragged the lady off?" Barber asked.

Derrick shifted. He'd put his friend off when he returned to the party, but Barber was too clever and too focused not to push and question and cajole. He was going to have to find an answer. And he couldn't let it be the truth. Barber would be furious that Derrick had brought an outsider into their case. He would be shocked that Derrick had tupped that very outsider against a wall in her brother's library.

"Miss Oliver has some insight into Lord Winford," he said with a shrug. "He's obviously interested in her."

"He's not the only one," Barber said softly.

Derrick jerked his gaze to him. His arms were folded across his broad chest and his brown gaze was unrelenting. "What are you implying?"

"I'm not implying. I know you, Huntington. I nearly died at your side. We're friends as well as partners."

"You are a true friend," Derrick said with no hesitation.

"Don't try to change the subject," Barber said, though he chuckled and his mood softened a fraction. "It's obvious the woman...entices you. You look at her like she's edible and you're starving."

Selina was most definitely edible. Derrick had been fantasizing about all the ways to taste her all day. But he pushed those thoughts away.

"You're seeing things," he said, but he could hear that his voice wasn't strong.

"I'm not, and the fact that you're denying the attraction concerns me all the more about it." Barber threw up his hands.

Derrick let out his breath slowly. "Very well. I will not deny that the woman is...she's very attractive. And that I have...I've noticed her finer attributes. How could one not? She's stunningly beautiful and alluring on every level. But that desire is not going to distract me."

It already had. He hated being a liar.

Barber pursed his lips and shook his head. "If you say so. After all, if you don't want to involve me in your thoughts, I can't force you. But you asked me about Winford."

Derrick nodded. "Yes."

"I think the man is pond scum embodied. He's a bigot and a bully. But he's also an idiot. The Fox is not."

Derrick sighed. "Yes. True. But I've been cross-referencing the parties the Fox stole from. The guest lists have all included Lord Winford but for two."

"Two is a great many," Barber said. "How would you explain his not being in two places where the Fox struck?"

Derrick shifted. "Because...er...well, these lists aren't always accurate, are they? A person could come to a party where they aren't invited. They could come in disguise. They could have altered the list."

Barber looked at him as if he'd sprouted a second head. "Why reach so high to put this man on the suspect list?"

Derrick turned away and walked to the window. He had no answer, at least none that would appease his friend.

"To protect her?" Barber said softly.

Derrick shrugged. "Perhaps I am compromised at that."

He heard Barber suck in a breath and turned to find his friend staring at him in surprise. Then his expression softened a fraction. "Miss Oliver is beautiful," Barber said. "And I admire her fire. I think her spirit could be a good match for your own. When this is over, I wouldn't tell you to ignore whatever this is between you two."

Derrick let out a long breath. Barber was talking about a future for him and Selina. He didn't even fully understand what their present was. The teasing, the flirting, the explosive passion...did that allow building something more? Especially since he never felt like he was on…solid ground when he was with her. Everything was constantly shifting and that was a wild adventure and a terrifying concept all at once.

Barber was oblivious to these thoughts as he added, "We *all* deserve to be happy, you no less."

"Can men like us be happy?" Derrick asked, shaking his head. "After what we've seen in war? After everything we've done?"

"Of course." It was clear Barber believed it. "We are more than our pasts. All of us."

"Perhaps," Derrick said softly.

Barber was quiet a moment. "Do you truly think Lord Winford would conspire to steal his own wife's jewels? Because our sources say *that* is the target."

"Our sources. An anonymous note received by one of the past victims," Derrick said. "Is that a good source?"

"We felt it was good enough to pursue this in the first place." Barber cocked his head. "The message contained information about past robberies that was never made public."

"And what if it were the Fox himself, trying to get us off the scent?" Derrick insisted.

"Then you're back to Lord Winford not being a suspect," Barber said.

Derrick scrubbed a hand over his face. He could admit, if only to himself, that he was twisting things in his mind to make them fit Winford as a suspect. Because he hated the man. Because he feared for Selina if she kept playing her games with the earl.

He pushed those thoughts away and tried to become the detached investigator again. Was there a reason he could find that *didn't* pulse with his personal vendettas and jealousies?

"Winford hates the fame the Breston necklace has given the countess," he said at last.

Barber considered that for a moment with a nod. "That is true. He mutters about it to anyone who will listen. They are a poisonous pair."

"Perhaps he'd steal the necklace just to hurt her," Derrick said softly.

Barber let out his breath in a long sigh. "It isn't the worst theory I've ever heard. I'll look into it."

Derrick lifted his brows. "Truly? Even though you suspect my motives aren't pure?"

"Pure motives or not, you always have good instincts. I'd be a fool not to listen to them after all this time." Barber got up and crossed the room to him, clapping a hand on his shoulder. "Personal involvements in cases like these could prove dangerous. Be careful, will you?"

"I'm always careful," Derrick said.

Barber smiled, but it was tight. "Yes, that was once true. I'll see you later."

His friend left him then, to think about what he'd said. To think about the woman who had created such a strange brew of emotions in his chest and chaos in the middle of his once-predictable life.

Selina dragged a gasp of warm air in and sighed as a sense of calm washed over her. Her life had always been tumultuous from the time she was a little girl. Consistency had never been a frequent caller, so she had learned to take care of herself and not depend on others. The problem was that always left her on edge, never completely at peace. Always at the ready.

But in this moment, as she walked in her brother's fine garden, admiring his beautifully tended grounds, she had a flash of...peace. Of belonging.

"Don't be foolish," she muttered to herself, trying to push the uncomfortable feeling away. It only clouded her judgment and made her question her plans.

It also took her thoughts to the garden party the previous afternoon. And what had happened in the library with Derrick.

She'd had lovers, she'd felt pleasure before, so she'd assumed when she began her flirtation with the man that she could control her reactions. That even if she ended up in his bed, it would only give her more control.

Only she didn't feel in control now. She felt tightly wound and needy and unfocused. All last night, she had dreamed of Derrick's arms around her, his mouth on her, his body surging with so much power deep within her own. She'd woken shaking, wet, and even bringing herself to release hadn't softened the need.

"Miss Oliver?"

She froze with her thoughts churning and slowly turned to find Mr. Barber standing there, watching her with an unreadable expression. She smiled at him as she took him in. He was really a handsome man, with his close-cropped black hair and warm brown skin. He was tall and lean, all angles, including high cheekbones, the kind most women in the ton would fight for. His lips were set in a perpetual near smile, and that gave him a kind air.

It would be easy to just see him as her lover's friend and not a man who hunted her. Only she couldn't do that. It wasn't possible. She had to play a game with him, different than the one she played with Derrick, but with the same goal: to keep him from suspecting her.

"Mr. Barber," she said, stepping forward with a smile. "I didn't hear you approach. Good afternoon."

"Good afternoon," he returned. "I was just taking a stroll through the garden, as is my habit every day at this time."

"I was doing something similar," she said. "These events get so hectic, especially as the shine wears off and having so many people around starts to be less amusing. There is nothing like a stroll amongst the flowers to clear one's head."

"Would you be opposed to company?" he asked.

She froze. He was watching her, appearing casual but actually reading her. And there was so much to read about the Fox, about Derrick, about the spinning confusion in her mind about the future.

She nodded. "Of course," she croaked out. He fell into step beside her, and for a moment they just slowly made their way down the garden path. She cleared her throat. "I hear from the Duchess of Sheffield that you are a gardener yourself."

He smiled. "A hobbyist, but yes, I do dabble in my own small garden in London. Roses are my passion."

She glanced at him from the corner of her eye. "Lovely to look at, but I've heard hard to maintain."

"Perhaps, but worth the difficulty, as are most things worth having," he said. His gaze settled on her for a brief moment, and she found herself wondering if they were still discussing flowers at all.

"You are likely right," she said. "I just haven't had the patience, perhaps, to learn to cultivate them properly. Your military discipline might help."

He considered that. "I suppose so. I wasn't as interested in flowers before I came home from the war, so you might be right. It is a fascinating thought I'll have to ponder more."

"I suppose after such a dangerous experience, it must be comforting to find something to fill your time," she said, careful not to reveal that she knew his true reason for being here. After all, she didn't know if Derrick had revealed her interference. The last thing she needed was to pivot Barber's attention more fully on her.

"Some men struggle to do so," he said, and his expression grew worried. "Some men lose themselves in drink or work and forget to make a life beyond their memories."

She frowned. "You sound as though you're talking about someone specific."

His gaze darted to her. "Perhaps I am. Or perhaps I'm thinking of a dozen friends."

"Is Derrick Huntington one of them?" she asked.

Now he stopped on the path and pivoted to look at her fully. His eyebrow arched. "I suppose after what we went through together, how close we have become as friends, as brothers, that I can't help but worry about him. Especially now."

She pursed her lips. "You are bringing this up to me and there seems to be a purpose behind it."

"You and he have been spending a bit of time together since our arrival," Barber said. "I think you may be...you might be learning about all of his excellent qualities."

"Yes," she said softly, because there was no use denying those facts. This man knew what he was talking about, and if it were only fears about Derrick that drove him to approach her, addressing them would send him away. Distract him from equating the Fox with herself.

And truth be told, she also wanted to see where he was going with this interrogation regarding Derrick. She wanted to know more from the facts he was carefully sprinkling at her feet.

"Does that worry you?" she asked, and tried to make her tone light and playful. "Are you here to ask me my intentions when it comes to your friend?"

He smiled at that quip, but his tone was still serious when he said, "It may not be my place, he might even be angry at me for doing it, but I am the closest thing to family the man has left. So I suppose yes, I am concerned about your intentions. Are you coming to Derrick in a real interest? Or are you a bored Society lass, interesting in slumming with a man you see beneath you? Because Huntington doesn't deserve to be used."

She flinched at the question and set her jaw. "I know you are a very intelligent man. I know you know about me, because I don't think you'd approach me without having at least ten moves planned out in this little chess match we've begun. So you must know, as everyone knows, that the last thing I am is a Society lass, bored or otherwise. I'm just a duke's bastard sister, Mr. Barber, brought here to assuage some guilt Robert has about the disparity of our upbringing. Or perhaps in some foolish attempt to match me with a man of substance, because my other half-brother recently married after receiving Robert's assistance."

She stopped talking because she realized she was rambling and giving out information she hadn't meant to share. Barber was quiet as she turned away, heat burning her cheeks, and stared at the fountain a few paces away along the pathway. She gathered herself and dared to look at him again. His expression was impassive.

"I suppose what I'm trying to say is that I know Huntington doesn't deserve to be used." She took a long breath. "He seems to be an honorable man."

"He is," Barber said softly, and then he took a step toward her. "As is your brother, Nicholas Gillingham."

She froze at the mention of Nicholas. She'd already slightly explored the connection between the men with Derrick, but Barber knew her brother, too. "You served with him," she said.

Barber nodded. "It was my great honor, yes."

She shifted. "And you said you and Derrick—Mr. Huntington— were among those with him when he was injured."

"Yes." Barber's expression went far away. "Our commander was a useless man, too important to make good tactical decisions. He set up camp in an area too exposed, near volatile munitions. Gillingham had no faith in him and saw the intense danger. He took over operations and moved the lot of us before there was an explosion. He was badly injured, as were a good many of us. Despite his own injuries, Derrick was the first man at his side. Your brother saved us. And Derrick saved him, in turn."

She could feel the blood draining from her cheeks with every word. Nicholas had been so close-lipped about the cause of his injuries. She knew he was being considered for a title, thanks to his saving of the very commander Barber maligned, the son of a viscount who was a close friend to Prinny.

"Derrick saved my brother," she whispered, and tears stung her eyes.

Barber nodded. "So you can see why I am protective of the man."

"Yes," she pushed out past pursed lips. "I knew you two served with Nicholas. I-I didn't know about the rest."

Barber shrugged one shoulder. "Huntington doesn't celebrate

himself. It's not his way. But now you know, so you'll do with that information what you will."

She glanced up at the house, knowing Derrick was in there somewhere. Knowing that she needed to go to him, as soon as possible and just...she didn't know what. Talk to him? Touch him and have it be unrelated to the Fox or his case? Just see him?

"The afternoon is getting late," she said. "I should go in and ready myself for supper."

"Ah, yes. It is nearly that time. Of course, Miss Oliver, I'll leave you to your preparations." He motioned toward the path with a partial bow.

"I'll see you tonight," Selina choked out, but she was already moving away from him, toward the house. Toward the man she wanted to see so desperately. Toward a connection she feared because it had nothing to do with the lies as the Fox and everything to do with the heart of the woman she truly was.

CHAPTER 12

Derrick stood glaring at the mirror, straightening his cravat for what felt like the tenth time since he'd tied it. It had been years since he had a valet, since he'd fully abandoned his grandfather's grander plans for him. A decade, perhaps.

He was well capable of shining his own boots and dressing himself. But the cravats...

"Bugger," he grunted as he unwound the contraption and started over in tying it.

Well, the cravats were still a struggle. He almost had it finished and was trying to find a place to tuck a sloppy end of fabric when there was a knock on his door. He crossed to it, still fiddling with the neckwear.

"Barber, if that's you, I'm going to need your assistance because you know I'm rubbish at—" He threw the door open as he spoke and then skidded to a halt. It wasn't his partner there waiting for him. It was Selina.

She was wearing another blue dress, another opportunity for her eyes to pop like fine sapphires. This one had short puffed sleeves, a scooped neckline and a gauzy overlay the cascaded over her curves like a waterfall.

"Selina," he whispered like a fool. "I...I didn't think, I'm sorry, I wasn't expecting you."

She slipped past him into the room without asking his leave, and she stood there in the middle of the small space, looking around her. He slowly shut the door, closing them in the same way they'd been in the library. His hands shook as he turned toward her, so he clenched them behind his back so she wouldn't see.

She met his eyes and there was something different to her stare. Something softer, something warmer.

"Selina?"

"You saved my brother," she whispered, her voice cracking and barely carrying across the room.

He caught his breath and couldn't help but stiffen at that declaration. A spoken fact, not a question. "Barber has been talking," he said with a shake of his head. When she nodded, he said, "I wish he wouldn't."

"I'm glad he did," she said.

He let out a long sigh. "Selina—" he began, but before he could finish, she crossed the distance between them in three long steps, wrapped her arms around his neck and pulled him in for a kiss.

He couldn't resist her, even if he'd wanted to try. But he didn't want to try. He just wanted this, so he sank into the kiss, angling his mouth to deepen it, exploring her mouth with his tongue, tugging her harder against his chest. Her fingers clenched against the back of his head, driving through his hair, massaging his neck, and he couldn't control the low moan that exited his lips at the sensation of her touching him.

"We don't have time to do this," he whispered against her mouth.

"No, not the way I want to," she agreed. Then she pushed back away from him and there was that wicked smile again. Intoxicating and maddening as it lit up her face. "But I can do this..."

She punctuated that statement by easing her hand between their bodies and cupping him. She stroked him, once, twice, and his head lolled back almost against his will as he groaned out her name. Pleasure streaked up his cock, into his balls, made his legs shake. It was more powerful than anything he'd ever experienced before.

He realized, somewhere in that fog of sensation, that she was unfastening his fall front. Her fingers closed around his bare flesh, hot and tight and certain as she rubbed him harder. Her mouth found his, her tongue tracing the crease of his lips, her breath hot against his mouth.

Then she stepped away and pointed to a chair. "Sit."

He blinked, dragged back to reality by the sharp order of a woman he could break with his passion if he wanted to. Except she kept breaking him, this petite sprite. And he liked it.

He sat as she'd asked, slouching a little to give her a place to perch as she fucked him. Only she didn't take it. She grabbed a pillow from his bed and dropped it between his splayed legs. She kept eye contact with him as she sank to her knees on the pillow and then leaned up to grab his cock again.

"Selina," he said, this time with more urgency. Only he couldn't do anything else because she was just so damned good at what she was doing with those magical fingers. And just when he thought it couldn't get better, she leaned in and traced the head of him with her tongue.

His eyes flew open and he stared down at her. She was watching him as she circled that pink tongue around and around the sensitive head, wetting him so that the friction of her hand disappeared. And then she took him into her mouth completely and stars burst before his eyes.

She sucked him gently, swirling her tongue over him as she sucked him in long, slow strokes. He found his hips lifting and she accommodated him, drawing him deeper and deeper into her throat as her pace increased. His legs shook, he gripped the armrests of the chair until he feared he could rip them from their moorings, and all the while, he was lost in sensation. Powerful pleasure unlike anything he'd ever felt rocked his cock, his entire body. His heart throbbed, his back arched, the pleasure built, brick by brick, until there was a wall ready to explode.

He lowered a hand against the back of her head and she smiled against his cock, increasing her pace.

"Selina, I'm going to—" he grunted. "I don't want to make you…"

She ignored his pleas, working him all the harder, and it was too much. It was everything. With a cry in the quiet, he came, his entire body rocking with pleasure. She took every drop of him, continuing to swirl her tongue around the exquisitely sensitive tip of his cock and drawing the intense sensation out further, even long after he'd been drained dry.

Only when he went limp in the chair did she let his cock from her lips with a wet pop and smile up at him. "That was…delicious," she whispered, and that same cock twitched with the wickedness of this remarkable woman.

"*That* was outrageous," he corrected. "I am no monk, but I've never come that hard before."

Triumph crossed her face. "Very good, then I suppose I win a prize." She pushed to her feet and walked to the basin across the room. She washed her hands and then looked at herself in the mirror where he'd been straightening his cravat earlier. She fiddled with herself, smoothed the fresh wrinkles in her gown.

"I won the prize, darlin'," he drawled as he got to his feet, testing his shaky legs to make sure he wouldn't fall over.

She grinned at him in the reflection of the mirror. "Why, Mr. Huntington!"

He cleared his throat as he tucked his cock away and straightened his own clothing. "Why did you talk to Barber about your brother?"

She froze for a beat and then faced him. "I didn't exactly," she said softly. "I saw him in the garden and we walked together for a while. The topic came up somewhat naturally. After all, Nicholas is something we share in common."

"I suppose," Derrick said, but wasn't certain of that explanation.

"I met Nicholas when I was eleven." Her expression was faraway. "He was sixteen and had only just found out that he was one of Roseford's bastards."

"Did the previous Roseford introduce you?" Derrick asked, clinging to this moment of vulnerability like a lifeline. She offered him so few of those—she was always on guard.

"No." Her laugh was brittle. "Certainly not. He didn't give a damn about any of us. My stepfather told me who Nicholas was, actually. Probably to hurt me."

Derrick wrinkled his brow, for her pain was just at the surface. Pain and anger. At her father, at her stepfather. And he began to understand, at least a little, why she had said she'd been on her own for most of her life.

"Why would he want to hurt you?" Derrick asked.

Her gaze darted to him, and for a moment wild terror lived in every flicker of her face. He could read it like a book. She'd said too much, revealed too much, everything was dangerous. She would do anything to escape.

"Why does anyone do anything?" she said, her tone back to breezy and without a care. She moved away from the mirror and past him to the fire, where she stared into the flames. "The point is that I later created a situation where I could meet Nicholas. I don't know what I expected, but he was...he was so kind to me. Like I was his true sister, not just half-blood. He has meant the world to me ever since. And I thank you for saving him. For saving the part of me that would have died with him."

Derrick let out a shaky breath and moved to her. He caught her shoulder and turned her back toward him. She stared up at him with those hypnotically blue eyes boring into his very soul, and for a wild moment he wished they could stay in this room together forever. Just the two of them. No one else.

"Your brother is the bravest man I've had the pleasure of know-ing," he said, his voice low and rough with emotion that always came when he thought of the war and those who had been lost and changed by it. "It was my honor to do even the slightest bit in keeping him alive."

Her lower lip trembled, and he thought she might talk to him more about herself, about her brother, about the truth that he could see now lived just below her surface. But then she cleared all of that from her expression and instead laughed as she reached up to touch his cravat.

"It looks like I ruined this with my ardor," she said, and it was apparent all other subjects were now closed.

He tried not to be hurt by that fact and instead smiled down at her as she started to untie the mess of a knot he had created. "I would not allow you to accept the blame for that. I am a notoriously bad cravat tier."

She smoothed the long swatch of fabric, then lifted up on her toes as she began to rewrap it around his neck. "You could have allowed me to take the blame. I never would have known the difference," she said softly.

He looked down at her with a laugh. "But that would have been a lie."

Her brow wrinkled partly in concentration, but he also saw that this subject troubled her. "And you've never told one of those in your life?"

He tensed, thinking about his upbringing. His stern parents, obsessed with honor and reputation. To the point they would select reputation over their own son, taking his grandfather's side when a choice was demanded. "I was raised not to do so. But I'm certain I have."

She smoothed the cravat gently and then her gaze darted from his. "There you are, Mr. Huntington. Fine as can be."

He pivoted to the mirror and found she had tied him the perfect knot. Even his valet long ago had not done such a superb job. "Fine as can be," he repeated.

There was a jingle of a bell in the distance, and she looked up at him with a smile. "And there is the bell to call us all to supper. We

JESS MICHAELS

must go."

"May I..." He hesitated. "May I escort you, Selina?" He held out
his elbow as he asked.

She stared at the outstretched arm, focused intently. Then she
lifted her gaze to his and nodded. "Yes."

She slipped her fingers into the crook of his elbow and he
guided her from the room, first being careful that no one would see
them in such a compromising position. And it had compromised a
great deal at that. Her perceived virtue, both of their positions in the
household...and the precarious hold he still had on control.

∾

"He's very handsome."

Selina jolted from her distracted state, staring down the
long supper table toward Derrick, and glanced toward the lady at
her side. The Duchess of Crestwood, Meg as she insisted all her
friends call her, was smiling at her with a knowing expression.

"Who?" Selina said, but her tone was weak, indeed. She'd been
caught ogling the man who had imbued her every fantasy with life
since his arrival here.

How could he not, after what they'd shared? Those moments
before supper had been highly charged. Even now she could feel
the hard, heavy weight of him in her mouth, taste him on her
tongue, the sounds of his moans were still loud in her ears. She had
loved stealing his tightly wound control with her mouth and her
hands.

She'd liked even more the way he looked at her after it was over.
With passion and desire, of course. But with more than that. He
looked at her like she was a fully formed person, a rare thing in the
world of men. So rare that she had gotten away with stealing under
their noses.

That fact sobered her.

"Mr. Derrick Huntington," Meg responded softly. "But you *know*

122

who I mean. You are just playing coy with me. It is your business, of course, but he is quite the catch."

"I'm not trying to catch anyone, Your Grace," Selina muttered as the footman took their plates away in preparation for the final course.

The duchess nodded slowly. "Yes. You are very independent."

"Is that a slur in your mind?" Selina asked.

"Not at all!" Meg set her fork down and pivoted slightly to face her. "Gracious, I have nothing but admiration for your self-sufficiency. I suppose it is a failing of our group of duchesses. We're all deliriously happy in our marriages, so we are always looking for ways to marry everyone else off."

"I do not think you would be very successful in marrying me off," Selina said with a smile to her companion, because she liked the duchess quite a bit. She'd watched Meg go through a scandal with her head held high and continue to fight for anyone bullied or treated badly. "And...yes. Mr. Huntington is very, very handsome."

Meg laughed. "And it never hurts to look."

Selina tipped her glass toward her. "That is something I can drink to."

They clinked their glasses, and for a moment Selina's humor improved. Until, that was, her gaze flitted past Derrick and found Lady Winford. She and her husband were chatting with the Duke and Duchess of Sheffield. That kind couple did not look pleased with the results in the least, but they were managing out of politeness.

Selina's gaze drifted to the countess's neck. She wasn't wearing the Breston necklace. Not yet, at any rate. Her palms itched at the thought of the piece. It was the reason she was here, after all. It was easy to forget that when Derrick touched her, but it remained true.

And perhaps now was the time to put aside her wild attraction to the man and instead focus on her job. That would make Vale happy, at any rate. She knew her partner was anxious that they just get this done and move on.

Tonight would be a perfect opportunity. Selina only had to lay the groundwork. She shifted in her chair and set her fork down with a little sigh.

Just as she had suspected would happen, Meg leaned forward to rest a hand on her forearm. "Are you well, my dear? You suddenly got an odd look."

"Just a headache," Selina lied. "It must be all the excitement of the past few days. I swear I am unaccustomed to these kinds of parties."

"They can be overwhelming," Meg said kindly. She glanced down the table toward Katherine, who was sitting beside Robert. Their heads were close together, and from the smile on Katherine's face, Selina's brother was saying something very naughty. "When we break from supper in a few minutes, why don't you sneak away to your chamber?" Meg said. "I'll make your excuses to the group."

"That is very kind, but I couldn't be so rude," Selina said, even though this was exactly what she'd been steering Meg to do. But she couldn't make it too obvious. The duchess was a sharp woman.

"It isn't rude to take care of yourself," Meg said. "I insist. I'll wager after a good night's sleep, you will be right as rain."

"Well…" Selina pretended to consider it. "I suppose I won't do anyone any good feeling as I do. If you don't mind, I would greatly appreciate it."

Meg squeezed her hand. "Of course. Anything for a friend."

Selina stiffened. A friend. Was she anyone's friend, truly? Could she be when she was scheming behind their backs?

She pushed the thought away as the final plates were taken. She settled back with a sigh as she awaited the signal for the guests to rise and split off with the ladies going to the large parlor and the men going to their port.

She had wiggled herself into an opportunity tonight. And she had to make it worthwhile by focusing on the task at hand. Not on regrets. Not on consequences. Certainly not on Derrick. And she *could* do it.

At least, she hoped she could.

CHAPTER 13

S elina glided free the lockpick that was hidden in her hair and
wedged it into Lady Winford's lock. The lockpick was ornate.
It had to be in order to fit in with the other decorative pins that held
her hair. She smiled at the sparkle of paste gems as she wiggled the
handle and heard a distinct click of the mechanism giving way.

She opened the door and stepped inside, then took a long, deep
breath. After days of feeling out of sorts, at last she was herself
again. Picking locks, sneaking through the dark, relaxing into the
role of Faceless Fox. This was much better than the confusion she
felt whenever she was around her family, whenever she was around
Derrick. When she questioned herself, her motives, her past, her
future.

She blinked as she realized she was still standing at the door,
woolgathering instead of focusing. And focus was paramount to
these things. She thrust her shoulders back and moved across the
room, letting her eyes adjust to the dim light of the low fire. Now
she just had to find wherever Lady Winford had put the necklace.

"Not in the open," she murmured, but still crossed to the little
box on top of the dressing table. She dug through the jewels there.
"Paste, paste...real..." She examined the piece closely and then

tossed it aside. Pretty, but not worth the trouble. "Paste, paste, real, real..."

There was nothing of material value in the jewelry box, certainly not the Breston necklace. But she hadn't expected it to be. Lady Winford would hide it, thinking that would protect her from the Fox or any other interested party.

Selina had marked several places where Lady Winford might put her jewels when she had been here with Derrick. She moved toward the false drawer in one of the dressers, but as she opened it and slid clothing around to find it, her mind wandered again. That night when Derrick had found her snooping here and they'd searched the room together had been one she'd never forget. Aside from Vale's assistance with research and pretending to be her companion, she worked alone, she lived alone, she'd resigned herself to being alone.

But when she'd stood in this very room with Derrick, she hadn't felt alone. She never felt alone with him. She felt comfortable and accepted. She felt worshipped and adored.

A false feeling, of course. Derrick Huntington wanted her body. His passion every time he touched her proved that. He would do or say anything to get that prize. When he was bored, when their time together was over, he would forget all about her. Other men had. Hell, she had done the same with plenty of lovers. Passion was transactional and once the price became too high, it lost its value.

Except that all around her were couples who didn't seem to fit the mold she'd come to expect. Robert and Katherine, for example. Robert had been as wild as Selina now was. Only he'd changed with love. He was faithful, and even all these years later, he seemed as drawn to and in love with his wife as he ever had been.

The Duke and Duchess of Crestwood were also exceptions to the rule she'd thought existed in the world. She knew their story, everyone did. Their passion for each other had broken Meg's prior engagement, destroyed a friendship for a time and sent ripples through Society for years. If ever there was a recipe for falling out of love, that was it.

But they hadn't. Just yesterday she'd caught them kissing passionately behind a tree in the garden, like they were young lovers.

And the Duke and Duchess of Sheffield? Also seemingly in perfect accord. Whenever they were near each other, it seemed they were bound to touch. Like magnets, drawn together. Or moths to a flame. Always holding hands or brushing fingers. Two becoming one in a constant reaffirmation of connection.

She blinked. She'd spent a lifetime telling herself that kind of lasting affection didn't exist. It seemed it did. She'd also told herself she didn't want it. And yet, when Derrick touched her, when he smiled at her from across a room, she felt the flutters of something more than mere desire. Something deeper than passion or pleasure.

"Little idiot," she grunted out loud.

She was truly a fool for allowing those feelings. After all, Derrick didn't know the truth about her, did he? He was seeking the Faceless Fox with unswerving devotion to his duty. He wanted to catch the thief and bring that person to justice. If he ever found out that it was Selina?

Certainly all the tenderness or sweetness or connection she sometimes saw in his eyes when he looked at her would be gone. He would despise her, not only for who she was and how she'd lived, but for the lies she'd told him. He would see pleasure as pain then. He would see seduction as manipulation.

He would hate her.

For a moment, deep, sharp pain gripped her at that idea. So powerful that she reached out to press a hand on the dressing table to keep herself from falling over. And it was in that moment that she heard voices in the adjoining room.

She gasped. She'd been so lost in thought, she hadn't heard the door in the adjoining chamber open. There were female voices, two of them, and they were coming right for the room she was in. She glanced at the door that exited to the hallway, but it was too far away. The knob was already turning.

She had no choice but to dive for the window, pressing herself behind the curtains as the adjoining door opened and she heard footfalls into the room.

"Well, the fire didn't die entirely, that's something," came a very Scottish voice. "Lady Winford wouldn't let me light it while she readied herself before supper. Something about the heat ruining her curls. Her *perfect* curls." There was mocking in the voice now. "But I'll stir these embers now and have it ready so she doesn't scream the house down later."

"Never can be pleased, that one," came a voice in the distance from the adjoining room. "I'd go if I could, but…"

There was a cackle from the other side of the curtain. "But we all know what happens to servants who leave her house, by force or by choice. Poor Mary had such a bad reference, I hear she's a barmaid now at the Lucky Swan in London."

"It don't have as much respectability, I guess, but the wages come at a far lower cost," the other voice added. "Oh drat, she's tangled up the knot on this dressing gown something fierce. I swear she does it just to make extra work. Will you help, Gertie?"

"Aye."

The voice in the room behind the curtain faded, as did the footsteps, and Selina sucked in a breath. She would only have the amount of time required to loosen the knot they were discussing in the other room, then the servant would return. It was likely she'd throw open the curtain just to check that the window was secured for the night. And then Selina would be cooked.

She had to get out. Right now.

She stepped from the curtains and glanced toward the door. The room was already brighter thanks to Gertie stoking the fire. Which made Selina's next moves all the more treacherous. She had to get across the room, crossing in front of the now-open adjoining door, and to the exit without being caught.

She drew a long breath and began to creep toward the wall opposite the open door. The farther she was from the gossiping

THE HEART OF A HELLION

servants, the less likely it was she would be caught. The more likely she could find some second hiding spot if one of them did come into the room.

"Penny, you're only making it worse!" one of the servants said with a giggle. "Heavens, you've wrapped it all around itself."

"You know that bitch will complain about the wrinkles, too," the other girl said. "And with no time to go press them out."

Selina shook her head as she eased around the foot of the bed, moving into the line of sight of the two servants if they looked her way. Lady Winford sounded like a terror to work for. She deserved whatever she would get when Selina finally took that damned necklace.

She inched along the foot of the bed, easing around it at last and back toward the wall, into the shadows. Just as she neared the door, she pressed her foot down on one of the floorboards and there was a loud creak that pierced the silence of the room.

"What was that?" one of the servants whispered to the other. "Did you hear that sound from t'other room?"

Selina was still a least a few feet from escape and there was nowhere else to hide except to tuck herself hard into the shadows and hope her dark blue evening gown would offer her some camouflage.

"Perhaps it's a ghost," came one of the whispered voices.

"Oh, don't speak of that, I'll be up all night with the terrors."

Selina reached for the handle of the door and glided it open softly. She kept her gaze on the other room, listening as the women debated which one of them should be responsible for going and checking to see if they were truly being haunted.

She stepped into the hall and shut the door with a quiet click. She heard the maids squeal from within and hustled away just in case one of them got up the gumption to check the hallway for their ghost.

Her heart throbbed as she staggered up the hallway, away from the room. She had been the Faceless Fox for years and never been anything close to caught. It was a matter of pride for her, really, to know that no one had seen more than a shadow of her. To the point they didn't even know she was a woman, not a man.

But tonight she had been distracted. More than distracted. And that made her sloppy. It put her in danger. And it proved, once again, how being close to other people didn't match with being a master thief.

So she was going to have to decide which thing was more important. The burgeoning relationships she was starting to forge? Or the life she had lived for so long that she hardly remembered another?

Derrick stepped into Selina's chamber and quickly shut the door so no one coming up the hall might see him. He looked around and his brow wrinkled. She'd left the festivities of the gathering downstairs with a headache, or so he'd been told when the gentlemen rejoined the ladies a short while ago. And yet she wasn't here in her bedroom, resting. He didn't hear her in the adjoining sitting room, either, but he went there regardless and opened the door.

He was startled to find Selina's companion, Vale, sitting by the fire, a book in her hand. She glanced up, and instead of panicking at the sight of a strange man in her mistress's chamber, she arched a brow at him and set her novel aside.

"Mr. Huntington," she said. "This is unexpected."

"Miss Williams," he said, trying not to shift with discomfort. "I apologize for disturbing you. I ought not have entered the room."

"No, I suppose propriety dictates such," Vale said, getting to her feet and taking a step toward him. Pale blue eyes swept over his face and down his body. "But Selina and I have never stuck much to the rules of propriety."

His brow wrinkled at the purr in her tone. The way she glided toward him. "*Selina* most definitely marches to her own beat," Derrick said. "And you two are obviously close."

"Very," Vale said. "So you can understand why I might be protective of her."

"You are well within your rights to be so. It's good to know Selina has someone on her side."

"Are you on her side, Mr. Huntington?" she pressed, arms folding across her chest. "Or are you just tupping her?"

His lips parted at the unexpectedly blunt question. Part of him wished to deny it all, to act as though he didn't know what she was talking about. But it was evident this woman did know what he'd been up to with Selina. Perhaps she'd told her friend. Selina had made it clear she didn't have a prudish mind when it came to sex and sin. Or perhaps Vale had overheard something, put the pieces together when tidying up for her mistress.

Or maybe they were just too obvious in their ardor. After all, he could tell Barber suspected them, as well.

"You would have to speak to your mistress about that," he said, refusing to reveal anything that Selina hadn't, herself, said out loud.

Vale arched a fine, blonde brow. "I'm asking *you*."

He frowned. So much for trying to go the gentlemanly route. Not that he could. He'd thrown gentlemanly out the window the moment he took Selina against the library wall.

"You are clearly a clever woman and I can see you know what you think you know. So I won't deny that Selina and I have grown...close...since our arrival here." He blinked. "More close than I ever could have imagined. But I'm not...using her, Miss Williams."

Her eyes narrowed. "You truly care for her?"

She acted as though that was a strange thought. Why? Did she not believe Selina warranted someone to care for her? Or did she just judge all such clandestine relationships harshly?

He hesitated in his answer. He hadn't told Selina he cared for her. Christ, he hadn't allowed that thought to fill his own mind all

JESS MICHAELS

that much. Caring for her was not in the cards. It wasn't why he was here.

Either way, he certainly didn't want her companion to be the one he told his feelings to.

He shrugged. "She is captivating."

Vale smiled, but it was on the edge of a smirk. "Oh yes. She is *that*. Everyone ends up captivated by her in the end. She's like a flame. She draws moths like us, Mr. Huntington. She draws us in and it's warm and lovely in her circle. But you must also be wary, lest you burn up in the fire."

He frowned. Vale was defending Selina, yes, as he would expect a friend to do. But it was all in a very backhanded manner. Why would she do that?

"Not a kind assessment of a friend," he murmured.

"Don't get your back up, Mr. Huntington," she said with a chuckle. "I'm only warning you to be careful. Selina is all the wonderful things you've seen, all the things you care about, even if you refuse to admit it. But she can be more. She can be less."

"Can't we all," he said, holding her stare.

There was a sound from the room behind him, and Vale stepped forward. "Sounds like your real desire is coming in now. I'll leave you two alone."

She pushed past him as Selina entered the room. He pivoted, watching as Selina's gaze flitted first to him, a combination of pleasure and confusion. Then to Vale. When she looked at her companion, she wiped her emotions away and gave a little shake of her head.

"Mr. Huntington has come to call, *miss*," Vale said as she stepped forward. "I'll leave you two alone." She glanced back over her shoulder. "Good evening."

"Good evening," he mirrored.

Selina was quiet until Vale had left the room and closed them in together. He took her in with her dark blue gown and her white gloves with the blue stitching along the seams. She was so utterly lovely.

"I-I didn't expect you," she said at last, taking a step toward him, then hesitating like she wasn't certain she should do so.

"I know you didn't," he said softly. "I was surprised not to find you here when I arrived. You called off the gathering with a headache."

She arched a brow. "Were you coming to check up on me?"

He laughed. "Yes."

She smiled at him. "Well, you know as well as I do that those events can become tedious. If I wasn't entirely honest about my needing to escape, perhaps I can be forgiven."

He saw the paleness of her cheeks, the tightness of her lips, tells of discomfort. But was it just that she'd lied about her headache, or was Vale's implication that there was more to her the reason?

"I've probably snuck out of a few parties with the same excuse, especially in my youth," he said, moving toward her. "I don't judge."

"Good," she said, reaching for him.

Their hands tangled. His bare one, her gloved one and a thrill of desire shot through him. Hardened him. This woman was a drug and he never wanted to be free of the influence.

He cleared his throat. "Your companion is…interesting."

Her fingers tightened a fraction on his. "She already knew about us," she whispered.

"I assumed so, by the way she talked," he said. "She's…blunt."

Selina's gaze flickered up to his face. Color had returned to her cheeks, but now it was a blush. "I suppose she can be."

"She isn't your typical lady's companion," he continued to press. Why he did it, he couldn't say. Only that his conversation with the other woman had aroused such…suspicion…in him. A feeling he didn't want, not when it came to Selina.

Her brows lifted. "Are you judging her because you think she might have a past?"

"No. We all have a past," he said. "Are you saying I've guessed correctly?"

She let out her breath in a sound of almost frustration. "Derrick."

"I'm simply curious."

She shook her hand from his and crossed away from him. She stood before the fire, a silhouette of curves and angles that was so achingly beautiful that he wanted to fall down on his knees and worship. That was the flame Vale had implied earlier. That beauty and allure that sucked everyone closer to this woman.

And at what cost?

She pursed her lips. "It isn't my place to share her past."

"Then tell me yours," he said. "How did you meet? How long have you known her?"

Her lips pursed, annoyance, he thought. Perhaps something more. Something darker. "How does anyone meet in these circumstances? She was looking for work. I was looking for someone to fill her position."

Derrick's frown deepened. And there it was, that cagey reluctance to tell him something that should have been so benign. Which meant one of two things. Either she didn't trust him enough to give him even the most harmless of information, or...it wasn't harmless at all. There was something she hid because it was worth hiding. Especially from a man like him who represented the law to her.

He didn't like either answer. He drew a short breath. "Selina—"

She interrupted him with a lifted hand. "I'll tell you that she's been a friend to me when I needed her most." Her gaze got distant. "Loyalty is hard to come by in my world."

He pulled away slightly at the turn of phrase. "Your world?" he repeated. "And what world is that?"

She stepped back in his direction, her blue eyes wider, her hands shaking ever so slightly at her sides. "Why are you here, Derrick?"

He knew she was changing the subject. Trying to distract him from the line of questioning she didn't want him to follow. Why, he couldn't say. As an investigator, it increased his doubts.

But in this room, with her standing so close, *was* he an investigator? When he stood before this goddess, trembling with need for her, was he the man sent to look for a thief? Or was he just a man? Standing before a woman who made his blood burn and his body ache?

In this moment he didn't want to be anything more than that. So he set his questions aside.

"Are you just here to interrogate me about my companion?" she continued.

"No," he murmured and he slid his fingers into her hair. He bunched them against her scalp, feeling her pins shift against his hand. One pricked at his skin, sharper than he'd expected, and he smoothed the locks anyway and the pins clattered to the floor around her feet. "You know why I'm here."

She shivered, an expression of surrender. Of desire. Of the need that burned in her as much as it burned in him. "Why?" she pressed, making him say it. Making him own it.

"To finish what we started earlier tonight," he whispered, and then he lowered his mouth to hers and claimed her lips.

She lifted her gloved hands to his face, the silky fabric stroking along his jaw as she made a soft groan of desire into his mouth. It wasn't enough. He wanted her skin on his.

He pulled back and met her eyes as he lifted one hand between his own. He kissed her knuckles, blowing steam through the glove before he unfastened the button at her elbow, gliding his thumb beneath the fabric and swirling a circle against her flesh with the pad.

Her eyes fluttered shut and she whispered his name in the quiet. He was going to make her groan it, scream it, offer it as a prayer.

He rolled the glove down. Her initials were stitched in the lining in a pink thread. He traced them with his finger before he leaned in and kissed a path along her inner arm as he inched the fabric lower. He nipped her flesh. Her hips surged, bumping his, asking for what would come in a moment. He ignored the demand, though it was almost impossible to do so, and instead exposed her wrist. There was a tiny scar there, and he swirled his tongue around it, feeling the raised flesh, tasting the lightly salty flavor of her.

He tugged each finger of the glove, and at last he tossed it away over his shoulder. He sucked her index finger between his lips, swirling his tongue around its length. When he allowed her finger to pop free, she rubbed it across his lips, her gaze wide and dilated.

He repeated every single action on the opposite hand, removing her glove the same way he would soon slowly and purposefully remove the rest of her clothing.

And she seemed to have the same idea. She grabbed his lapels and used them as leverage to drag him to her mouth. Their lips collided again in rough, powerful passion. She devoured, driving her tongue with certainty, biting his lip gently and then less gently, pulling him as close as she could while her fingers tugged the cravat she had only helped him tie a few hours before.

It felt like a lifetime since they last touched.

She unwound the long swatch of fabric and tossed it to the ground with her gloves. Continuing to kiss him, she tore at the buttons on his shirt, freeing enough of them that he could push away from her and tug the contraption over his head. He was ready to step back into her, but her stare stopped him.

"What is it?" he asked, breathless.

She was staring at his chest. At the scar that slashed across his left pectoral, the other one on his stomach, marks of war and sacrifice. She lifted a shaking hand and pressed it to the hot flesh, and he felt like he would die from it and it would be a happy death.

"I've never seen you naked," she murmured.

He nodded. "Neither one of us has seen the other unclothed. We've always been too...rushed."

"Well, we have all night now, don't we?" she whispered, her gaze fluttering up to his. "And I'd like to savor every moment of it."

CHAPTER 14

I t was a funny thing, vulnerability. Selina hadn't really felt the emotion when this man had taken her against a library wall or when she had sucked his cock until he spent in her throat. But now, fully clothed, staring at his bare chest and admitting she wanted to revel in everything that would happen next…

That was vulnerable. Because it revealed too much of what she'd begun to feel without wishing to feel it. It revealed that this was more than some fun little tup with a near stranger.

There was connection here now. Something deep and powerful that had meaning she didn't want to analyze.

So she didn't. She pushed it all away and returned both hands to his chest. She shivered as she touched him, all hard muscle and bright scars. Scars that proved what he'd been through. Scars that were linked to the near-death of someone she loved dearly. Derrick had saved Nicholas. And she could never repay him for that.

No matter how many times they did this.

He watched her as she rubbed her hands over him, fingers clenching through the curly hair across his pectorals, thumbs teasing his nipples, palm flattening across his toned belly. He was a god, only not made of stone or legend.

He was made of flesh and bone, and that flesh and bone was moved by her. Wanted her. She wasn't about to waste it.

She lifted her gaze to his, challenging him as she always did because she knew he liked that moment when his practiced control snapped. Even now she saw him wrestling with it. Trying not to become the animal who rutted with her. And both of them anticipating the moment when he'd be just that.

It was all just a game of how they would get there.

She unfastened the fall front of his trousers for the second time that night. And for the second time, she found a hard and ready cock hot against her hand. She stroked him and his eyes fluttered shut.

"Do you know how much I wanted you before supper?" he asked.

She smiled as she leaned in to nuzzle his neck, still rubbing his cock with long, firm strokes. "I could hazard a guess," she whispered.

"So much that I could hardly control myself," he growled, nipping her ear and sending a shockwave of pleasure through her body. "But do you know the funny thing that you sucking me dry does?"

She lifted her head and found his gaze again. "What's that?" she asked, wary now, because there was a wickedness in his tone that she'd never heard before. One that called to her, made her stomach clench, made her hands shake.

"You make me all the more capable of maintaining control so I can torture you for hours. I can make you beg for *hours*, Selina. I can make you come over and over until you're weak and shaking for me." His brown eyes glittered in the firelight, a predator, she his prey. "So let us begin."

"Derrick," she whispered, but he didn't answer. He just swept her into his arms and carried her to her bed. He tossed her there, motioning her to lie on her pillows as he stripped out of the rest of his clothing.

She was still dressed, and she stared at him now. Naked. Good God, so beautiful in every way. She wanted to trace her tongue along every line of him. She wanted to rub herself on him like a cat. She wanted to touch all those hard curves and valleys until she knew him as well as she knew herself.

And she hated herself for wanting those intimate things that went far beyond mere sex.

He braced his hands on the bed and caught her ankles. She squealed as he dragged her down toward him with one yank. She splayed out because he forced her to and leaned up on her elbows to see what he would do.

He held her gaze as he removed one slipper, driving his thumb hard into the arch of her foot through her stocking, and she threw her head back with a hiss of pleasure-pain combined. He repeated the action on the other foot, and then his hands dragged up her calves, pushing her dress up, digging his fingers into her stockings. And she was lost in sensation.

Sex had been a favorite pastime of hers from the first time she'd surrendered her virginity. But this was different. It was *always* different when it was them. He woke something in her that wasn't like anyone else. He dragged something from her that she wasn't even certain she wanted to share. And when his hands cupped her kneecaps, she made a sound unlike anything that had ever squeezed from her throat before.

"You make it so easy to know where to torture you," he laughed.

"Is that the kind of interrogation you like to participate in, Mr. Huntington?" she asked, wishing her voice wasn't so breathless. "Torture?"

"Not the worst idea." He leaned in and pressed his mouth to her knee as his hands moved higher under her skirts. He found the top of her stockings and tugged, rending the fastenings away with a tear of fabric. "Confess."

Her mind was spinning so fast, she hardly had the ability to feel anxiety at that demand. Confess. Right now she might be so foolish as to confess anything.

"I have done no wrong," she lied, squirming when he pulled her torn stockings down, baring her thighs, her knees, her calves.

He tossed the stockings away and pressed his hands on her thighs. His fingers dented her flesh. "I doubt that, Miss Oliver. Confess to me."

His voice was so deep, so hypnotic that it was almost impossible not to obey. "What do you want to know?" she panted. "A little more specificity, if you please, sir."

He laughed before he shoved her skirts around her stomach and pushed her thighs open wide, exposing her to him. He shuddered as he looked at her, her sex glistening, her legs already shaking. "Confess that you want to come," he demanded, his gaze lifting to hers. "Confess that you want my mouth on you."

She heard the garbled sound choke from her throat and nodded. "Oh, I most definitely confess that. Freely. I want your mouth on me, your tongue in me. I want you to taste my release."

"Christ, Selina," he grunted, and then he settled between her legs, cupped her backside and lifted her so he was granted better access. "Your wish is my command."

His head dropped and she felt his breath on her sex. Hot and steaming against flesh that felt almost too sensitive. She lifted toward him, seeking and begging without words. But he didn't deny her, even if he had promised erotic torture. His mouth found her as he peeled her open with his thumbs, and he licked her hard from the rosette of her bottom to the tingling nub of her clitoris.

She settled back into the pillows, letting her body go limp and focusing only on sensation as he lavished her with his tongue, awakening every nerve in her sex, spreading pleasure through her limbs. He did that for a long time, just licking and teasing, tasting her like she was fine wine he wanted to savor. But as time drew on, endless and limitless, he began to focus his tongue on her clitoris.

And he was as proficient at this as he was at everything else. He sucked her, swirling his tongue around the swollen nub, flicking the hood back so that the pleasure got sharp and heady. She lifted into him, grinding against him as she tried to find more, more of anything. More of everything.

He gave it. He watched her as he licked, changing his pace when she sucked in her breath, angling his head when she covered her mouth with her hand so her moans wouldn't ricochet through the house.

And just when she thought she might go mad, he slid two fingers deep within her sheath, pumping into her slowly and gently. The pressure of his tongue increased, the pace of her hips joined. She began to shake as she edged herself toward the cliff of pleasure, needing it as much as she needed breath or water in this moment.

And then the waves hit her. One after another, they washed over her and she rode them as she bit back screams and dug her fingers into the coverlet so hard she feared she'd rip the fabric. He tortured her through it all, as he'd promised he would, sucking her as she quivered, pulsing his fingers into her as she clenched around them. Taking and giving in equal measure until she was weak and gasping, her vision blurred and her ears ringing with the most powerful orgasm she'd ever experienced.

She felt him moving, but couldn't lift her head to watch. Felt his fingers withdraw from her, felt his mouth release her. The weight of him bowed the bed as he kissed a path to the buttons along the front of her gown. He unfastened her and tugged her to an upright position to pull the dress away.

She was naked beneath it. She'd never seen much value in a chemise except to make lines where they didn't belong. He chuckled as he tossed the gown over the edge to join the rest of her abandoned items. She waited for him to just slam into her, to ease his own ache, but he didn't. Instead, he lay on his side, tracing her curves with his fingertips as he stared at her as if he were in no rush to claim her.

"You are lovely," he murmured, leaning in to press a kiss to the side of her throat. "So lovely."

"I bet you say that to all the ladies you shatter with your tongue," she teased, an effort to take away the power of what he whispered.

He didn't lift his head but nibbled a path down her throat, lower to her breast. He licked one taut nipple and she gasped in pleasure.

"I don't remember the last lady I shattered," he said. "I'm not sure I'll ever remember another. There will only be you and that amazing display I just witnessed."

She squeezed her eyes shut as she lowered her hands into his crisp hair and held him at her breast. When he was licking and sucking her, he wasn't just pleasuring her. He also wasn't looking at her. He couldn't see how he moved her and how much she wanted to believe this attraction between them meant something.

Even though she knew it couldn't. She shivered, both from the stimulation of his mouth at her breast and from disappointment at that truth. That it wouldn't last. It couldn't.

So she was going to live every moment of it now.

She cupped his chin and turned his face toward her. His pupils were dilated to almost pure black, and there was a slight smirk on his face that made him look far less honorable than she knew him to be.

"I want to taste myself on you," she whispered, pulling him toward her.

He growled like an animal seeking its mate and lunged up, smashing his lips to hers. They were still slick, sweet with her release, and she devoured them and him until there was nothing in her mind but pleasure. She opened her legs, welcoming him to settle there. His cock was hard at her entrance, heavy with desire as he nudged her with it.

"Yes, yes, yes," she murmured, over and over until he reached between them and pushed himself into place. He lifted his head, watching her as he glided forward, deep into her body, claiming her and filling her and making them one, if only for a little while.

He surged then, thrusting hard and deep. She clenched against him, grinding up to stimulate her already sensitive clitoris all over again. His eyes went wide and he stroked a second time, his hands gliding up her sides. He dug one hand into her hair, holding her in place, and the other he wrapped gently but firmly against her throat.

She spasmed in pleasure, nodding against him so he'd know she wanted this. With that permission he transformed into that wild animal again. He took and took, his fingers pressing gently into her flesh, his cock not gentle at all, but probing and claiming in a way she'd never known she wanted.

The second orgasm erupted almost without warning and she lost all control. He caught her mouth with his, swallowing the sound of her pleasure, sucking her tongue as she jerked against him helplessly.

She was still reeling with pleasure when he withdrew from her body and rolled her over. She positioned herself on her hands and knees and he chuckled again, this time possessive and low. His mouth burrowed against her, his tongue piercing her, tasting her, wetting her as she pushed back against him and moaned. She pushed her hand between her legs, rubbing herself to the edge, then withdrawing, to the edge, then back again to draw out the pleasure this time as he licked her.

And then he pulled away and she felt his cock at her entrance. She pushed back, forcing him to the hilt as he grunted out a curse that echoed in the room. He gripped her hips, digging his fingers in hard enough that she would surely bruise, and then he fucked her. Hard. Fast.

She continued to touch herself, gripping him, grinding against him and her own fingers, and the third orgasm nearly caused her to lose consciousness. She pushed her face into the pillow, screaming as her entire body convulsed, milking him. He let out a low moan and then he was gone from her twitching body, his hot seed splashing across her lower back as he came with a trembling cry.

He collapsed over her, his sweat mingling with her own, his

arms hard and strong around her, his mouth against hers as they panted together in sated bliss.

She allowed herself to relax into him, let her breath match his. This wouldn't last. She knew it. But she was going to bloody well enjoy every moment until the last.

~

He left hours later, in the middle of the dark night, sneaking from her bed with whispered promises and heated kisses. And as her door closed, Selina snuggled into her covers, reveling in the beauty of what they'd shared. It had been perfect and lovely and unforgettable. It had changed her, but she could accept that change because it was for the better. She would never again be the Selina she'd been before that night.

She didn't want to be.

She was about to lean over to snuff out the candle he'd lit to help him find all his scattered clothing when the door to the adjoining chamber came open. Vale stood there, leaning in the jamb, staring at her.

"Well, that took long enough," she murmured.

Selina felt heat flood her cheeks and tucked the sheets higher around her breasts as she struggled to a seated position. "Please tell me you weren't sitting in that room listening to us the whole time."

One of Vale's fine eyebrows arched. "Why? Are there things you told him that you wouldn't want me to know?"

"I could ask you the same," Selina returned. "I *know* you spoke to him about me. Enough so that he had a lot of pointed questions about you. About me and our past."

Vale's brow lowered. "He had questions about *me* after I spoke to him?"

"Yes." Selina let out an exasperated breath. "Which you shouldn't have done at all, Vale."

Vale speared her with a glare. "Well, he snuck into your chamber

THE HEART OF A HELLION

and found me there. What was I supposed to do? Blush and bow away and leave it at that?"

"Yes!" Selina pushed from the bed and grabbed for a dressing gown she'd draped across the back of her chair a few hours before. "That would be more fitting a servant."

"I'm not your bloody servant," Vale snapped.

Selina was brought up short by the sharpness of her partner's words and pivoted to face her. She'd known Vale a long time. Even before they began working together. Vale had a bite to her. A hardness that could cut or maim if the other woman wished it to.

When it flashed, it was instant and heated. But it was always short-lived. Vale could erase the anger from her face with a blink, just as she had now that she had aimed that anger at Selina. It was gone from her face, leaving impassive boredom in its wake.

What Selina had never understood was whether Vale continued to stoke the anger in her chest in those moments or truly let it go.

"I'm sorry," she said, reaching for Vale's hand. Her friend allowed her to take it. "I'm not trying to imply you are my servant. But *he* thinks you are. Everyone here does."

"I suppose you are correct," Vale said. "But you must know how dangerous he is if he's turned his investigative mind to you and to me."

Selina worried her lip. Yes, when she thought of Derrick, she thought dangerous. Just not in the way Vale thought it. But it wouldn't do to reveal that to her partner. She had to be managed, manipulated. Good thing that was Selina's specialty.

"That mind was easily turned away by my bedding him," Selina said, and the fact that it was true stung. She'd bedded him because she wanted him. And yet part of her knew that it had also been to control him.

And she hated how that fact tainted those powerful moments between them.

"There may not be a way to fuck him every time he suspects something about us," Vale said softly.

JESS MICHAELS

"But—"

"No!" Vale's tone grew sharp again. "No buts, Selina. This is threatening us both. You were supposed to get that necklace tonight from Lady Winford, but you didn't. I've never known you to miss your shot when you took it."

Selina shifted. Christ, she didn't want to have this conversation right now. Not when she was still warm and tingling from the night with Derrick. The pleasure faded with every moment she talked to Vale, replaced by cold, hard realities she didn't want to face just yet.

"I mistimed the entry, that is all," Selina said. Lied. After all, it had been her distraction that had kept her from her quarry as much as bad timing. "The maids haven't gone into the room until ten-thirty for a few nights, so I assumed it was their pattern. Tonight they were in at ten-fifteen."

Vale folded her arms, and Selina could tell she was wary of that explanation. "If you're not careful, you're going to end up transported. And friend or not, I'm *not* going down with you."

Selina flinched. "I'd never ask you to."

Vale crossed the room to her and caught her hands. Her expression gentled at last. "If I'm hard on you, it's because I'm worried. Let's get Lady Winford's necklace and *get out*. Stop pretending there's something in this world for you, in this family. Stop getting seduced by handsome investigators or some vision that you could ever be truly accepted by the duke and his wife."

Selina bit her lip hard enough that she tasted the faint hint of blood. It was better to have that physical pain than the emotional one Vale was causing with her words. After all, she wasn't wrong, was she? Selina didn't belong here. And if any of the people who claimed to care for her ever found out what she truly was...

Well, they wouldn't love her anymore, would they?

"I know," she whispered.

Vale sighed. "I hope you do. Now I'm going to bed."

Selina kept her back to her friend as she slipped past her and left the room. When she was alone again, she lifted her hands to cover

146

her face. Vale had only said exactly what she had to hear. Only reminded her of what she already knew deep in her heart.

That this place, that these people...they were all an illusion. And reality was that she was the Faceless Fox.

But it was also that the moment she took the necklace, every dream she'd been living in would be over. And there was a place deep within her chest that didn't want that moment to come.

CHAPTER 15

Derrick stared at the pages of the journal before him and the list he had begun to compile in it. Although the list had to do with his investigation, he was not writing it in an official capacity or within the pages of the reports he and Barber were keeping. This was his private journal.

He frowned at the handful of items in the list. What was he doing? That was the question of the week, it seemed. And could be addressed to a dozen circumstances. What was he doing hiding this information from Barber, his partner and friend? What was he doing asking these questions? What was he doing going to Selina Oliver's room and taking her until her legs shook?

What was he doing leaving afterward instead of staying with her until dawn, until noon, until a new year, until a new decade?

He shook his head. His mind felt like a maze and he a helpless rat trying to find its way to the goal. Only he didn't know what the goal was and the maze kept changing.

"Mr. Huntington?"

He jolted at the sound of a voice at the door and looked up to find the Duchess of Roseford standing there, watching him.

"I'm so sorry," she said as he lunged to his feet. "I didn't mean to startle you. I tried saying your name a handful of times."

Derrick blinked. In his profession, it was dangerous not to always be aware of one's surroundings, and this woman had managed to surprise him without even meaning to do it. *That* was how distracted he was. How compromised.

"I should be the one to apologize, Your Grace. I was obviously overly involved in my work." He motioned her into the makeshift office the Duke of Roseford had provided for them during their stay here.

"I had forgotten what a pretty view of the stables this room has," the duchess said as she moved to the window and looked out over the expanse of green outside. "I hope it is a comfortable space for you and Mr. Barber."

"It is, Your Grace," he said with an inclination of his head. "And a very kind offer from you and your husband that we be allowed to use it. I happen to agree about the view. I do love watching your man train the horses in the paddock there."

She smiled as she fully faced him. She was a truly lovely woman with her dark hair and bright eyes. She had a kind face, open and welcoming, never judging. He understood why Roseford had fallen in love with her, for both her external and internal beauty.

"Was there something you needed, Your Grace?" he asked, trying to refocus on matters at hand.

"Yes." She sighed and trouble flickered across that face now. An emotion she wasn't capable of covering any more than any of the others. "I had rather hoped you and Mr. Barber would be together."

"Barber is currently…" He cut himself off. The lady might know the generalities of his investigation, but there was no reason to inform her of the specifics and frighten her. "He's in the middle of something. But I promise I will share whatever you tell me with him."

She nodded. "Of course. This morning one of Lady Winford's maids approached our housekeeper with an item she had found in her mistress's chamber while she was making the bed. A glove, Mr. Huntington, but *not* one belonging to Lady Winford."

She dug into her pelisse pocket and withdrew a long, white satin glove, and held it out. Derrick stared at it a fraction of a moment, his heart sinking. He didn't want to touch it. He didn't want to take it, but he had no choice. The satin caressed his fingers as he whispered, "I see."

"Now, under normal circumstances, I wouldn't think much of it," the duchess said, her face drawn and lips pinched. "Laundry sometimes is done together in the washroom and items are mixed up, someone could have dropped it and it was mistakenly returned to the wrong room, a dozen other scenarios I cannot think of in the moment. And perhaps those reasons are still valid. But since you and Mr. Barber are here to investigate someone wanting to steal from Lady Winford, there are also more sinister explanations, so I thought it important to turn the item over to you."

Derrick nodded. Everything the duchess said, every other explanation rang true. They could have been the answer to almost any other item of clothing being misplaced in Lady Winford's chamber.

But they didn't explain this one. Because he recognized the glove. He had peeled it and its partner from Selina's slender hands not twelve hours before. He peeked surreptitiously in the inside lining when the duchess bent her head, and there were the initials he'd seen the night before that confirmed he was correct.

Selina's glove found in Lady Winford's chamber. She'd had them both when he seduced her, so the only time this one could have been left there was *after* he departed her bed in the middle of the night. Not left by a laundress or lost by a careless partygoer.

He swallowed and pushed the glove into his pocket. "You are right, it is probably nothing," he choked out. "But I appreciate you bringing it to me. Barber and I will look into it."

That was a lie. He had no intention of showing Barber the glove. Just as he had no intention of sharing the list he would add the glove to as evidence. The one in his journal that organized every tiny shred of evidence that could possibly prove *Selina* was the Faceless Fox, not some bored nobleman or angry footman.

Selina. *His* Selina.

"Was that all, Your Grace?" He heard the tension in his voice, but hoped the duchess didn't know him well enough to hear it too.

She shifted and her smile grew a little tighter. "I suppose it isn't, especially since Mr. Barber isn't here."

His heart dropped. God, had the duchess guessed the glove was Selina's too? Was she suspecting her sister-in-law, as well? What would that do to their family? To the fragile bonds he could see Selina creating with her brother and his wife?

"You have been spending a great deal of time with my sister-in-law, Mr. Huntington," she said at last. "I would be remiss as a friend to her and a guardian of sorts if I didn't speak to you about it."

He blinked as those words sank in. This wasn't about the Fox at all. The duchess was inquiring about intentions. And that was just as fraught a conversation, wasn't it? What were his bloody intentions beyond merely stripping Selina naked and pleasuring her until they were both sated? That was as far as he'd ever taken it in his mind, never allowing for more, no matter how she captivated or tormented or matched him.

And now he had to take into account his suspicions, as well. His poor mind was more of a jumble than ever.

"Mr. Huntington?" Her tone was more concerned.

He shook his head. "I apologize, Your Grace," he said. "I suppose I should have been expecting this line of questioning. I just assumed it would come from the duke."

The duchess laughed. "Robert is observant about a great many things, but with relationships it's sometimes impossible for him to see what is right in front of him."

"And you haven't pointed this out to him," he said.

She inclined her head. "Not yet. If I do, he'll decide to become protective, and that might not be the best course of action. I'm trying to determine what that is myself."

"Well…" Derrick shifted. "I think I would be a fool to deny that Miss Oliver and I have become friends since my arrival here." He drew a long breath to calm his heart and make himself use his skills to read her. "Do you disapprove?"

There was a hint of a smile that tilted the corner of her lips, a brighter quality to her expression. Happiness, joy. She liked the idea of Selina having someone show an interest. She liked the idea that it was him.

And his heart, regardless of everything else, warmed. The expression said a future with Selina could be accepted by her family. Immediately he regretted the feeling. What future could they have?

"I don't," she said softly. Her mouth twisted. "I wonder how much she's told you about…" She trailed off. "Selina hasn't always had the…the easiest life."

Derrick caught his breath as he thought of Selina's offhand comment that she had been alone for a long time. Her similar suggestion that in her world loyalty was hard to come by. Both those statements were on his list of reasons to suspect her, but they also sat heavy in his heart.

What had happened to her to make her think and feel those things?

It was as if the duchess read his mind. She shook her head slightly. "That is her story to tell, not mine, but the crux of it is that she shouldn't have had to endure what she did. Perhaps she hasn't always made good choices because of it. But I think she deserves happiness and joy and love more than anyone I've ever known. She deserves a future."

Derrick stared at his hands, clenched before him. "A future," he repeated. "I cannot tell you that I know the future, Your Grace." He waved around the room at the piles of paperwork, evidence. "Obviously, I have a complicated life."

"Everyone has a complicated life, Mr. Huntington," the duchess said with a soft smile. "If I've learned anything in the past few years, it's that. Even the duke and I had a rather fraught past."

"You did?" He could not hide his surprise at such a notion. The two always seemed in such perfect accord, it was hard to imagine them otherwise.

She laughed. "Oh yes. Before we married, I *despised* Robert. I might have even wanted a little revenge on him."

His eyes went wide and he stared at her. "What?" He shook his head. "I beg your pardon, that was rude of me."

She shrugged. "I brought it up. And it's true. I thought him the devil. And he is, as he'll proudly tell you if you ask him. But he's not the devil I once thought him to be." Her expression softened. "And he is my heart."

Derrick shifted. He'd heard other friends in love describe their objects of affection as being their heart. It had never rung true to him before. The heart had always been a muscle to him, an organ. It was only poetry that labeled it as more.

But something had shifted in him. When the duchess said it, it felt more real to him, both because he had observed her with her husband and also because he was beginning to understand the concept. Selina was making him a convert.

And he suspected her of being a thief.

He rubbed his eyes, wishing he could scrub away his doubts as easily.

The duchess took a step in his direction. "All I'm trying to say is that complicated is not insurmountable. But only if you decide to overcome it."

"Yes," Derrick said softly, for there was nothing else to say.

She shook her head. "Don't mind me, Mr. Huntington. I'm a romantic at heart and I like you. It makes me a bit more meddling than perhaps I should be."

He forced a smile for her to ease her mind. "That you like me means a great deal, Your Grace. It's obvious you're an excellent judge of character. And I do appreciate, once again, all of your assistance and that of the duke."

She held his gaze a beat, then inclined her head. "I should leave you to your work. If you'll excuse me."

He gave a slight bow. "Good day, Your Grace."

She slipped from the room, leaving him alone once more. He moved to the window and stared out again at the stables and the training yard and the endless green grass of the grounds, but he hardly saw any of it now. Not when there was so much weighing on him. Selina's glove. Selina's heart. Selina, Selina, Selina.

He didn't know how long he stood there, contemplating the complication of his life after meeting her, but eventually he was drawn from his reverie by the sound of music in the distance. He jerked his head toward the door. The music room was on the opposite side of the big house. So where was the sound coming from?

He closed his journal, tucked it in a drawer so that Barber wouldn't find his list, and set out down the hall toward the sound. A few twists and turns, and he found a door that had been left ajar. The music came from behind it.

He pushed it open a fraction and drew in a breath. It was a small parlor, unused if the dust cloths over the furniture were any indication. The only thing uncovered was a pianoforte in the corner. Selina sat at it, her fingers moving over the keys gently, then passionately, then softly as she played a song he didn't recognize.

He stood mesmerized for a moment, his hand dipping into his pocket, finding her incriminating glove. He stroked his fingers over it like he was caressing her skin.

How had it gotten in that room? What had Selina done? Or was this some kind of way to frame her? But to what end? What purpose?

She crashed her fingers over the keys again, and he felt the passion of her playing through every nerve of his being. He stepped closer and cleared his throat. "Selina."

She jerked her head up, her fingers smashing on to the keys in a discordant note as she noticed him standing there. She leapt to her feet with a gasp of "Oh!"

He held up a hand. "Oh no, please don't stop. You play beautifully."

Color filled her cheeks and she broke her gaze from his as if she were shy. He'd never seen that little look from her before. Selina was normally so brave, so bold, so unapologetically herself.

"I suppose it is one of the few ladylike pursuits I have any grasp of," she said, breathless and still not looking at him.

He paced a little closer, looking around. "What is this room?" he asked.

That blush deepened. "I believe it might have been the private parlor of Robert's late mother. The last Duchess of Roseford." Derrick raised his eyebrows and she bent her head. "Yes, I know she would hate me being here."

"Why is that?" he pressed.

She shrugged. "I'm her husband's by-blow. She would have surely despised me. Certainly she wouldn't have wished for me to play her pianoforte."

"Then why choose to play here?" he asked. "Why not go to the more public music room?"

"Because I didn't want to exhibit," she said with a huff of breath. "And that room is all about people hearing you play and watching you. Judging you. I just wanted to play for myself. For...for..."

"For what?" he pressed, reaching out to take her hand. It was softer than the damned and damning glove in his pocket.

She let out a shuddering sigh. "Atonement."

He drew back a fraction. "What do you have to atone for?"

Her lips parted and she shook her head. "I don't know. My existence? My life? My boldness?"

He let his eyes come shut for a moment. Whatever was troubling Selina, it was opening a door for him as an investigator. He ought to take that door without hesitation, but with her there was nothing clear-cut. He wasn't just a man bent on finding the truth about the Faceless Fox. Not anymore. He was this woman's lover. He was becoming more than that with every moment he spent with her.

The truth of that nearly set him back on his heels, but he managed to keep himself calm and in line. He had questions for her. And yes, those questions would help his investigation, perhaps. But he wanted to ask them for far more personal reasons. He wanted to ask them because he wanted to know her and understand her and protect her from whatever might come in a day or a week or a month.

"Selina," he whispered.

There must have been something in the way he said her name, because she flinched. There was a flash of vulnerability and pain, fear and regret, that cascaded over her expression in a horrible waterfall.

"Selina," he pressed, holding tight to her hand when she tried to back away. "Why were you on your own?"

CHAPTER 16

It felt like everything in Selina's world froze in a flash as Derrick asked that question. The question that revealed everything. The question she'd been running from for years. But this man asked it so sweetly and so gently and without any ulterior motive to it. And she desperately wanted to explain it to him.

She desperately wanted to run away, too.

"Derrick," she murmured, at last freeing her hand from his. Now she *could* run, but she didn't. She stayed, looking up at him, lost in him and everything he offered with his presence in her life. Everything he threatened.

"You told me before that you've been alone since you were a child. And I need to know why." He reached out and cupped her cheek, stroking his thumb over her lower lip gently. *"Please,"* he whispered.

Her eyes closed and a sigh ripped through her, ragged and broken, just like she was broken under the surface she tried to present as a protection. This had been her burden to carry and hers alone for many years. She'd never shared the whole truth of it with anyone.

Showing him that vulnerability was dangerous, and yet she

yearned to do just that. To open herself just a fraction and let this honorable man past the gates. Perhaps if he heard her past, he would understand why she'd become what she was. Perhaps he'd hate her less if and when he figured out she was the very thief he despised and hunted.

And perhaps she just needed to say it to see if he was as good and decent as he pretended to be. To test his mask and see if it fell or if it was his true face.

"My mother was the daughter of a baronet," she whispered. "She met the last Roseford at some party in London. She was staying with an aunt as chaperone, sampling the delights of the Season. But the aunt was very old and mostly deaf and easy to escape. So when the duke crooked his finger..."

Derrick nodded. "It was easy for her to make her escape and meet with him."

"Yes." She sighed. "He was married, of course. But he was also handsome and, from all accounts, quite persuasive. I have no idea what he said to make her love him, to make her give herself to him when she had to know there was no future. But she did. They carried on an affair for months, with him whispering promises of protection and faithfulness and a lot of other lies she was foolish enough to believe."

"What ended it?" Derrick asked, no judgment in his tone.

She shrugged and then lifted her gaze to his. "Me," she whispered. "She discovered she was breeding and the duke was livid. He accused her of a dozen awful things."

"How do you know that?" he asked.

"Oh, we'll come to that," she said with a false smile that felt as brittle as glass. "Don't rush the crescendo, Mr. Huntington."

"Selina," he said, taking her hand again.

She stared down at their intertwined fingers. Felt the weight of them against her palm. The comfort of them. This man made everything so easy, even this story that was so damned hard.

She cleared her throat and continued, "He sent her back to her father, all his promises broken in one sweep. She tried to hide me for a while, but in the end how could she? Her pregnancy became obvious and it revealed the truth of what she'd been up to when her father thought her safely chaperoned to parties and teas like a lady above her station."

"He must have been furious when he found out the truth," Derrick said.

"Yes," she said with another humorless chuckle. "But with her, not Roseford. My grandfather arranged a marriage to a merchant within days of discovering the truth. He paid the man handsomely to claim her bastard as his own and never spoke to my mother again."

He winced. "So you never met him."

"No," she said. "I saw my grandfather once. At a party at the Earl of Grangerfield's London estate. I froze, staring at him. I have his eyes, you see. But I never got up the nerve to talk to him."

"You, not have the nerve?" he teased gently, his fingers smoothing over hers. "I don't believe it."

"You should," she murmured as she pulled away and paced to the window. "I wanted to confront him, to rip him to shreds, but instead I just stared at him, like a gaping fish."

"I'm sorry," he said softly.

"Save those platitudes until the end, Derrick," she said, staring out the window without seeing anything in her line of sight. "The story doesn't get better. You see, Peter Oliver, my stepfather, was willing to overlook the bastard he didn't sire for the tiny fortune that came along with his bride—in theory. But in truth?"

Derrick flinched. "He was cruel to you?"

"Sometimes. Never physically. I think there might have been some lingering fear that the Duke of Roseford would materialize and punish him if he laid a hand on me. But he certainly took great pleasure in hurting me in other ways." She sighed. "He *despised* me, and that only grew more potent as he and my mother established a real relationship. He loved her, in his own vague way. And she accepted anything he did to me because he sometimes brought her flowers."

Derrick's jaw was set now, his anger lining his face plainly. "You were a child."

"But not *his* child. The first time he told me that, I was six. He pointed out Roseford getting out of a carriage on the street near a market and told me that was my real father. My world was shattered. Once he saw he could hurt me that way, he did everything he could to cause more pain. *He* was the one who showed me the letters from Roseford to my mother, calling her a whore, calling me her bastard. He *helped* me find letters from my grandfather, too, the ones that cut us both off."

"Son of a bitch," Derrick bit out. "Tell me he is still living so I may give him the beating he so roundly deserves."

She shrugged. "What would be the point? The past is in the past. I've moved on. And he did settle down in the end. Ultimately the peace they came to was to ignore me. Both of them ignored me most of the time. And that gave me remarkable freedom. Even more freedom when they had their own children."

"You have other half-siblings?"

"Oh yes. I have nothing full and everything half," she said with a shake of her head. "Clara was born when I was ten. George when I was twelve. And I adored them, but I was always kept separate. The real children and the bastard one."

"Did you ever seek out Roseford?" he asked.

"The previous?" she said. "My father? Yes, the same year George was born I tried to reach out to him. I found his address and snuck myself into the house. He was enraged I'd sought him. I'd *dared* to defile to his home. He made it clear I wasn't wanted either, but that I would have a settlement when I came of age. Then he made me leave through the servants' entrance."

Her breath felt constricted in her throat and she fought to remain impassive and flat and unaffected as she always pretended to be.

"I learned to live with it," she added once she could actually speak again.

Derrick's fists were tight at his sides, his shoulders shook with righteous rage on her behalf. "You shouldn't have had to."

"But I *did*," she insisted. Then she forced a smile, praying the mask made her look wicked and not broken. "And you cannot mourn for me completely. When I was eighteen, I received my father's promised settlement. A large sum at majority and a healthy monthly allowance ever since. I bought a little house and got a companion and have lived happily ever after in my own way ever since. I do what I please, with whom I please and how I please." She stepped up to him and placed a finger on his lips. "You've benefitted from my freedom, I think."

"I would have rather not if it would have spared you one moment of that pain," he said. "You can be flippant about it, you can dismiss it and disconnect from it, but you must have been broken-hearted by these events as they were occurring."

She dropped her hand away. "What do you want, investigator?" she asked, her tone harsher than perhaps she had intended. "Do you want me to pour my blood onto the floor in front of you? Do you want me to weep and gnash my teeth and relive every—"

She cut herself off because her eyes were stinging with tears she didn't want to shed in front of this man. Memories she didn't want to recall. Emotions she had told herself were long put away.

"No. Of course not," he said. Softer, gentler now. Like he was trying to soothe a rabid beast. Perhaps that was what she was in the end.

"They didn't want me," she whispered past a tightness in her throat. Even after all these years, there it was. "I cannot complain. It made me strong, it made me independent, it made me—"

She cut herself off then. If she spoke too much, she'd reveal the truth. She'd reveal how she'd created the Fox for revenge and for safety and for a thousand reasons that had everything to do with what she'd endured.

And then he would hate her. And then he would leave her, too.

He drew a long breath and then took a step toward her. Another. Another. Until the distance between them was erased. Until he stood before her, a wall between her and the pain. He reached out and touched her face, cupping her cheeks. His thumbs stroked, and he was wiping away tears she hadn't realized she was shedding.

"I have nothing but utmost admiration for you, Selina Oliver. I did before. I do now. I always shall."

"You can't promise that," she whispered.

He arched a brow. "I do promise it. Nothing could change it."

She almost laughed at that idea. Of course that could be changed. He wouldn't care for her once he wasn't in the same space as she was, let alone once he knew the truth about what she'd done. What she still intended to do.

This was going to be over, and sooner rather than later.

"Do you want to do something for me?" she whispered. "Do you want to help?"

He nodded slowly, solemnly, a man of honor. A man of goodness and kindness and gentleness. A man unlike any she'd ever known in all her life. "I do."

She shivered at the low timber of his voice, the intense eye contact, the fact that he was still cupping her face, staring down at her like she was treasure of far more value than any she'd ever stolen.

Everything about this man made her quake. That was dangerous and desperate and she didn't care. She wanted him. All of him.

"Then take me to my bed," she whispered. "And help me to forget again. Help me to pretend all of that never happened."

His lips pursed, as if he didn't completely approve of that method of dealing with her past. But he didn't argue. He didn't fight her. He just took her hand and led her from the room.

THE HEART OF A HELLION

Derrick drew Selina into her chamber and released her hand. She crossed to her bed and stood there as he closed and locked the chamber door. He gave her a half-smile before he moved to the dressing room door and locked it, too.

"No interruptions," he murmured, then looked around. "It's funny how different a room looks in the day than at night."

She nodded. "I've often thought the same. There's something very scary and romantic about a darkened chamber, especially one where you don't belong."

"Scary *and* romantic?" he asked with a smile.

She returned it, and he was pleased that this time the expression actually looked real, not as forced as what she'd worn as she told him about her horrible childhood. "Scary can be romantic," she explained. "Just a tiny bit of a scare is thrilling. Uncertainty is thrilling. *You* are scary, Mr. Huntington."

He arched a brow as he moved toward her, drawn to her, yet again, like the moth to the flame her companion had spoken about a lifetime ago. "Am I?" he whispered. "I don't try to be."

"If you tried to be, you wouldn't be," she said, and chuckled as she wound a hand up into his hair and guided his mouth to hers.

He kissed her as she demanded, tasting remnants of tears on her lips, deepening the kiss to erase them all. She melted against him with a little moan, her fingers gripping his forearms, her body molding to his from chest to hip, her skirts tangling around his legs.

He could have stood like that forever, just holding her and tasting her and being in her presence. But she had something else in mind if the way she lifted into him was any indication. Today he had no intention of letting her down.

He broke the kiss and smiled down at her. The one she returned was shaky, not the usual confident display that normally brightened her face and drove him mad. Confession had made her vulnerable. He wanted to honor that.

He turned her so that her back was to him and flicked each

button of her gown open one by one, revealing her bare back, the arch of her spine. He chuckled. "Do you *ever* wear undergarments?"

She shook her head and leaned back against his chest with a little sigh. "Never."

He wrapped his arms around her, holding her tightly to him, then leaned in and kissed the side of her neck. She arched a little, granting him greater access, making a soft sound of pleasure as her shaking body relaxed against him.

He reveled in the surrender. It was not easily won with a woman like Selina. Normally when he made love to her, it was a battlefield, all passion and fire and parry and thrust. Today he wanted to give her something different.

He slid his fingers into the gap of her dress, dancing the tips along her soft skin, eliciting a hiss of sensation from her. Then he pushed the gown forward. She tugged it away, giving her hips a little shake so that it pooled around her feet.

She turned into him, rising on the balls of her feet, wending her arms around his neck, kissing him hard. It was so easy to get swept up in her, just as she intended it to be. But he managed to keep his wits about him. When she thrust her tongue, he caressed gently, slowing the kiss, pushing his fingers into her hair to angle her for better access, deepening and tasting and exploring like they had all the time in the world.

She made a little sound, almost of confusion, in the back of her throat, but then she slowed herself. And the kiss went on and on until every nerve in his body was on fire.

"Please," she whispered against his lips, her fingers digging into his back. "Please, please."

He nodded and cupped her backside, lifting her to him. She wrapped her long legs around his hips, rocking against him as he carried her to her bed. He laid her down and covered her, fully clothed as he continued to kiss her.

"Hurry," she mumbled as she dragged her hands down his back and cupped his backside, tugging him hard against her with a tiny moan at the abrasion of his rough trousers against her soft, wet sex.

"Not this time," he growled against her neck before he began to lick and kiss a trail lower. He nipped at her skin, sucking, tasting, savoring her flavor. She writhed beneath him, whispering incoherent sounds of pleasure that ripped through his veins and burned in his blood and his gut and his cock. He wanted to tear the flap of his trousers down and just take her, but he resisted.

Today wasn't simply about claiming. Today was something more. He needed it to be about more because she'd given so much a short while ago.

So he continued the path down her body, pausing at the sweet swell of her breasts. He pressed them together, licking a trail back and forth, sucking hard on one nipple, then the other. He watched her as he pleasured her, watching the twitch of her mouth, the flush of her skin, felt her hips rub and rub against him, trying to find release that he wouldn't give. He loved that responsiveness, that utter disregard for anything but sensation. He wanted to keep her there, cut off from anything but these good feelings, for as long as he could.

He dropped his mouth lower, across the smooth expanse of her stomach. He nudged the sensitive flesh with the rough beginnings of stubble, and she actually arched up, her toes flexing against the bed beneath them.

"Please!" she cried out, this time with more aggression. "Derrick!"

He shook his head as he lifted it. "Miss Oliver, you may control a great deal. But not me."

Her pupils dilated and her nipples hardened a bit more. She liked when he took control. He understood why now. Her entire life she'd been balanced on a precipice of despair. She'd never been able to depend on anyone.

Would that have turned her to crime?

No. He wouldn't think about that. Not when he was covering

her naked body with his, steeped in her warmth and her surrender. He refused to think about his suspicions.

He wanted to take even a fraction of the load for her. By controlling even a little of her experience, he hoped it would be like a pressure release valve.

"I could control you if I wanted to," she purred, but she made no effort to do so and simply relaxed back on the pillows, her eyes coming closed as he edged his way between her legs.

He could already scent the sweetness of her desire, heady and powerful. He pushed her legs wider and her outer lips parted, revealing her slick opening. He swept a finger across her and she moaned.

"You probably could," he agreed softly. "But today you won't."

"Mmm" was her only response, and he smiled as he lowered his head and licked her.

He loved her flavor. That heady sweet and saltiness of her sex was better than any wine. He wanted to memorize all of its notes, all of its expressions. Savor it like a dying man's last meal.

Perhaps it would be. The party was coming to a close in a few days. Whatever his worries about her role as the Fox, this would end. They would end.

"Selina," he breathed against her, pushing everything else aside and diving into pleasuring her. Because in that moment, he felt too desperate to do anything else.

CHAPTER 17

S elina felt the shift in Derrick as he began to lick her in earnest. Where when they started he'd been slow and steady, in no rush, now there was a purpose to the way he stroked her with his tongue. Something had changed, but her mind was too blurred by pleasure to figure out what. He swirled his tongue around her clitoris with the perfect pressure, and the effect sizzled through her entire body. She was weightless and boneless, rendered helpless by his mouth on her, his fingers sliding into her sheath and pumping as he sucked her. Harder and harder, faster and faster as she lifted her hips into him.

The orgasm came hard and heavy and fast, washing over her, stealing her breath. She covered her mouth with her hand, crying out against it as the waves continued to wash over her like a never-ending sea. Her entire body shook when he finally released her and made a lazy trail back up her body to kiss her. She tasted her release on his tongue, warm and sweet, and it made her sex twitch all over again, needing more than just his mouth to be satisfied.

But he seemed in no hurry, just as he'd promised earlier. He simply kissed her, his arms coming around her, tucking her into his still fully clothed body. She arched a leg around his hip, grinding against him as the kiss deepened.

He chuckled and pulled back, his handsome face just inches from her own. "You are unstoppable."

"A force to be reckoned with," she whispered back with a smile, her first real one since she confessed her past to him.

"I hope that never changes," he said, kissing her nose before he got up and left her in her bed.

She sat up in a jolt. "You're not leaving?"

His eyebrows lifted as he turned back toward her. He motioned to the hard line of his cock, pushing insistently against his trouser front. "You think I could? No, I'm just going to divest myself of my clothing before I finish what we started."

Her eyes went wide and she settled back on the pillows. "Show me. Undress *for* me."

His stare grew more focused and then he laughed, that sound another tug both to her heart and between her legs. "Unstoppable," he repeated.

But he didn't deny her. He reached up and slowly untied his cravat. Unwinding the fabric as he maintained eye contact with her. He dropped it away and pushed his jacket to the floor next. He took his time with his shirt, unbuttoning every button with a seductive flare.

Her breath caught as he tugged the linen from his waistband and slowly pulled the shirt over his head. His stomach muscles flexed with the effort, revealing fascinating lines of his body that she'd never seen on any other man she'd bedded. She inched to her knees and crawled to the edge of the bed so she could explore further. Her fingers trembled as she reached out, gliding over the toned flesh, tracing her nails over the ridges, into the valleys. He watched her as she did it, gaze focused on her face rather than her hands.

She leaned in and brushed her cheek against his stomach, turning to press her lips to the exposed skin. He touched her hair, his fingers clenching against her scalp like they had when she took his cock in her mouth. She licked him, tracing the muscle, loving how it contracted against her tongue when his breath shortened.

"What were you saying about not letting me be in control?" she murmured against his flesh as she looked up into his face.

He was smiling and her breath caught. How could one man be so beautiful? So perfect in form? But better than that, how could he have such honor? Be so kind? So intelligent? She'd never imagined such a man could exist, let alone could walk into her life.

Of course, he was there to destroy her, whether he knew it or not. And that was why this was all hopeless. That was why she couldn't let the skip of her heart lead her down foolish trails.

She could fuck this man. Nothing more.

"If you want control, then direct me, Selina," he said, placing a finger beneath her chin and tilting her face up for a kiss. "I'm at your command."

Her breath quickened at that idea. Derrick had always been so forceful when he took her. Always in command, always drawing her where he wanted her to be. She loved that. Loved every powerful, passionate moment of it. But the concept that she could do the same to him?

That was magic.

She pointed to the settee before the fire. "Take off the rest," she said evenly, "and sit there. Better yet, sprawl there like you men like to do, looking all dark and dangerous."

He laughed again, then bowed slightly. "As you wish, my lady."

He moved to the settee and she slid off the bed, padding around to stand before the fire as he sat down and pulled off his boots. Then he stood and unfastened his trousers, met her eyes and pushed them from his hips to land in a pile at his feet.

She shivered seeing the whole of him naked. Somehow she'd thought that would stop moving her once she'd seen it the first time. But he still made her tremble. He still made her weak and wet and ready without doing much more than simply existing in her world.

After this was over, she would still know he existed. She had no doubt that knowledge would haunt her, as would memories of these stolen moments in his arms.

She shrugged off the thought and waved him toward the settee with one hand. "Slouch."

He shook his head as he sat down on the velvety cushions and then splayed out there, slouched as ordered, legs the perfect perch for her, arms rested on the back of the settee as he watched her.

"Now what?" he asked, his voice low and rough with a desire that matched her own.

"Now you're mine," she murmured, and slid over to him. She eased over his lap, aligning her still-wet sex to his hard cock. She gripped his shoulders as she glided down over him, taking him fully inside of her inch by wonderful inch. When she was filled to the brim, she rested her forehead on his with a trembling sigh.

"God, what you do to me," he moaned on her throat, licking there gently, sucking until she shivered and flexed over him almost against her own will. Even when she was over him, he still directed her. That puppet on his string.

So she broke the string and began to ride him. She moved hard and fast, grinding down over him to stimulate herself, drawing almost fully away so she could receive the full benefit of her body.

He grunted, his neck straining as he cupped her backside and rocked her harder. She tilted her head and kissed him, everything lost focus, nothing mattered but this. And she rode and rode, pleasure arcing and spreading and warming and teasing through her whole body.

His breath was rough, he moaned her name with pleasure and she loved it. Loved that he was just as lost as she was. Loved that there was only one way to be found and that was when the pleasure overflowed.

Hers was just about ready to do that. Again the pressure built between her legs, hot and heavy and insistent. She needed release, she burned for it. She burned for him and only him now and forever. That thought scarred her entire being just as the pleasure took over and she jerked against him with a cry he caught with his tongue.

His fingers dug into her hips and she pressed hard against him, grinding her flesh to his body as she came and came and came until she felt like there was nothing left of her. She was a shell, stripped clean by their joining, weak and limp in his arms.

He picked her up then, holding her legs around his waist, keeping their bodies joined as he took her back to the bed. He leaned her against the edge, his hands clenching into fists in the coverlet on either side of her hips.

And then he took her hard and fast. Her still-twitching body rushed back to life, the orgasm rekindled by the passion of his claiming. She scratched his back with her nails as she tried to maintain purchase, her thighs clenched around his hips tightly.

He let out a cry in the quiet and then he withdrew, his hot seed pumping between them as he sank his head into the crook of her shoulder, teeth scraping her skin, sweat mingling.

And for the moment, there was nothing else but this.

Selina had no idea how long they'd been lying together in her bed. Too long, certainly, but none of it mattered anymore. If anyone was looking for them, they could keep looking. She wanted nothing more than to be in Derrick's arms, her head on his chest, listening to the beautiful sound of his heartbeat as it thudded beneath her ear.

His fingers threaded through her hair, smoothing over her scalp, dancing over her shoulders. It was perfect. Too perfect. Too close.

But for once in her life, she didn't feel like running.

"I need to ask you a question," he said, his voice rough in the quiet.

She tensed in his arms. A question. Great God, could it be *the* question? The one other women tittered and cooed and squealed over? The question she had always avoided in her lovers because none of them had ever meant more to her than a bit of fun?

Was it possible Derrick Huntington was about to ask her a question that would change her life? What would she say? How could she answer at all, knowing that she was nothing more than a lie?

"Selina?"

She lifted her head and looked at him, struggling to keep her expression passive as she nodded. "Yes, sorry. What is it?"

He looked nervous, and that made *her* all the more nervous. Great God, he really *was* going to ask her *the* question. Right here in this perfect moment in her bed.

He drew in a deep breath and let it out slowly. "Why was your glove in Lady Winford's chamber?"

Over the years, Selina had developed the talent to keep her reaction from her face. Being too honest, too open, in her expression was a very dangerous thing for a woman like her. Perhaps for a woman in general, given the power men held over their sex. She was proud of how she'd developed the ability to keep all emotion at bay and confuse anyone who tried to read her.

But in this moment, she couldn't use that skill. Her jaw dropped open and her eyes went wide even though she didn't want them to do so. She pushed away from Derrick's chest and sat up, tugging covers with her so that she wouldn't be physically revealed as much as she was emotionally revealed.

"What are you talking about?" she choked out. "My glove?"

His brow wrinkled. "This morning one of the maids found your glove on the floor in Lady Winford's chamber. Do you know how it might have gotten there?"

Selina shook her head, trying to find any kind of explanation for this incriminating news. More so, trying to understand the answer herself. How *had* her glove come to be in the Winford chamber? She had no idea! Had she been so careless as to leave it there? No. She'd been wearing both gloves when she returned to her chamber and she'd never gone back.

THE HEART OF A HELLION

"I must have lost the glove the night we first searched the chamber together," she said, barely keeping the tremble from her voice. "Perhaps it was kicked under the bed somehow and that delayed its discovery."

He shook his head slowly. "No, Selina. They were the gloves you were wearing last night."

She swallowed hard. "How could you possibly know that?"

He leaned a little closer and his hand stirred like he wanted to touch her. But he didn't. He didn't, and her heart hurt. "Because I remember peeling them off your fingers," he whispered. "I remember seeing the little embroidered initials inside. I remember your scent clinging to them, vanilla and cinnamon, the same one that clings to me when I've spent any time at your side. They were the gloves you wore last night, Selina. And you had both of them when I came to your chamber to make love to you. Aside from the fact you weren't wearing gloves the night we searched the chamber. So the one had to have been left in Lady Winford's chamber *after* we parted company."

Selina pushed from the bed, hating how exposed she felt physically and emotionally. And also how compromised she was by her lack of knowledge. If she knew how her damned glove had gotten into the chamber, she could have probably created a passable lie. But since she had no idea...

"Selina." His tone was sharper. No longer the voice of her lover who had comforted her and pleased her and held her. No, this was the voice of Derrick Huntington, investigator. She wasn't his bed partner anymore—she was a suspect.

And she stung from the loss of connection as much as she trembled from fear that he was about to uncover all her secrets.

"I don't know," she breathed, because that was the truth and he would see that. "I don't know how the glove could have possibly gotten into the room, because I never went there."

"Not even to help me?" he pressed. "Not to take part in the investigation against my wishes?"

She shook her head. That wasn't what he thought. She could tell from his voice. He really did suspect her. And she had to get him to change his course right now.

"No, I never went back," she said, strong with that truth again. "But...but perhaps the Fox did it."

One brow arched and he stared at her. "How?"

"He could have gone there looking for the necklace and dropped my glove," she said, desperate for the answer that would make Derrick stop looking at her like she was a liar. She *was* a liar, but seeing it on his face was like ripping her heart out.

"Why would he have your glove?" he pressed. "How could he had gotten it if you never left your chamber last night after I departed?"

She worried her lip, trying to come up with an explanation. She walked away from him as she did it and crossed to her dressing table. She opened her top drawer, trying to find something to do with her hands and saw her few pieces of jewelry there. It was funny, she rarely wore any. She just stole it from other people.

Most of her pieces weren't worth much, except for a pair of cameo earrings that Robert had given her at Morgan and Lizzie's wedding the previous year. And looking at them, she developed a plan. Not a perfect plan, but a plan nonetheless.

She made a show of digging in her drawer and used the distraction to palm the earrings. "Derrick!" she cried out. "Derrick, my earrings are gone!"

"What?" he said, getting out of the bed and coming to her side.

When he stared into the drawer, she took a moment to drop the cameo earrings into the pocket of her robe. How she hated herself for it. And for all the lies she would now tell.

"Robert gave me earrings at our brother's wedding a few months ago," she explained. "And they're gone. *That* could be how he got my glove. Derrick, I seem to be a victim of the Faceless Fox!"

CHAPTER 18

Derrick fastened his trousers and tucked his shirt into the waistband as he watched Selina pace the room. Every step was restless, shaky. She was certainly no longer the intensely confident woman who had tested his every boundary.

She was also still clad only in a flimsy dressing gown, going on about her lost earrings in fits and starts. He wasn't sure if the near-nudity was truly because she was distressed and hadn't realized she was still unclothed...or if it was nothing more than an attempt at distraction.

It certainly worked as one, for he couldn't stop staring at how her body shifted beneath the silk, even now when everything in him told him she was a liar.

He shook his head as that word ricocheted through his brain, not for the first time since confronting her about the glove. He hated that word. Hated that he aimed it at her, even as a question.

And hated that he now had to put himself into his role as investigator with her. But he did it, even as his uneasy heart throbbed. He watched her rather than listened. Every tic, every breath, every flutter of her hand was a tell. Together they told the story, whatever truth she might try to hide. Whatever truth he might not really want to reveal.

She was afraid, *that* was clearly true. He could see it in the way she moved, in the elevated pitch of her voice, in the way her hands shook ever so slightly at her side. She *was* afraid.

What he didn't know was the reason for the emotion. Was it because she thought a criminal had slipped into her chamber and stolen from her while she slept a few feet away? That could engender fear in even the most confident and brave of people.

Or was it because she *was* a criminal and Derrick had nearly caught her by the fluffy fox tail?

He found himself praying it was the first. Because if she'd truly been victimized by the Fox, she couldn't *be* the Fox. And that would make everything easier, bearable...

"Derrick, that would explain everything, wouldn't it?" she asked, drawing his attention back to her in this moment and not all the ways he was trying to absolve her in his mind. No, not his mind. His heart.

"I suppose it would," he said slowly. "Though the Fox's modus operandi is a bit...different."

Her gaze fluttered away from his. "Oh? How so?"

He shook his head. This was not a conversation he should be having with a suspect in his investigation. In fact, considering how compromised he was, perhaps he shouldn't be having a conversation with her at all.

He cleared his throat and tried to clear his mind so easily. "Come, we must speak to Barber."

Her eyes widened. "But...why?"

"Because if you have been robbed by the Fox within the last twelve or so hours, that means he's on the move and Barber needs to be kept up to date." He dropped his gaze from hers. "Get dressed."

She stared at him a beat. He felt those blue eyes boring into him even when he didn't look at her. She even drew a breath as if to say something. He waited for her to do so, waited not knowing exactly what he *wanted* her to say. A denial? A confession? Neither one would satisfy.

But then she shook her head and instead went looking for her stockings in the mess on the floor around them.

It felt like an eternity as she dressed, though it couldn't have been more than a quarter of an hour, in truth. Selina was efficient— she even was able to fasten herself. Perhaps that came from how she'd grown up. He wanted that to explain it. He wanted not to wonder how she was so practiced when she now had a companion to help her.

He tried not to add it to the growing list of reasons to think her the Fox. He also tried not to stare as she wound her hair up in a loose bun and pinned it in place. Gone was the woman he'd made love to. She now looked as pulled together as she was when he'd found her playing piano a few hours before. As if that woman were a mask she wore.

He feared she was.

He cleared his throat. "Is there anything else you need?"

Her gaze dropped to his lips, but she shook her head. "No, I'm ready. But you might want me to peek into the hallway to ensure we won't be caught leaving my chamber together. Not everyone has such a liberal-minded view of unmarried people making love all afternoon. We wouldn't want you caught up in something you didn't want."

She slipped past him as she said it. He stared at her as she looked into the hall. She meant he might be forced to marry her. There was a thought. *Marrying* her. Being with her every day for the rest of his life.

Knowing she might be lying to him every one of those days.

She gave a strained smile from the door. "All clear. Let's go before that changes."

He followed her into the hallway, and they walked in silence back downstairs toward the workspace provided for him and Barber. Tension coursed between them with every step they took, but for the first time it wasn't merely erotic tension. For the first time he truly felt like an investigator with her.

Perhaps he should have been all along, given what he now suspected.

As they entered the study together, Derrick's eyes found Barber sitting at the desk, his dark head bent over the timeline he and Derrick had been formulating together the past few days. Derrick's heart sank. In some small part of him, he'd hoped they wouldn't find his partner. That he'd be able to put off this inevitability for a little while longer.

But he wasn't so lucky, it seemed. Barber looked up from the desk. His gaze flitted over Selina and then swung to Derrick. He held there for a long moment, and Derrick saw him analyzing the situation. Barber knew what he'd been doing and from the deepening frown on his face, he didn't approve.

At last, he rose to his feet with a sigh. "Miss Oliver," he said. "Good afternoon."

"Mr. Barber," she said. "I'm so sorry to intrude on your work."

"My work?" Barber repeated, his eyebrows lifting toward Derrick again. "I'm merely a visitor in your brother's home, miss. I assure you I was doing no work."

The room spoke otherwise, of course, with its papers strewn about, notes written on them, desks pushed together in the middle of the space.

Derrick bent his head. "Selina knows," he said softly.

Selina caught her breath, as if she only just realized they were outing her knowledge of Derrick's true identity. She rushed forward, hands raised in a gesture of surrender. "Mr. Barber, you must understand, I rudely eavesdropped on the conversation you and Mr. Huntington had with my brother last week. You were never betrayed by your partner."

Derrick flinched. Selina said he hadn't betrayed Barber, but of course he had. He'd kept her knowledge about their work secret for over a week. He'd kept his suspicions about *her* secret for days. And judging from Barber's expression, they would be having words once Selina was gone.

Barber arched a brow. "I would never assume my partner betrayed me, I assure you. I trust him." Those words were pointed, thrown toward Derrick like a casual bomb. A piercing reminder. "Tell me, Huntington, how much does she know?"

"That we're here after the Fox," Derrick said.

"I see," Barber said. "And how many people have you told about our true reason for being here, Miss Oliver?"

"No one," Selina said. She swallowed. Derrick saw the working of her throat, caught the hint of pink that briefly swirled on the exposed skin on her collarbone. Then it was gone. The tell erased. But he'd seen it.

Was she lying about telling others? Vale, perhaps? Her companion? Why? Idle gossip of a lady to her trusted servant? Or a thief to her partner? Vale, after all, was part of why Derrick's suspicions had been raised against Selina in the first place.

Barber folded his arms and his expression was blank and unreadable. Derrick frowned. Barber was too good at hiding his reactions. He couldn't tell if his partner believed her or not.

Believed *him* or not.

The second stung like a bullet.

"You two look as though you have something quite important to say," Barber said. "Otherwise, why would you barge in here and suddenly confess Miss Oliver's knowledge of our case?"

"Yes!" Selina burst out, hands clasped before her. "Something has happened, Mr. Barber."

Barber leaned back in his chair. "And what is that?"

"Selina has had something of hers stolen," Derrick said, and nearly choked on the words. "We think it might have been the Fox."

Barber paced away from the desk to the window. He stood there for a moment, staring out at the yard. Gathering himself? Derrick couldn't tell. Barber was methodical in all things. It made him a good investigator.

He turned back at last. "Very well, sit down, Miss Oliver. And tell me all about what the was stolen from you and why you believe it was the Fox."

~

S elina's hands were shaking. Normally she would have fought to maintain control over that reaction. Physical reactions could easily reveal too much, especially to close observers like Derrick or Barber. But today she allowed it to happen. She hoped the men would read the fluttery reaction as fear over being robbed by an infamous thief. It could easily lend credence to the story she was telling. The lie.

However, she wasn't certain of what either of them thought at present. It was frustrating to the highest degree. Barber sat at the desk across from her, fingers steepled before him, occasionally taking a note on a piece of paper before him. His expression was utterly blank.

And Derrick sat behind her, perfectly positioned so that she couldn't see him at all. But she felt him there.

Oh, how she felt him.

"And so I opened my drawer and discovered my earrings were missing," she said as an end to her short tale of the supposed robbery. "They were a present from my brother, Robert. You would have to ask him their worth, but I believe they were not an inexpensive gift."

She frowned at that thought. She had loved those earrings. She mourned that she would likely never be able to wear them in public again thanks to this lie.

Robert would be upset, he would worry over her. She didn't deserve that care. Or the replacement he would surely offer. God, but she hated this. Hated that she had been cornered into displaying her worst side. Hated that she had to lie to so many people she loved.

"And why would you think this was related to the Fox?" Barber asked, interrupting her thoughts.

She blinked. That was a good question. Derrick had mentioned something earlier about how the robbery of her earrings hadn't fit into the style of the Fox. Of course it hadn't. She knew that full bloody well. She had made the suggestion out of pure terror, just a quick way to get Derrick off her scent.

Luckily, she didn't have to come up with an answer. Behind her, Derrick cleared his throat. "I meant to mention this to you, Barber. The Duchess of Roseford found me this morning while you were out and mentioned that a mysterious glove was found in Lady Winford's chamber this morning. Selina's glove. It was during our discussion about how it could have been found in the countess's chamber that Selina discovered her missing earrings."

Selina nodded. "I thought perhaps this Faceless Fox person had come to my chamber first and taken my earrings and my glove. That would explain the transfer of the glove to Lady Winford's."

Barber's lips thinned. "Indeed, it does explain it perfectly."

Selina almost flinched at the dry, flat tone. It was impossible not to like Barber, even as he all but stalked her across the room. He was a clever man and normally that sparked her interest in a person. There were far too few clever people in the world.

Only this clever person was hell-bent on turning his brilliant mind on her. Her lies. Her truths. And she could tell he had his doubts. Unlike Derrick, he wasn't looking for a reason to believe her. He wouldn't bend the facts in her favor.

"Funny that Lady Winford hasn't reported anything stolen yet," Barber added, leaning back in his chair and folding his arms.

She stiffened. "Well, as you say, *yet*. Perhaps she hasn't noticed whatever was stolen. Or perhaps the thief—"

"This Fox person," Barber added helpfully.

She swallowed. "Yes. Perhaps he was interrupted."

She was talking too much. And she knew better. Silence was a great weapon against curiosity or suspicion. And yet she couldn't stop talking. She actually bit her tongue to keep herself from continuing to explain herself into a corner.

Barber leaned over his papers and wrote a few sentences. How Selina wished she could read his notes, but they were in a small, tight hand, upside down and too far away to be deciphered. When he was finished writing, he glanced up at her, almost dismissively.

"I think that's all for now, though we may have more questions for you later." He stood and she staggered to her own feet. "I would like to speak to Mr. Huntington alone for a moment, if you don't mind. Perhaps you'd like to go talk to the duke about this update yourself, as it is his gift to you gone missing."

She barely kept herself from flinching as guilt ripped through her yet again. "Y-Yes. I suppose that would be a good idea. Thank you, Mr. Barber."

She moved toward the door, and Derrick stood and walked behind her. When she reached it, she turned back to look up at him. Would this be the last time she could do it without irons around her wrists? Without him scowling at her as if she were a stranger?

He leaned closer. "All is well," he reassured her beneath his breath, though his smile didn't reach his eyes. "We'll…we'll resolve this, I swear to you."

She forced her own false smile, even though she didn't want them to resolve anything. Resolution was ruination, for everyone. Because of her.

"Thank you," she whispered, and slipped from the room.

Only she had no intention of going to Robert. No, she had someone else to speak to. Someone else who might have the answers to how she'd ended up in this trap.

CHAPTER 19

Derrick quietly closed the door as Selina stepped into the hall, and leaned his hand against it for a moment, unready to turn and face the barrage he was sure was about to come.

"So..." Barber said, dragging the word out too long. "Let me see if I understand. You discovered Selina Oliver knew about our true identities upon our arrival and you didn't tell me."

Derrick finally pivoted and faced his friend in silence.

"And then," Barber continued as he stepped around the desk and came closer, "you found out about her glove in a potential victim's chamber and spoke to her about it before me, as well."

Derrick forced himself to hold Barber's stare. He owed him that. "Yes," he said softly.

"Also you're fucking her," Barber added.

Derrick flinched at the bawdier term. One meant to raise his ire, he thought. Barber was using investigation tactics against him, it seemed. "I won't lie to you. I've taken her to bed."

"You won't lie to me *again*," Barber corrected. "Because I think we both know you have been lying to me. Over and over for the past week or more. I assume there's even more you haven't told me between 'she eavesdropped on a conversation' and 'her glove was found in a suspicious location'."

Derrick scrubbed a hand over his face. "You have every right to be angry with me."

"Oh, thank you for that." Barber snorted. "And I *am* angry. I'm also concerned. You don't involve yourself with suspects, Derrick. You never have."

Derrick blinked at Barber's use of his first name. It was a rare thing. Something that highlighted the seriousness of this infraction. "Is that what she is now? A suspect?"

It was said weakly, and Barber rolled his eyes. "Of course she is. And I can see from your eyes that you bloody well know she is."

Derrick walked away to the window and stared out at the stables so Barber wouldn't see how much further he'd already gone with his suspicions. He wasn't fully ready to share them. To say out loud what echoed in his head. To say out loud what would doom her, and them, forever.

"Why have we always believed that the Faceless Fox was a man?" Barber asked.

Derrick bent his head and gripped his hands at his sides. This was a snowball let loose at the top of a hill. It was already rolling, gaining momentum and mass. It was inevitable that it would crush everything in its path.

And yet he still struggled to slow it down. "Barber," he said in a weary tone.

"Answer the question. Why?"

He pivoted to face him, arms folded. "Because that's always how others have referred to the Fox," he said through gritted teeth.

"But he was never more than a shadow," Barber said. "An outline slipping from a window in the night. No one ever saw him...or her...clearly enough to name their sex with certainty."

"And I suppose because many of the victims would not believe a lady capable of such a crime," Derrick added reluctantly. "They see women as fitting into a certain category. Helpless victim, not clever thief."

"That would give a woman far more freedom, wouldn't it?" Barber pressed. He dug around in the papers on his desk and came up with one. "Here it is, the descriptions given by those who got a glimpse. Shall I read them?"

"No," Derrick whispered.

Barber ignored him. "'Slim.' And here's another: 'Moving with an unexpected grace.'" He glanced up at Derrick. "And this one is perfect. 'Quick as a fox.'" He set the papers down. "I could go on and on. Perhaps we've thought of this wrongly, to the benefit of our quarry."

Derrick fisted his hands at his sides. "So you are determined that the Fox is a woman now."

"And you are desperate for her not to be," Barber said.

"I'm desperate not to falsely accuse someone," Derrick said, throwing his hands up. "Selina is not the Fox."

Those words felt weak coming from his lips. They tasted bitter and false.

"Because you don't want her to be," Barber said softly, almost gently.

"Because she isn't," he insisted, even though it only served to dig a deeper hole in the sand for the water to fill. He was already up to his neck.

Barber moved toward him and caught his arm, holding tight as he looked up into Derrick's face. Barber's eyes were kind, but they offered no escape. "Do you really believe that?"

Derrick shook away. "I was not truthful with you, I admit that. And perhaps I let my feelings...my attraction...interfere in my investigation. That was wrong. All those things were wrong, and I admit that. But you won't accuse me of protecting a criminal. I-I wouldn't."

He pivoted on his heel and left the room before Barber could respond. But just because he'd ended the discussion didn't mean that it didn't hang in his mind, his doubts and Barber's doubts merging and taunting him. Like poisonous eggs laid and now hatching, spreading the venom through every part of him. Threatening a future he'd never dared to hope he could have.

A future he could see fading away with every step he took.

～

Selina burst into her chamber and slammed the door behind her. "Vale!" she called out into the empty room as she crossed to the connected door. "Vale, where are you?"

As she reached the door it opened and she staggered back as Vale entered the bedchamber. "You needn't call the house down. I'm here."

"Why was my glove in Lady Winford's chamber?" Selina asked. It was blunt, but she had no emotional energy for anything else.

Both of Vale's eyebrows lifted in surprise and she shook her head. "What are you going on about?"

She strolled past Selina into the main chamber and settled onto the settee before the fire. Selina pursed her lips at seeing her there, where she and Derrick had made love such a short time before. That was a sacred place, and Vale was lounged across it like it was nothing.

Selina hated being irritated at her friend. She hated doubting her when Vale had always been loyal.

She shut her eyes and drew a long breath to calm herself and then forced herself to explain better. "One of the gloves I was wearing last night was found by a servant in Lady Winford's room. It was ultimately turned over to Derrick. How did it get there?"

One of Vale's hands clenched and her gaze narrowed. "Perhaps you've forgotten as you traipsed around here all lady of the manor, but I'm not your actual servant, *Selina*. It's not my bloody role to keep track of your things, no matter how we've asked the world to see me."

186

"But—"

Vale interrupted her. "Perhaps you're just getting careless in your distracted state and left them there while you were fruitlessly searching the room."

"No," Selina insisted. "No, that's not it. I had the gloves on when I came back here last night. I was wearing them."

Vale pushed to her feet. "How do you know?"

"Because—" Selina felt blood rush to her cheeks as she recalled Derrick peeling each glove off, his mouth on her palm, on her wrist. She blinked away the images and the emotions they forced in her. "I just *know*. And I never returned to Lady Winford's room afterward. I cannot think of many ways they could have been transferred to that chamber."

"Wait," Vale said, stepping closer. She folded her arms and there was a spark of deep anger...rage...in her eyes. "Are you asking me or *accusing* me of something after all we've been through together?"

Selina stared at her a beat. Vale had been her friend, her partner for years. She'd depended on this woman with her life and her secrets and never doubted that decision because Vale had always kept them close.

But right now everything she knew and felt and understood felt...shaky. Probably because the person she distrusted most was herself.

"No," she whispered. "I-I'm not accusing you. I'm asking for your help in determining how the glove could have possibly gotten there, especially if you truly don't know."

Vale moved closer again, and Selina fought the desire to step an equal distance away. Vale extended a finger and pressed it against her sternum, jabbing not entirely gently. "Have you ever considered that your lover has already guessed your true identity? That perhaps *he* took your damned glove and planted it in the room himself because he hasn't figured out how to prove your guilt otherwise?"

Selina's lips parted at that horrible idea. Derrick was certainly hunting her, but until today, until the incident after they made love, she'd never felt his suspicion fall on her.

"No," she whispered. "He wouldn't do that."

"But you thought, at least for a fraction of a moment, that I would," Vale said. "I can see you're certain in this, though. I see it all over your face. You know him so well after fucking him a few times?"

Selina turned away, moved past Vale to the fire and stared at the flames as she tried to gather herself. "I do know him," she insisted.

And it was true. She knew his good heart, his brave soul, his honorable actions. She knew how he made her feel, that flutter she'd never believed could move her. She knew how he looked at her, passionate and protective all at once. And she knew how much he respected her. He thought her clever. He thought her bold. He liked those things, even if many in Society would ask her to be different. To be quieter. To be smaller.

And in that moment, as she easily listed the many reasons she had for having faith in him, another fact became powerfully and completely obvious.

She loved him.

An audible gasp escaped her lips at that realization, and she gripped the mantel before her with one white-knuckled hand to stay upright. She loved Derrick Huntington, despite the fact that he hunted her, despite their short acquaintance, despite the fact that it was all doomed. *They* were doomed. They could never be, and that shook her as much as the realization of her heart did.

Everything hurt. And she had to pretend it didn't. But then, she'd been doing that all her life.

She drew in a long breath, wiped all her feelings from her expression and turned back to Vale. "It wasn't him," she insisted. "There has to be another explanation."

"Fine. There's some other mysterious explanation," Vale spat. "I'll let you live in your fantasy world if that's what you insist upon.

How did you explain it to your lover, then? How did you keep him from putting you in irons, and not the fun kind?"

Selina explained her "missing" earrings and the discussions that had followed, and Vale nodded slowly. "I'm impressed, Selina. That's the old you, jumping quick and not worrying about who you hurt with a lie."

Selina flinched again. Was that the old her? In some ways, certainly.

She shrugged her tangled thoughts away. "We must formulate some kind of plan for how to deal with this turn of events."

Vale wrinkled her brow. "You steal the fucking necklace and we get out of here. Today, tonight. Grab and go, Selina. That's the plan and it's always been the plan."

"No." Selina shook her head. "The necklace is a loss now. If I take it and disappear, everyone will *know* that I'm the Fox."

"Why does that matter?" Vale breathed. "You'll be *legendary*. Stealing the jewel out from under the noses of two investigators at your own brother's party? They'll talk about it for decades. We'll sell the necklace at an even higher premium and use the spoils to move on. London is a bad market for us regardless. The Fox is too well known. The mavens actually hope for your arrival at their parties. We go to the continent. We move from country to country, never in the same place more than a few nights. *That's* the next step in the evolution of the Fox."

Selina blinked. "But...but that would mean never seeing my family again."

"What family?" Vale snapped.

Selina turned her face, for it was almost as if she had been slapped. "My—my brothers," she insisted, but oh, those words sounded weak.

Vale's expression turned to something almost like pity. "Selina, you can't be so soft. They're your *half*-blood brothers. You want a connection to them, but you must consider them with open eyes. The Duke of Roseford has his own past, certainly. But he'll disown you the moment he realizes who you are. Hell, he might do it just because you're a suspect. That lot doesn't care about family if it makes them look bad."

"No," Selina whispered.

"Yes," Vale said firmly. Not unkindly, but without quarter. "And as for your other two brothers? Morgan might have once stood by you. He was as desperate as you were, running the streets and making trouble. But he's different now, isn't he? He married to a lady of the highest order. He'll follow Roseford's lead. And I've heard Gillingham is up for a title, himself. He'll take his army friend's side if only to cover up what you did. You don't have any family, Selina, no matter how much you want it. People like us never do."

Selina flinched, for Vale had just laid out exactly her worst nightmare. That this persona, this Fox she had created to protect herself, to exact some tiny justice...would destroy all she loved in the end.

It would destroy her family. It would destroy whatever sliver of a future she might have once hoped for with Derrick.

"You're asking me to start over," she whispered.

Vale tilted her head. "I'm *telling* you not to go soft."

There was an edge to Vale's voice now and Selina wrinkled her brow at it. "Or what?"

Vale drew in a long breath and shook her head. "Just don't."

Vale said nothing else, she simply turned and left the room. Left Selina to stand by the fire, her hands shaking, her pulse throbbing, her heart breaking. She realized now that the point of no return had gone by a long time ago.

And that meant every choice she had to make now was bleak. No matter what she did, she wouldn't win. In fact, she would surely lose.

Lose her life. Lose her freedom. Lose her family. Lose love.

And she sank to her knees, rested her cheek on the settee, and wept for the damage she had created.

CHAPTER 20

Since he walked out on Barber the day before, Derrick hadn't left the table in his chamber. He hadn't eaten, he hadn't slept, he hadn't shaved. He'd just gathered, compiling evidence on a long chart, putting together elements he'd feared to bind.

And now he looked at the fruits of his labor. The facts of his own obsession. All of them pointed to one truth. One bitter end.

He had no doubt that Selina Oliver was the Faceless Fox. No one else fit the profile so exactly. No one else had so much evidence that pointed to them.

He leaned back in his chair with a heavy sigh and rubbed his eyes. It was a truth he'd suspected, of course. Something that had made him hesitate, that had made him question. But *knowing* his suspicions were correct...that was something different. That was something final.

Of course, all of it was different than knowing what the hell to do with the truth. Duty said to march up to Barber, show him what he'd gathered, admit Barber's accusations were correct. Derrick's duty said to pursue her. To put her into custody. To turn her over to the guard, along with the evidence, and be a part of her downfall. He'd done it with other criminals in the past. He'd been proud of his part in their trials, convictions. Justice was important in a world where sometimes there was very little.

But watching Selina burn didn't feel like justice. Not to him.

His heart screamed at him to protect her. To find out why she had created the Faceless Fox. Why she had robbed the first time, why she had continued to do so over the years. Mostly, his heart wanted to figure out a way to save her from the consequences the truth would bring when it came out.

Because it *would* come out. Barber was as hot on the trail as Derrick was, and he would figure out the same answer.

There was only one night left at the gathering. Tomorrow the first of the guests would begin to leave. The rest would follow in the next day or two. That meant the Rosefords were hosting a final ball tonight. The perfect place for a Fox to strike.

Or to fall into a trap.

So he needed to figure out exactly what he would do before Barber overtook her and everything ended in destruction and tears.

~

"Selina, I've been looking all over for you."

Selina started from her position seated on a garden bench, looking over the rosebushes, and stared up to find Robert coming toward her down the winding garden path. His expression was worried and her heart sank.

"You've been looking for me?" she asked weakly, scooting down to give him room.

He nodded as he took a place beside her and drew in a long breath. After he exhaled, he smiled. "You know, if you had told me even a few years ago that I would be contentedly observing my garden during a country party, I would have challenged you to a duel."

She laughed despite the concern she had over this encounter. "I think you might have. You were very convinced that your roguish life was perfect and you never wanted to leave it."

He shrugged, and his expression darkened as he glanced up toward the house. Toward Katherine, she supposed. Toward the life he had built for himself here.

"I'm not sure I ever thought it was perfect, no matter what I said and did," he said with a sigh. "I understand now that some part of me believed emptiness was all I...I *deserved*. That it was all there ever could be for a man like me."

This vulnerable side of her brother was one she hadn't seen. Robert smiled and laughed and still played the rogue, if no longer the rake. But this was different. This was her brother opening his chest and showing her his heart.

A gift, to be certain. Perhaps one she didn't deserve, considering how duplicitous she, herself, had been.

She turned toward him and reached out to squeeze his arm. "I'm *glad* you were disabused of that foolish notion. Watching you with Katherine is a joy. You're happy, anyone with eyes can see it. And you *do* deserve that, Robert. You truly do."

"Thank you." He smiled at her. "So do you, you know."

She shifted. He had no idea. "Hmmm," she murmured in what she hoped was a noncommittal tone.

They sat in silence for a moment, both staring out at nothing, though she thought with very different reasons. Finally, his voice cut through her spinning mind again. "Do you ever intend to tell me the truth?"

She jolted and glanced over at him. He was still staring away from her.

"The—the truth," she stammered, as she pondered what truth he could be referring to. Did he know about the Fox? Had Derrick told him, or perhaps Barber? Was everything about to end, including her relationship with this man she had come to see as truly her brother? She mourned that intensely in a moment.

"Your cameo earrings," Robert said, and looked down at her

sternly. "I was informed last night that they were taken by the Face-less Fox. Imagine my surprise when Mr. Barber spoke to me about it because he assumed *you'd* told me about the theft."

She sucked in a breath. Barber would surely count that fact against her. Rightly, of course. Her lie that she would tell Robert about the fake theft would only be more evidence in the pile against her.

"Oh, yes," she whispered when she realized Robert seemed to be waiting for an answer to his statement. "*That.*"

He caught one of her hands and held it gently. "You and I weren't raised together. We didn't really know each other at all until very recently. That was *my* failing, amongst a great many other failings."

"No," she interrupted as she pulled away from him. "I won't let you say that. Our father is the reason all of us were kept apart. You have been nothing but kind and accepting, probably more than all of us have deserved. Please don't judge yourself too harshly."

He smiled at her. "I appreciate that. My marriage put a great deal into perspective for me. I realized how much I feared getting to know you all. And how much I was missing out on by avoiding you. I've tried to make up for my shortcomings. Now I wonder how good a job I've done. Selina, *why* didn't you tell me about the earrings?"

She swallowed and ducked her gaze because she didn't trust her brother not to see through her. He and Derrick were very similar in that way, actually. Two men who could read a person down to their soul. Perhaps for different reasons, but the result was the same.

"I didn't want you to worry," she said, and that was true. As was what she said next. "I didn't want you to be angry."

"Angry?" he repeated. "How could I be angry when you were a victim of a thief? One who came into your room while you slept in your bed." He shivered. "I shudder to think what he could have done that would have been far worse."

She flinched. "The Faceless Fox has never been violent," she whispered. "I don't think I've ever been in danger from that person, if that helps."

He rubbed his hands along his thighs, his jaw set with emotion. "I don't share your assessment. I was *always* concerned about this investigation coming into my home, threatening those I love. Now it has come to pass and I hate myself for allowing it. For ignoring my instincts when Nicholas asked for my assistance. And when Mr. Huntington and Mr. Barber presented their case to me to allow things to play out."

"Well, if it helps, I doubt Katherine is in danger," she said. "Surely the Fox will go to ground now that he's taken a trinket. So those you love won't be in danger."

"I'm talking about you," he said, blinking.

Her lips parted. "Me?"

"Of course," he said. "I'm not always good at...at expressing myself. With Katherine it's easy—I have practice, plus she demands nothing less of me."

"She *is* tenacious," Selina said with a smile.

He returned it, but then he shifted. "But I sometime still struggle with words when it comes to others. Like my siblings. God knows Morgan and I were at loggerheads a dozen times last summer when I came to his aid. It was a struggle, but coming to an understanding, being able to see each other as brothers...as friends..."

He caught his breath, and she was shocked at the emotion that crossed her brother's face. "Robert," she said softly.

He smiled, blinking back tears. "It means a great deal to me. Selina, I want you to know that even if I haven't said it, I am immensely proud of you. Your independence and self-sufficiency in the face of a difficult past are admirable beyond belief."

Now it was her eyes that stung with tears. "I didn't know you thought of me so much."

He nodded. "Of course I do, and I have for some time. I remember the first time I reviewed the whereabouts of all my siblings. Seeing that you took your settlement and obtained a home for yourself, that you refused to back down from what you wanted...I was proud then."

She gritted her teeth. How proud would he be if he knew the truth? She could see he didn't...not yet. So Barber had not revealed his suspicions about her. Perhaps that was a kindness. Perhaps it was something else, a part of his investigation.

Whatever it was, it gave her time, though not very much of it.

"Thank you," she whispered.

"And beyond that," he continued, "I do love you, sister. We may be only half blood, but that is with my whole heart."

She was shaking from the power of that statement. She, who had never been wanted, never been loved by her family. And now, on the cusp of having her identity revealed, she realized how much she had to lose.

But perhaps she didn't have to lose everything at that. If she took the truth into her own hands, if she offered atonement along with confession...perhaps she could show her family, along with the man she loved, that she was worthy of their regard. That she wasn't a monster they feared, but still the woman they cared for.

But she couldn't do it alone. She would need help and there was only one man who she could receive that from. The one man who might hate her all the more for it.

Derrick.

"Well, this has been mightily maudlin," Robert said with a chuckle as he got up and tugged her to her feet. "And I would much rather enjoy my last few days with you as houseguest."

She smiled, pushing away the inevitable for a little while longer as she linked arms with her brother. "I agree. You know, I have heard you once played a lot of dirty tricks on your friends when you were a lad."

"Oof, Simon was talking, eh?"

She giggled. "He and Baldwin, both. But I'd like to hear *your* side of the story. Is it true you tricked them all into swimming naked at some party?"

"Not exactly," he said with a moan. "It was rather the other way around…"

They strolled off, with Robert regaling her with tales of his misspent youth. But even as she laughed at his outrageous stories, she plotted her own next move in the back of her mind. One that could end this happily, or simply rush along her jump off a cliff.

CHAPTER 21

The ball was in full swing, but Derrick hardly noticed the swirling couples on the dancefloor or the brightly liveried servants offering drinks as they floated by. His attention was locked, as it had been for half an hour, on the door to the ballroom. He was waiting for Selina. He'd had a wild thrill ten minutes earlier when her companion, Vale Williams, had entered the room. But Selina had not been at her side, nor had she joined the party since.

He hadn't seen her since the previous afternoon with Barber. And now he longed for her. And feared meeting her. Because what would happen next would change everything. It would decide everything.

In that moment, that desperate moment when he feared and longed for her in equal measure, she appeared. His heart stopped and his breath caught with the sight of her. It was a strange thing, her beauty. He could always convince himself that it wasn't as powerful as he remembered. That it wasn't as bewitching. But then she'd walk into a room and he'd realized she was even more stunning than he'd recalled.

Tonight was no different. Her sleek black hair was done up with elaborate twists, her cheeks pink, her lips warm. She always wore impeccable fashion, but tonight she looked like a queen. Her gown was gold brocade and she shone like the sun as the candles glinted off the fabric. The eyes of the room turned on her, women whispered behind their fans, men tracked her as she entered the room, smiling at her family, waving to friends.

She was everything, and he burned for her. He burned for what could be destroyed in a few moments.

Her gaze swept across the room and found him. He saw her jolt a little when she did. He waited for her to run, to avoid him. Only she didn't. She set her slender shoulders back and then she moved across the ballroom toward him. Her bright blue eyes held to his, a trap. A freedom. A boon he had never deserved.

She'd been his for a moment. And that might come to an end tonight.

"Selina," he breathed as she reached him. The vanilla and cinnamon scent of her wafted to his nostrils, the warmth of her curled around him, and he very nearly lost his nerve.

But she didn't seem to have that problem.

"Derrick," she said. Then she leaned in. "Have we been...avoiding each other?"

That directness made him smile even though there was nothing pleasing about what was happening at present. Still, he couldn't help but be drawn by her directness. It was in such contrast to the duplicity he now knew she was capable of. She had so many remarkable facets, and he knew he hadn't begun to learn them all. That was a loss in itself.

"I think we have been," he said. "It would be foolhardy not to acknowledge that truth."

"Obviously things...*changed* after yesterday afternoon," she said.

Her expression softened with those words. Became sad. Was that a game or the truth? Could he even tell with her? Was he so compromised that it all blended together?

"Yes," he admitted.

She swallowed and her fingers stretched out. She touched his hand. She wasn't wearing gloves, nor was he. Skin on skin, just the hint of it, but it was intoxicating.

"We need to...to talk," she said. Her voice cracked. Tension poured through her. Fear and anxiety and need and pain. "Privately. Because we both know there is a great deal to say and I can't do it in the ballroom where fifty pairs of eyes will be watching."

He nodded slowly. "Yes. I think you're right. In this instance, we need privacy."

Her shoulders rolled forward just a fraction. A surrender. An acceptance and his heart lurched. She looked determined, but also defeated, and now he wondered what she would say the moment they were alone.

"The library," she said. "It only seems right to go back to where we began. Will you meet me there in—"

She didn't get a chance to finish the sentence because in that moment there was a scream from across the room. Both she and Derrick pivoted toward the sound. The Duchess of Roseford stood in the middle of the ballroom floor, one hand clasped to her lips while she held the other shaking one in front of her.

"My bracelet!" she cried out. "Someone has stolen my bracelet!"

The Duke of Roseford raced across the room as the crowd parted even farther from the duchess, as if the theft were somehow contagious. As he reached her, he called out, "Shut those doors! No one comes in or out."

He wrapped his arms around his wife, clutching her close to his chest. She leaned into him, still trembling as he spoke words of comfort close to her ear.

"Katherine," Selina breathed.

Her voice shook Derrick from his haze and he rushed forward. He could see Barber approaching from the other side of the room, his face lined with similar concern. They reached the couple at the same time and exchanged a look. Questions flowed between them, but Derrick had no answers.

"Are you harmed, Your Grace?" Barber asked.

"N-No," Katherine stammered. "But I was wearing a bracelet and someone has slipped it from my wrist. It was an anniversary gift. Priceless to me. Robert!"

Derrick watched as Roseford tucked her even closer. He looked furious, but also deeply protective. As if he could wrap himself around his wife like a cloak and somehow erase the harm that had been done to her. The fear she now felt.

"You are certain you were wearing the piece when you entered the ballroom?" Derrick asked gently. "It couldn't have fallen off before or even while you were dancing?"

"It couldn't have," Katherine said firmly. "I always double check the clasp before I go anywhere wearing it."

"What does it look like?" Derrick asked.

"Rubies and diamonds, Mr. Huntington," Roseford said, his voice vibrating with tension.

Derrick flinched. While Selina's cameo earrings were not the usual type of jewelry the Faceless Fox stole, the bracelet sounded more her speed. And he glanced toward Selina from the corner of his eye to see her reaction.

She was at his elbow, looking just as worried for Katherine's well-being as everyone else. And he thought a little confused by this turn of events.

Roseford, though, looked nothing resembling confused. He looked increasingly enraged.

"This is enough," Roseford growled toward Derrick and Barber.

"Your Grace," Barber said, a warning to his tone.

But Roseford seemed beyond listening. He lifted his voice. "For the past ten days, I have remained silent, but I will do so no longer. There is a criminal within these walls and I will not stand for it. He has already taken from my sister, and now he has slipped the bracelet from my wife's wrist here in this very ballroom."

There was a collective gasp from the crowd, which murmured toward each other in concern and excitement. For most of them, this was just a game. Something they would gossip about later. Something they would crow about being a part of.

For Derrick, for Roseford, for Selina...it was something more.

"Your Grace, perhaps this isn't the time—" Barber began.

"Bollocks!" Roseford interrupted, eliciting another excited ripple through the rapt crowd. "It is the perfect time. Katherine, how long has the bracelet been missing?"

"It couldn't have been longer than a moment or two," Katherine said. "Helena was just complimenting me on it."

The Duchess of Sheffield moved forward in the crowd and caught her friend's hand. She was pale as paper. "I did. Oh, Katherine, I hope my compliments aren't what drew the attention of some thief."

"No," Robert growled. "You needn't accept any of the blame for this, Helena, I assure you. This isn't some common thief, and I'm certain this was part of their plan all along. Ladies and gentlemen, among us is the Faceless Fox."

That declaration caused even more than a mere ripple, and the crowd erupted in gasps and whispers as they looked at each other.

"The Fox?" came a voice from the crowd. "Here?"

"How thrilling!" This time it was a female voice. "I've always heard tales of him."

"But this time they've gone too far," Roseford continued. "I don't think they've had enough time to escape the ballroom. I want everyone to turn out their pockets and reticules. I'll search you each myself if you refuse. I will have this villain on shanks before this night is through."

The milling crowd seemed mesmerized by Roseford's declaration, but Derrick waited for the pushback. Surely none of these Society mavens and straight-laced lords would be willing to turn out their pockets, not even for the duke. But to his utter surprise, they did.

It started with Roseford's friends. The Dukes of Sheffield and Crestwood both turned their pockets out, showing they were empty, and that set off the floodgates. As the two dukes shifted silently through the crowd, people couldn't seem to move fast enough to be the next to prove they weren't the Faceless Fox and then leer at the next partygoer to see if they were the one.

"This is ridiculous," Barber whispered. "Whoever did this might not have put the bracelet in a pocket at all."

"I agree," Derrick said. "But it's still an interesting exercise. Watch the faces. Watch the reactions before they make their move. It's telling."

He said it, but his gaze kept flitting to Selina. She was standing beside her brother and had not yet emptied her own pockets. Of course, her beautiful gown probably didn't have them. If she had taken the bracelet, it could be in her cleavage or passed to someone else. Who knew what she might have done?

At any rate, her expression was impassive, free of guilt. She seemed to have no fear about this intense search of the partygoers. And as the number of guests who had revealed themselves dwindled, she stepped forward.

"I have nothing to hide," she said softly, and reached into the unexpected pockets that were hidden within the beautiful golden skirts of her gown. One was empty, but as she overturned the other, a glittering line of red clattered to the floor.

The room as a whole froze, staring at once at the ruby-and-diamond bracelet that now lay on the floor. Katherine's bracelet.

And then all hell broke loose.

Robert's fingers dug into Selina's arm as he all but dragged her into the closest parlor. She staggered away from him, checking the room for exits as it filled with staring, judging faces. Katherine's face, streaked with tears and betrayal. She was followed into the room by Mr. Barber and last was Derrick. He shut the door and stared at her, pain lining every part of his expression.

But not surprise.

"How could you?" Robert gasped out, his breath shot as he paced in circles around the room. "How *could* you, Selina?"

She opened her mouth to speak, but Katherine moved toward Robert, catching his arm and stilling him. "I'm sorry, I'm sorry, my love. But please, let us consider there may be an alternate answer than that your sister did this." She turned toward Barber and Derrick. "Gentlemen, you have been investigating this Faceless Fox thief for months. Would he try to divert attention in this way?"

Barber straightened and cast a quick look toward Selina. She could have withered beneath his judgment. She knew he wouldn't protect her.

"I am sorry, Your Graces. Deeply sorry. But I have come to suspect that the Faceless Fox is, indeed, Miss Oliver," he said softly. "There is a great deal of evidence supporting that fact, not the least of which is your stolen bracelet tonight."

Katherine wobbled in her place and Robert's hand shot out to steady her. Or perhaps to be steadied. The way they clung to each other, it was clear they both sought comfort in the eyes of this betrayal. Selina bent her head. At least they would have each other.

Even though she would lose them.

She felt Derrick's stare on her. Even and steady from the door. Everyone else was talking at once, their upset and hurt and confusion crackling through the room like lashes across her skin. But Derrick only watched her.

Until he stepped forward and said, "Selina."

That one word silenced the room. Or perhaps it was that commanding tone of his voice that had always dragged her to him like a puppet on his string. Even now she leaned toward it and toward him, seeking comfort he could no longer give.

She cleared her throat. "I did *not* take Katherine's bracelet."

It was true, of course. Just as she hadn't left her glove behind in Lady Winford's chamber, she hadn't done this thing. She would *never* betray Katherine that way. Not just because she was family, but because it would violate her code of ethics as a thief. Katherine had never harmed another creature. She helped those around her regularly. She didn't *deserve* punishment.

"You had it on your person," Barber said. "It is hard not to think you are lying when every other fact matches."

She shut her eyes. She had lied so many times, of course she couldn't be believed. And that was *her* punishment, doled out at last by some faceless person who had discovered her secret. Doled out by a cruel universe that would offer her a family and a love and then snatch both away at the last moment.

Robert released Katherine and crossed the room toward her. His dark gaze held hers—and stung her. Gone was the man who had declared himself proud of her just a few hours before. The man who had said he loved her like the sister she'd never been allowed to be until now. The man who joked with her and welcomed her into his life. Now he was a stern duke, judging her for what she'd done to the love of his life.

She was nothing else.

"Selina," he said sharply.

"Please," she whispered. "Please, believe me. I've done many things, but I would never do this."

His nostrils flared as he stared at her. "You've done many things. What does that mean?"

Her lips parted and she struggled with what to say. She'd meant to make this confession, first to Derrick and then to her family. But not like this. Not when it felt like an excuse, not an olive branch. Not when it was too late.

"What does it mean?" he repeated, loud enough that it felt like the room shook with his question.

She was shaking as she dropped her gaze to the floor. Shaking as she swallowed hard, and then the words fell from her lips. "Mr. Barber and Mr. Huntington's suspicions are correct. I-I *am* the Faceless Fox."

CHAPTER 22

"Selina..."

It was Katherine's voice that said her name this time, soft and shocked and hurt. Selina couldn't bear to look at her. To see the expression that went with that tiny tone. She'd lost so much already in such a short span of moments.

"I am the Fox," she continued. "But I would never hurt my family."

Robert turned from her, walked away and tossed over his shoulder, "But you did, Selina. You did."

She nearly crumpled at that. That dismissal she had earned through her own actions. That tearing away of affection that had come to mean more to her than anything else in this world. And when she looked up at Derrick, her heart broke even more.

His expression was shattered, both for her and by her. The future she'd once seen, a tiny glimmer in his beautiful eyes, was gone. Everything was gone.

Barber cleared his throat, his discomfort clear as he stepped up to her. "I appreciate your candor, Miss Oliver," he said softly. "And I apologize for everything I will now be forced to do."

THE HEART OF A HELLION

She lifted her chin and made herself meet his eyes. "I don't blame you for that, Mr. Barber. You have a duty to uphold. I would not expect less from a man of honor such as yourself."

He inclined his head slightly, surprise on his face. He had not thought she would accept her fate.

"What exactly *does* come next?" Robert asked, his tone numb, still refusing to look at her.

"It is very late," Barber said. "But tomorrow Huntington and I will transport Miss Oliver back to London. She will be turned over to the guard and we will report back to the victims of her crimes who hired us. After that, it will be up to the magistrate what will happen. Miss Oliver's sex and her connection to an important family might be swaying factors in protecting her. And if she is willing to return any items she might still have in her possession."

"I will hire a defense counsel," Robert said in that same cold tone. "Perhaps you two can recommend someone of good reputation."

"You...you would do that?" Selina whispered.

He glanced at her briefly. "To protect my family from further harm, I would do so. Nicholas, especially, could be damaged by what you've done. I would hate for him to lose his chance at the title he so desires, thanks to you."

She flinched. So it was not out of love, at least not for her, that he would help her. "I see. Of course."

"If you do not mind, Your Graces, I will take Miss Oliver back to her chamber now. She will remain there under guard until the morning." Barber motioned to her. "Come now."

She didn't resist. How could she? What was happening was what she deserved. She would see it through, however it played out. Her life as she knew it was now over. And she would have to face uncertainty alone, because that was what she had earned.

D errick didn't speak as he followed behind Barber and Selina through the winding halls of the estate. If they passed by a servant, the person stopped to stare. He heard whispers behind doors. This was a scandal of epic proportions, thanks to the dramatic revelation in the ballroom.

And it would not stop.

But even though all evidence pointed to Selina's guilt, even though she had quietly admitted to being the Faceless Fox in the parlor a few moments before, Derrick had a nagging feeling that something wasn't right.

Why would Selina turn out her pocket, a *hidden* pocket that no one would have guessed was in the gown at all, so casually if she knew the bracelet was there? She'd made no obvious effort to hide the piece from view or protect herself from what was to come. And she admitted she was the Fox, but declared herself innocent in the robbery of her sister-in-law. The crimes of the Faceless Fox were far more severe, so why deny this one small crime that had already seen its jewels returned to their owner? Except to protect her relationships.

But if that were the case, then he circled back to why she would do it in the first place. The robberies the Faceless Fox...*Selina*....had committed in the past had never seemed driven by compulsion, but were targeted events. Something carefully planned with a very specific kind of victim. Katherine didn't fit that profile, even if her bracelet did.

Just like with the matter of the glove, Derrick felt uncertain. And he wouldn't have true answers until he spoke to Selina alone.

They reached her chamber and Barber waited for her to open the door. She paused there, standing quietly to await orders. She didn't argue, she didn't declare anything. It was as if some of that beautiful spirit Derrick had come to admire had been broken by tonight. And his heart ached for her.

Even though he knew he shouldn't feel empathy or heartbreak or...or anything else for a criminal he had hunted.

"There will be someone outside your door all night," Barber said. "To ensure you don't take it in your head to escape."

"Certainly," Selina whispered, her chin dropping. "I understand."

Barber's brow wrinkled at her capitulation, as if he, too, were expecting more of a fight from the famous Fox.

"Is that all?" Selina asked, her gaze sliding to Derrick.

Barber followed the motion and his frown deepened. "Yes. Goodnight, Miss Oliver."

She sighed. "I realize everything will have to change after tonight. So I'd like to tell you thank you, Mr. Barber, for being so decent about this. I do appreciate your kindness, because I know it isn't required." She looked at Derrick again, and tears filled her eyes before she ducked into her room with a quick, "Goodnight."

As the door closed behind her, Derrick moved toward it, but Barber lifted a hand, pressing it to his chest and keeping him in place. "Don't," he said softly.

Derrick backed away, trying to retain some control. It felt impossible. "How can you say *don't*? You must see there's more to this than what she said."

Barber inclined his head. "Perhaps. I don't deny the circumstances are...odd. But Huntington, you cannot involve yourself in this matter anymore."

"Why the hell not? We're partners, aren't we?" Derrick snapped. "I still have a say in it, don't I? And if I feel something is amiss, why shouldn't I further pursue it?"

"Because you love her," Barber said.

The words, stated as fact, not a question, slapped through the air and hit Derrick so hard he nearly staggered from them. Loved her. Love her. He couldn't deny that those words rang in his head like a bell. They explained the unfettered desire that coursed through him every time she came near, the intense interest he felt in her past and her present and her future. The fact that the idea of losing her had become an actual, physical pain that kept him up at night.

"No," he whispered, and it felt so false that he couldn't maintain the lie. "Perhaps," he clarified.

Barber nodded slowly. "I have no idea of the heart of the woman behind that door, friend. We've chased her for months, I've studied her ways and so have you. What you've shared could be real. Or perhaps you were being used—"

Derrick lunged toward him, catching Barber's collar in both hands and giving him a shake. "Shut up," he growled past clenched teeth.

Barber sniffed as he carefully extracted himself from Derrick's grip and took a step closer to the door. "As you have just proven, yet again, you are compromised. Go to bed. *I* will manage who watches her."

Derrick gripped his hands at his sides as a red rage pulsed through him. But more powerful than that was fear. Fear for her. Fear for himself. Fear for what would happen next that would destroy everything for them all.

And he turned and walked away. But he knew this wasn't the end of it. He wouldn't allow it to be.

Vale was seated before the fire when Selina staggered into the room. Her partner lifted her gaze and held there, judging. And Selina was too weak to hide.

"Something happened," Vale said, a statement of fact.

Selina nodded and then the dam broke. She collapsed forward, bracing herself on all fours as the torrent of emotions rushed over her. Vale stared at her as she wept on the carpet and then silently came beside her. She tucked Selina into her side, rocking gently as she poured all her pain and fear and heartbreak into this person who had known her secrets for years.

Well, almost all of them. She'd never revealed all of herself before. The closest to that was what she'd shared with Derrick. And now he had to hate her just as her brother now hated her.

"Tell me," Vale insisted as the tears eased.

"I owe you that," Selina hiccupped, getting to her feet slowly and brushing off the beautiful dress she'd put on with such hopes and fears a few hours before. "Because it will affect us both in the end."

She did tell Vale then. Told her everything about the night and the bracelet and the horrible confrontation.

"You *admitted* you were the Fox," Vale gasped in horror. "Selina!"

"I have heard my name whispered as a curse, said as an admonishment by people I love all night," she said, rubbing her eyes. "Please spare me it one more time. I had no choice, don't you see? I'm cornered. I'm caught. But you don't have to be."

"How could I not be?" Vale said, pacing the room, her hands rubbing in front of her with nervous energy. "Christ, Selina, these two men must already suspect I'm far more than your companion. They'll come for me, even if it is just to lessen the heat on you."

Selina couldn't argue that. Derrick and Barber were too clever not to see through all her lies now that they'd begun to unravel.

"And there is also the danger to you from whoever framed me for Katherine's jewels," Selina added. "Whoever put my glove in Lady Winford's chamber. Well, whoever did that clearly knows who I am and wanted to punish me."

"A victim, perhaps?" Vale suggested. "Or a rival?"

"Possibly one of those things," Selina said on a shuddering sigh. "But how can I protect you now that I'm trapped in this chamber, ready to be marched to London tomorrow?"

"There is a guard watching the doors," Vale said slowly. Then she paced to the window and threw open the curtains. She lifted the sash and a burst of cool air filled the room. "But I'm assuming he doesn't know your skill with windows."

Selina walked to the window and stared down. It was a long climb, fraught with danger. It wouldn't be an easy descent for them, that was certain. Equally certain was that she could manage it. She'd escaped many a manor home exactly this way.

"If I run, it will destroy any hope I have to reconcile with my family," she said. "It will make my confession look self-serving."

Vale pivoted and caught her arms. "It should be self-serving! Why allow yourself to be caught? Why allow yourself to be punished? No. We run."

Selina stared again into the night. She had done this to Vale. She owed her partner a chance at freedom. Together they had it. If she could get back to London, she could give access to funds to her friend, see that she escaped punishment for her part in Selina's crimes.

And then Selina could turn herself in. Vale wouldn't approve, but what would it matter then? She would have saved the last person she didn't want to damage. And she could accept her fate.

"Fine," she said, and turned her back. "Unfasten me. I can't climb in this contraption."

Vale laughed softly and rushed forward to unfasten her, but Selina felt no joy or thrill in this decision. Just another disappointment she would create in Derrick. In her family.

And she couldn't imagine how much more they'd hate her when this was finished.

~

Derrick stepped from the protection of a doorway at the end of the hall. Barber wasn't at his post. Of course, at four in the morning, he hadn't expected his friend to be. They needed to be well rested for all to come, so he had probably assigned a footman to watch the door in the wee hours. Derrick moved down the hall toward Selina's room and from the shadows stepped one of the servants, just as he had guessed.

"M-Mr. Huntington," he stammered. "What business do you have?"

Derrick stifled a curse and smiled at the boy. "I'm taking over for you on watch."

The young man glanced down the hall. "I dunno, sir. Mr. Barber and the Duke of Roseford were clear I wasn't to leave my post."

"Not to leave your post unattended," Derrick reassured him. "Which you wouldn't be."

"I—"

Derrick straightened his shoulders and snapped into a military tone that he knew as well as his own name. "Boy, I've given you a direct order. I'm in the service of the King in this matter. To defy me is to defy your sovereign. Is that what you would like to do tonight?"

"N-No," he responded, lifting his hands. "Of course, sir. I leave you to it, sir."

Derrick felt bad as he watched the boy rush away. But in the end, Barber would blame him, not the young man. Derrick could take it. He had to because he needed to see Selina and resolve this.

Her door was locked, but it didn't matter. He slipped a lock pick from his boot and popped the lock open with a few twists of his wrist. He settled his hand against the flat of it, opening it slowly so it wouldn't creak.

He stepped into the room. The fire had burned low in the night. He saw the shadow of Selina's form in the bed, but she didn't stir as he entered and shut the door behind himself. He moved toward her, his breath almost nonexistent as he reentered her space. He needed to see her. To touch her.

To get some kind of explanation so he'd know what to do next.

He reached out a hand, watched it tremble as he set it where her hip should be on the bed. But instead of encountering the firm lines of her body beneath the covers, his hand sank into softness, deeper and deeper.

He yanked his hand back and stared. The lump still hadn't moved. His stomach dropped.

"Bloody fuck, Selina," he grumbled as he threw the covers back and revealed an expertly positioned group of pillows beneath. Selina was gone.

And all that was left was a note on her empty pillow that read *I'm sorry.*

CHAPTER 23

W hen Selina had come to Roseford from London, she and Vale had traveled a direct route on good roads. But the way back was far different. She knew there were two bloodhounds on her trail, working together to find her and make her pay for her crimes. So the past two days she and her partner had traveled carefully, on back roads, stopping at nondescript inns and hiding their carriage so it wouldn't be seen.

Now Selina sat in the sitting room of their chamber at a rundown inn on the outskirts of the small city they'd stopped in. She didn't even know the name as she stared at the wall with a blank, unseeing expression. She was so tired. She'd hardly slept in the time since she slipped from her brother's window. She didn't want to eat.

She just wanted to get Vale to safety and then turn herself in.

She reached into her pocket and pulled out the cameo earrings Robert had given her all those months ago. The ones she'd lied about to save herself. As she looked at them, she felt the cameo face glaring at her. Digging into her skin and her heart.

"Stop staring at those," Vale snapped.

"How can I not?" Selina asked, glancing up at her. Vale had been increasingly annoyed with her as they traveled. She couldn't blame her partner, really, but she also couldn't change what she felt. "My brother gave me these."

"And he could have afforded to give you emeralds," Vale growled. "Pearls. Rubies as fine as those in the bracelet that wife of his wore. Instead he gave you something with half the value."

Selina shook her head. "Not half the value to me."

Vale threw up her hands. "Come, we'll go to the finer inn down the lane to sample their fare. Food will put you to rights. I've heard they'll have music tonight, too."

"No," Selina said, turning her face away from her friend. "I'm not hungry and I don't need any entertainment. You go. Enjoy yourself if you can."

Vale pursed her lips. "*Fine*. I'll be gone a few hours. I hope in that time you'll reconsider your life and remember who you really are."

She flounced out then, leaving Selina to ponder those words, she supposed. What Vale didn't understand was that she'd been doing just that for days and had come to the realization that her life had been very...empty before she went to Roseford. Derrick had changed that. Derrick had changed everything. But it was ruined now. It had to be.

There was a knock at her door, and she started. She hadn't asked for anything to be sent up for her. But then, perhaps it was Vale, back to force Selina to her will. She trudged to her feet and called out, "I don't want to go to the entertainment, I swear to you I just need—"

She threw the door open and her words caught in her throat. It wasn't Vale there waiting for her—it was Derrick. A scruffy-faced Derrick who looked like he hadn't shaved since she last saw him. A messy-haired, wild-eyed Derrick who clasped her wrist and yanked her against him before he dropped his mouth to hers and kissed her.

She melted, only vaguely aware that he was pushing her into the room, closing the door behind himself, locking it. Trapping her, she supposed, but it didn't matter. If it meant being with him, she'd take trapped for all eternity.

But at last he released her and stepped back, panting as he stared down at her and she up at him. "I found you," he whispered.

She nodded. "Yes. You found me, though I have no idea how. Except that you are very good at what you do. And I expect you'll be returning me to London for all the trouble I deserve."

He reached out and she froze, watching his hand extend toward hers. Only he didn't take it. Instead, he slipped the cameo earrings from her hand. She flinched as he stared at them, another lie revealed.

"They're pretty," he said.

"Yes," she agreed.

He continued to hold the earrings, even as he folded his arms. Her lover, her love, he was gone. This was an investigator come to call on her. A man bent on truth and reconciliation. On crime and punishment. Justice, or some version thereof.

"You need to stop lying to me," he said.

She caught her breath, looking up at that handsome face that had drawn her toward him for weeks. Looking up into those eyes she had fallen in love with, eyes that could read her soul like no one else had ever been able to do. And she nodded because she didn't want to lie anymore. Not to him. No matter what.

He looked relieved that she didn't argue and he touched her cheek, perhaps as a reward. She leaned into his warm, rough palm, memorizing the weight of every finger on her skin.

"You're the Fox."

"Yes," she whispered. "I wasn't lying when I admitted it three nights ago. I am the Faceless Fox."

His lips pursed as he turned away from her and paced across the room. He set her earrings down on the table and stood at the window, staring out at the busy street below without speaking for what felt like an eternity. She waited, because what else could she do? She was owed no demands. She could ask him no questions after all her lies.

"Tell me everything," he ordered, and faced her at last, his gaze narrowed. "Don't lie to me. If you can."

Her breath caught. "Derrick—"

"Now," he interrupted.

She let out her breath slowly, trying to calm her racing heart, her fluttering body. She needed to have her faculties for this, the final confrontation and whatever would come next. He was owed her calm, not some display of hysteria that would require him to comfort or worry.

She lifted her chin. "What I told you about my family, that was true. They didn't want me and they did offer me enormous freedom, perhaps in the hopes I'd disappear and they would no longer have any responsibility at all."

Derrick's jaw set, just as it had when she first told him about her past. But he said nothing.

"I used the freedom as any young person would, I suppose. I ran positively wild. I drank too much, I gamed too much, I learned about pleasure."

"The Fox," Derrick said softly.

She nodded. "I'm getting there. This is my villainous monologue, Derrick. Allow me my gothic moment." She saw his mouth twitch a little despite himself, but he didn't stop her from continuing. "One night I snuck into a party. The one I told you about where I saw my father."

"That was the first time you stole," he said.

She flinched. "How do you know that?"

"When I'm not being seduced by my quarry, I'm actually a very good investigator. Well able to put together evidence, my love."

She froze at the endearment that gripped her heart in its fist and squeezed. Tears stung her eyes and she blinked at them, trying to rein in the reaction. Trying not to give too much or ask for too much in that moment.

"Am I your love?" she whispered.

He hesitated, his gaze holding hers. "Continue your story, Selina."

She bit her lip hard enough that she tasted blood, and it did what she wanted—it dragged her back to the present. Away from the dreams she didn't need to have. Away from whatever future she never could have had in the first place.

"I was upset after my encounter with the late Duke of Roseford...my father," she continued, wishing her voice didn't shake. "I had snuck into a parlor to have a good cry when there were voices. I hid behind the curtains, and there was this horrible woman who dragged a servant into the room. She was screaming at her and screaming at her, berating this poor, shaking girl who was begging for her own life. This wretched woman, revered by Society, slapped the girl and left her sobbing in a pile on the floor as she laughed and went back to her party."

"What did you do?"

"After the servant left, I went back into the ballroom, found that bitch and did exactly to her what I am accused of doing to Katherine. I slipped a yellow diamond bracelet right off her wrist without her even noticing I'd done it. And I was terrified and thrilled in equal measure. It was spontaneous, I should have been caught by all rights, but it felt...*good*! As if I'd taken back control not just for myself, but for that girl left crying on the floor. Also, it was before I got my settlement from my father, so the money helped."

"Selina." The way he said her name, she couldn't tell if he was angry, disappointed, sad...or some combination of them all.

She folded her arms, a poor shield against what just his look did to her. "You can judge."

"I won't be the one judging in the end." He let out a shaky sigh. "Why didn't you stop?"

She shrugged, because that was a question she'd asked herself a dozen times over the years. "Because it was..." She struggled for a word to explain it. "It was safe."

"Safe?" he burst out, his control wavering as he took a long step toward her. "How the hell was that safe, Selina? You could have been caught, abused, even worse if the wrong nobleman found you with your hand in his wife's drawer. You could have been arrested—"

She moved toward him, and now they were nearly touching. "By you?"

He shut his eyes, his breath coming in and out of his nostrils like a riled bull. She reached up, letting her fingertips stroke over his rough jaw. Watching his eyes come open, heavier and more focused. He didn't step away, but he said, "How was it safe?"

Her fingers fell away as her heart throbbed. She'd promised the truth, but it was so hard to say. So vulnerable to admit. But this man was the only one she could truly be vulnerable with. The only one she trusted with her secrets, her heart, even though she knew he had to take her away in the end.

He'd never lied about that. He'd never lied at all.

"If I could do it...if I could take from those who deserved to lose...then I didn't have to depend on my father and his whims. Or my brother, who I didn't know at the time. My future was my own." She dropped her head. "And it also helped me...balance the scales."

He hesitated, and then he whispered, "Justice. You saw it as justice."

"Yes," she said. "I know you don't understand."

"I understand," he said quickly. "I've built a life around justice, haven't I?"

She nodded. "I suppose you have. May I ask you a question?"

He shrugged, but she saw the wariness enter his posture and his expression. She hated that she put him on guard. She deserved it, but she hated it.

"How did you know it was me?" she asked. "Even before the ruby bracelet in the ballroom, I know you suspected me. Maybe you even intended to confront me about it when you and I were going to be alone in the library that last night in Roseford."

"I did," he admitted.

"How did you know?"

He stepped away from her and put his hands behind his back, widening his stance. A military posture. A posture of a man of discipline. Of the control she so enjoyed taking away. In this moment, he didn't look as though it could be taken.

"I gathered evidence I didn't want to see," he explained. "A list of things that, when put together, pointed to you as the culprit. First"—he ticked one finger off—"I caught you at Lady Winford's room that night when I came to search it. You had your explanations and they weren't bad."

"Thank you. They were off the cuff and I was terrified you'd arrest me then and there," she said.

His lips pursed as if that answer gave him no pleasure. But he continued, "Later you mentioned a party with Lady Winford, another time when you chose a victim thanks to her treatment of a servant."

She lifted her chin. "I've seen servants, especially woman, treated worse than one would treat shit on a shoe. People, Derrick. Deserving of respect."

"Yes, you are their champion, it seems. I can't fault you for that. But your mention of the party sent me to look at some of the lists we had compiled from the Fox's...from *your* history."

"Really?" she breathed.

"It wasn't that hard. Your targets were public. We crosschecked guest lists because we thought some gentleman was perhaps the culprit. We'd thought the robbery of Lady Rendleman's bracelet was probably an early strike by the Fox. When you mentioned the party with your father, I could guess your age and glean the facts from some details."

"I always knew you were brilliant," she said. "So you tracked me via the parties. What else gave me away?"

"You once told me I had no idea what you were capable of. An off-the-cuff comment, but one that added to my suspicions. And your companion... I suppose she isn't a companion, though, is she?"

Selina froze. It was one thing to give this man all the details of her own misdeeds. Another to force Vale into prison along with her.

"She is a companion," she said.

"Selina," he said, his tone sharp.

She folded her arms. "I won't do something that will send her to gaol along with me. I won't lie about my own life, but I won't reveal hers."

He sighed. "Fine," he said through clenched teeth. "But the night I came to your room, when I found her there. She said something about you being...fire. That you have to be controlled so you don't burn out of control."

She wrinkled her brow. "Vale said that?"

"Yes." He sighed. "And lastly was your hairpin. Though that was after you disappeared, after you admitted the truth, so perhaps it doesn't count."

"My hairpin?"

He tilted his head. "I was taking your hair down one night when we made love and scratched myself on your pin. I thought it was oddly shaped then, but was too distracted. But when we searched your rooms after you disappeared, I found the pin. It's a lockpick. You didn't leave a great many clues, Selina. But they were there, waiting to be collected."

She nodded. "And I suppose you would have to be the one to collect them. I got so much more careless after I met you. I knew you were tracking me but I kept...failing. Being reckless. If you punish yourself for being distracted by me, know that I was also distracted by you."

He stared at her a long moment, his gaze unwavering on hers. Then he stepped closer. "One last question. Was *anything* between us real?"

CHAPTER 24

Derrick was holding his breath as he waited for the answer to the only question that had ever mattered to him. His chest felt like it was collapsing around his heart, squeezing it. His hands shook like leaves in the fall.

She moved toward him, her own trembling hands cupping his cheeks as a tear slid down her face. She held firm there, keeping her eyes on him, revealing herself to him in ways she'd never fully allowed before. This wasn't just confession or vulnerability—this was surrender. It was bittersweet and he could see she felt that, too.

"There wasn't a moment I spent with you that wasn't true." Her voice caught and she struggled to compose herself. "I told you things, gave you parts of myself, that no one else has seen. Ever."

"Not your brothers?" he asked. "Not your friends?"

"Never anyone but you. *I* am a lie, Derrick. But what I feel for you isn't."

He covered her hands with his, smoothing his thumb along hers. Her skin was satin and he wanted to roll himself up in it forever. But he needed her to say the words, to go further. To go all the way now. "What do you feel for me?"

She licked her lips, he felt her tremble, he saw her fear. But she was stronger than all of that. Stronger than anything or anyone he'd ever met.

"I love you," she whispered.

A thrill crested over him, a joy, an utter peace. But it was followed by heartbreak. She gave, but it would all be taken away, and soon.

"I love you with all my heart, and it scares me," she continued. "I am so afraid of it, of you, of what you can do to me with just a look, with just a touch. And mostly I'm afraid because I know what I've done, I know what I am, and those things will steal any future we might have been able to make together."

He pulled her closer, letting his arms come around her as he molded her body to his with a ragged sigh. She was right, of course. He might not be able to save her. There was too much at their backs now. But he still had to try.

He kissed the crown of her head, breathing in her vanilla scent, dragging it deeply into his lungs and making it a permanent part of him. "You said you didn't take Katherine's bracelet at the ball," he murmured.

She looked up at him. "I would never do that. I'd never hurt her or my brother that way."

"I believe you," he said. "I always believed you."

She sagged in relief and he buoyed her up with his strength. Everything about her had softened with those words. His faith meant something to her. She'd experienced so little of it in her life, given or received. He knew that was part of why she'd become what she'd become. He knew it was why she could change herself if she wanted to do so.

"But if you didn't do it, that means someone wanted to make it look like you did," he said. "They knew your secret, Selina. And they used it against you in an attempt to destroy you."

She pursed her lips. "Yes. I've thought of that, myself. The same person who left my glove in Lady Winford's room, I suppose, was the one who went further with Katherine's necklace. Little trails left to damage me."

"Do you have any idea who?"

She sighed. "There could be many people. A person I robbed, another thief who hates my infamy or wants it for their own."

"What about a friend?" he asked.

Her eyes went wide and it was clear she took his meaning. "Vale?"

He nodded slowly.

"No, I don't...I don't *want* to believe it." She backed away a fraction, though she kept his hands clasped in hers. Like she was afraid to let go. "She and I have known each other for years. I helped her off the street."

"That's how you met?"

She shifted and he waited for her to push back, just as she always had when he'd asked about Vale in the past. Only this time, she didn't.

"I was gaming one night in a nasty underground club." Her voice barely carried. "The bet was...unconventional."

"Christ," he muttered, trying not to picture what unconventional meant.

She shrugged. "I would win his money, he'd win a night with me."

He flinched at the idea she'd be so desperate as to make such a wager. Selina liked pleasure, he didn't begrudge her that past. He certainly benefited from it. But this was something...different.

"I won," she continued. "*He* was angry. And he followed me. He had me cornered in an alley and it was clear my body wasn't all he'd take. And then this sprite leapt out of the shadows and bashed him in the head with a piece of wood she found laying there. Knocked him out cold."

Derrick shuddered at the dangers this woman had experienced in her relatively short life. Things that had almost kept him from ever knowing her. "She saved your life."

"Yes." She dropped her chin. "It created an instant bond between us. I came to trust her. Enough that I told her my secret about The Fox. She has never come close to letting it slip. We don't always agree. She believes her way is the only way, and she can be hard. But I can't believe she would betray me. Try to harm me."

"Selina…" he said, more uncertain than she was. After all, Vale had access. She had means galore to frame her friend.

"I'm her golden goose," she insisted. "At the minimum, why would she destroy me and deplete her means of income?"

He pursed his lips. Selina wasn't wrong, of course. But he wasn't certain her faith was perfectly placed. "I recognize that you don't want to hear Vale as a potential suspect. But if she *had* betrayed you, tell me, would she harm you? Physically."

"No," she said instantly. "*No.*"

That gave him some small relief. "Then I'll keep looking into who could have done it," he said. "But you must understand that Barber won't back down. He's riding for you."

"As he should," she said with a sigh. "He's a good man."

"So you don't blame him for his singular dedication?" Derrick asked, genuinely surprised by that answer.

She smiled. "I knew what kind of man he was the moment I looked at him. I knew his heart because he's too honest not to show it. Of course, he feels a need to complete his duty. To bring the villain to justice. That's his role—I would never blame him for it. Or for my own failings. Where is he now? Waiting for you to finish with me?"

He shook his head, guilt rising in him. "We knew you wouldn't take the main road to London and were left with two viable options. He took one, I the other. I found you. We're supposed to report to each other what we found when we meet up tomorrow. But I…I won't."

She gasped and her fingers clenched against his. "Derrick, I would never ask you to betray—"

He lifted their hands to her lips, stopping her from continuing. "I know you wouldn't. I'm doing it, myself. Because I love you, Selina. You must run because I love you."

She caught her breath and the tears returned to her eyes. "You do? How? How could you love me knowing what I am?"

"You are my heart," he explained, that heart nearly bursting in his chest. "And I do know what you are. Not the Faceless Fox, though she is part of you. You are Selina Oliver. You are strong and independent and infinitely frustrating and funny and beautiful, and I could go on and on. I *know* what you are. And I love every part of you."

She was shaking now, not just trembling. "I intended to get Vale to safety and then turn myself in."

He flinched. "If you must, then we'll face that together. But for now, just hide. Hide away in London and I'll try my best to fix this. If I can't...if I can't, I'll find you and we'll determine what to do next together."

She sagged against him with a shuddering sigh. Then she glanced up at him. "Do you really love me, Derrick Huntington?"

He smiled through the pain. "Oh, I do. I do really love you. I'd like to prove it. How much time do we have?"

She wrapped her arms around his neck and drew his mouth toward hers. "An hour or two."

"Hardly enough time at all. But I'll take it," he murmured before he brushed his lips to hers.

His body pushed him, screamed at him in the language of desperation and need and fear. But he ignored it. If things went wrong, this would be the last time he took this woman to bed. And he didn't want to make this joining about fear or pain or regret.

He wanted to make it a promise. To her. To himself. So he deepened the kiss as he eased her toward her bed. She didn't resist, she just lifted into him as he lowered her back and covered her body with his.

She moved beneath him like the ocean, lifting into him as he kissed her, as his hands stole down her body and memorized her lines, as he unbuttoned her gown and let his fingers dance beneath the fabric against her warm, bare skin. They had done this so many times, so many ways. It had bonded them and united them even when they were worlds apart.

But now...now it was different. He knew she loved him. He loved her. So when he tasted her skin, he was tasting the future he so desperately wanted. When he parted her gown, it was parting the way that seemed so impossible.

He loved her and this meant so much more.

She pushed at her dress, managing to yank it down around her waist despite his weight on her, and he smiled. "Always in control," he said on a chuckle that dissipated some of the tension in the room between them after her confessions.

"Never with you," she promised as she kissed him again. He cupped one breast, flicking his thumb over the nipple, measuring the weight of her in his palm. She whispered his name against his mouth and he felt the tug of it like she had cupped his cock.

Need took over again, washing away everything else as he slid down her body and tasted her breasts, teasing her with his teeth and his tongue until she writhed beneath him, her cries echoing in the room around him like music. He pulled her dress lower, over her hips. She kicked the fabric away and spread her legs to give him a place to rest. He took it, pushing her wide as he trailed his tongue over her stomach, her hip and finally stroking her sex in one long lick.

She spasmed against him, already on the edge of release. He raced her toward it, sucking her clitoris over and over, fingering her gently and then rougher until she jolted against him and the flavor of her orgasm coated his tongue.

"Please," she murmured, tugging at his jacket, pulling him toward her. "Please, please."

He nodded as he cast the coat aside. As she tore at the cravat beneath. The shirt. He unfastened the placard on his trousers and she caught his hard cock, stroking him until his vision blurred and he couldn't wait any longer.

He tugged her lower on the bed, rubbing his cock back and forth over her as she mewled in pleasure. And when he took it was a hard, long stroke that filled her slick body completely.

Tears streamed down her face as he claimed her. They merged in their kiss as she held him to her, her fingers tangled in his hair. She lifted to meet him, waves on that same ocean, and he lost himself in sensation. He lost himself in her as pleasure built. She came again at last, her sheath milking him hard with tremors, and he could hold back no longer.

He moved to pull away, but she gasped and cupped his backside, holding him tight as they locked eyes. He could have moved. Could have refused what she wanted. But he wanted it too. So he poured himself into her with a roar and then collapsed over her, sweat mingling as he kissed her and kissed her and kissed her.

~

Selina curled her fingers against Derrick's chest, loving how his arms felt around her in the quiet of this sanctuary. Knowing she was selfish for wanting this night to never end. And for what she had encouraged him to do. He'd come inside of her. He might have created a life by doing so. That life could save her from the hangman's noose and perhaps that's why he'd done it.

Even if it didn't, she still loved the idea that a child with his eyes and her smile might exist because of their love. The idea of him or her was beautiful enough to make the next few weeks bearable.

He had been combing his fingers through her hair for what felt like a lifetime, but now he stopped. The tension re-entered his body as he moved a little, forcing her to roll from his chest onto her side. He was frowning, not at her, but into nothingness.

"I don't want to go," he whispered.

"I know." She ached for what she had to say next. "But it's time. Vale will be back soon."

"Be...careful of her, Selina."

She frowned at his continued doubt. He wasn't wrong in his assessment of the situation, of course. On paper, Vale looked to be a good suspect. But Selina couldn't believe her partner, her friend, would turn on her. Their bond might be strained at present, but she believed it was powerful enough to withstand the troubles Selina had brought down on them.

"How will I give you my location in London?" she asked.

He got up, and she stretched as she watched that remarkable body move through the small room. Muscle and sinew, grace and command. Scars brought by war and life that told a story he rarely spoke about. She loved it all. She wanted to know all the details of it all.

He scribbled down a place to address her letters on a piece of paper on the table, then dressed, his gaze slipping to her. When he was finished, he sat on the edge of the bed and traced her face with his hand once more. "I'll never stop looking for a way to fix this," he promised.

Her heart stung. Fix what she'd broken. Fix what she'd done. "I don't deserve that," she whispered.

He didn't answer, but leaned in and kissed her. Then he went to her door. One last look, a long one, and he said, "Goodbye, love."

She couldn't bring herself to say the same as he left her room. *Goodbye* felt final. She knew it might be, despite his hopes and promises. She knew how the world worked, perhaps even a little better than he did. It was a dream that she could be saved.

But it bought her time.

She rose slowly and dressed herself, though when she looked in the mirror, she appeared well loved. She could fix her hair, but didn't. She wanted to leave it, to feel that feeling a little longer. To know it was his fingers that had run through her curls.

The door behind her opened and she pivoted with a gasp. But

her fear subsided as Vale came into the room. Her friend had a slight scowl on her face as she looked around.

"You're back early," Selina said, happy Vale hadn't come even a few moments sooner or else she would have walked in on quite a scene. "Was the music not good?"

"It was passable," Vale said, folding her arms. "And how was your love?"

Selina froze, staring at her friend. "My love?"

"I know Derrick Huntington was here, Selina," Vale said with an exasperated shake of her head. "I saw him. You ought to thank me for giving you the chance to talk. Or whatever you two are calling what you did."

Selina bent her head. "He did come to me. Why should I lie?"

"Because that's how we're built," Vale said with a sigh. "Women like us move through the world and protect ourselves with lies. We tell men what they want to get what they'll give in return. To keep them from taking what we don't want to provide. We *lie*, Selina. And when you stop lying, you don't just endanger yourself. That man is a hunter, sent here to find you."

"That man was hired to hunt me, yes," Selina said. "But that's not why he came. We love each other, Vale. Truly love each other."

Vale frowned. "And where does that leave me?"

"I'm getting you to London, just as I promised," Selina said. "You'll disappear into the world, like you've wanted to do for so long. But I...I won't. I can't anymore. I have too much to protect. I'll stay. And I'll accept whatever punishment comes."

"You idiot," Vale murmured. And then she reached into her pocket and pulled out a tiny pistol, which she aimed at Selina's heart.

Selina cried out, staggering back even though there was nowhere to go in the small room. "Vale," she said. "What? *Why?*"

"I wasn't going to do this until we got to London. But if you're going to blow up our lives, I don't see any reason to wait even a moment longer."

CHAPTER 25

D errick had let a room at the finer inn in the little village and
he trudged through the main hall and up the stairs, barely
marking his surroundings or the loud music thundering through
the packed hall below. All he could think about was Selina, all he
could do was make plan after plan about how to save her.

But he was a strategist, he always had been. And he feared that
all those plans would play out with her in Newgate or transported
or...or hanged. He could do nothing to stop it.

He tried to focus on breathing as he unlocked his chamber door
and stepped inside. But before he could close himself in, perhaps
even allow for a collapse before he shored up his strength, he heard
a voice from the fireplace.

"I knew you wouldn't be able to stop yourself."

He spun on the voice and found Barber standing there, the Duke
of Roseford at his side. Both men were watching Derrick closely,
guarded in their expressions.

"Bloody hell," Derrick grunted. "We're supposed to meet
tomorrow at the crossroads. And why is he here?"

Roseford arched a brow. "*I* am here because Selina is my sister.
She's in trouble and I need to help her. And *we* are here because

neither of us is a fool, Mr. Huntington. It's clear you're in love with her. It's written all over your face."

Derrick's shoulders rolled forward because he was just too tired to fight. "Yes," he whispered.

"You're compromised," Barber said, more gently than Derrick deserved. "Just as you have been from the moment you first laid eyes on her. So yes, I did my due diligence on the other road, and then we circled back here because it made sense this would be her stopping point if she took this path. This would be where you found her." Barber moved closer. "*Did* you find her, friend?"

"She didn't steal Katherine's bracelet," Derrick said, an answer to a different question. The answer to the one asked, as well.

Roseford's jaw set and twitched. "She said as much a few days ago."

"And you didn't believe her," Derrick said. "You broke her heart."

"She broke mine," Roseford said, his fists clenching at his sides. "The moment that bracelet fell from her pocket, I...I knew what she would be condemned to."

"To be fair, Huntington, she admitted to being the Faceless Fox. How can we believe that she didn't steal from the duchess?" Barber said.

Derrick scrubbed a hand over his face. "Because she admitted to what she'd done. Taking something from her family, from Katherine, never made sense. She has a code. She's always had a code and you know it, Barber. She steals from ladies of the *ton* who make other lives miserable. She exacts a strange...justice. And she says she'd never hurt you that way, or your wife, Roseford, so I believe her."

Roseford watched him carefully for what felt like an eternity, then smiled slightly. "I think if you are going to so passionately defend my sister, you perhaps should start calling me Robert."

Barber turned toward the duke. "So you believe him."

"I do," Robert said with a sigh. "I was so shocked when that bracelet fell from her pocket, I could only see what was in front of

JESS MICHAELS

me. But over the past few days, I've come to doubt my initial reaction. And I think you have, too, Mr. Barber. I have marked your increasing discomfort with the subject of my sister as we rode."

Barber straightened his jacket with a tug. "I know what awaits her in London, Your Grace. I can't imagine the pain it will cause your family if she is tried and convicted as a criminal."

Derrick and Robert exchanged a glance, sudden partners in fear and a desire to save Selina. He would take that partner.

"Let us set aside the fact that Miss Oliver is the Faceless Fox," Barber said slowly. "She's admitted that, it is not up for debate. But we *can* examine the attempt to steal Her Grace's bracelet and frame Miss Oliver. If that is true, then someone is trying to harm her."

"Yes," Derrick said. "The person planted a glove in Lady Winford's room first, the one Selina denied leaving there, and then this bracelet. We'd be fools not to believe it was the same person."

Robert nodded. "I agree. Someone who knew her true identity."

"Which would narrow the field considerably," Barber said. "At least at first glance."

"Her companion," Robert said softly.

"That is what I tend to believe, as well," Derrick said. "But she doesn't want to think ill of her friend, a woman she's trusted for many years. Still, the means is there. The knowledge of Selina's true identity."

"And the simplest answer is often the truth," Barber said. "But what would be the motive?"

"She's benefitted from Selina's actions if she's been with her a while," Derrick said. "If she felt her changing, pulling away from that old life, she might feel threatened."

"Yes," Robert said. "When our brother Morgan married last year, I sensed a change in Selina. But it...it might be more than that." He paced the room. "Selina has independent control over a portion of her inheritance. The bulk of it pays for her home and its upkeep. But there's a not insignificant fund that sits mostly untouched. She recently asked my solicitor to change who would inherit if she passed."

"Who?" Derrick asked. "Who would get those funds?"

Robert shook his head. "Vale Williams."

Derrick nearly buckled as motive slapped him in the face. Not just for framing Selina, but for far worse.

"So she might be angry that Selina is pondering her future without the Faceless Fox," Barber said. "And knowing she would inherit if Selina were out of the way, she destroys her in the eyes of her family, her protection. Which isolates her. And would give Miss Williams every opportunity to—"

Barber cut himself off, but Derrick had already started for the door. "We have to go back. We have to find Selina and make sure that if Vale is our culprit, she won't do anything before we can stop her."

He was out the door, Robert and Barber at his heels, but as he raced down the hall, he had the worst feeling. That he was going to be too late. And then nothing else would matter.

Selina's feet hurt as she staggered through the brush in the darkness of the night. Vale hadn't allowed her to put on shoes. Of course, that was a method to control her, to keep her from being able to easily mount an escape.

Not that the gun in her back didn't do the same.

"Why are you doing this?" Selina said. "I'll protect you, Vale. I've *always* protected you."

"Always used me," Vale corrected, nudging her forward without regard for her physical wellbeing. "The Faceless Fox was all for you, Selina. I was just a cog in the machine."

"You are...*were* my friend. My partner. We helped each other. And I shared the wealth, didn't I?"

"When you harvested it. But you were always so much more

worried about your damned code of honor. Picking and choosing your marks, as if every person in the Upper Ten Thousand didn't deserve to be maimed. You ignored prizes worth ten times the ones you chose and you patted yourself on the back for doing the 'right' thing. I knew you'd go soft eventually. I saw it happening last year, and I knew I had to act."

Selina tripped over a rock, pain jolting up her body from where she'd stubbed her toe. Vale shoved her forward, ignoring her staggering and swearing as she pushed them forward, through the darkness.

"What do you mean, last year?" Selina asked, trying to keep her former friend talking both to uncover her motives and to develop some kind of response.

"When Morgan went with Roseford," Vale said, rolling her eyes. "Waste of a handsome man that he married some spoiled toff's sister. But you were...*jealous.* I saw how jealous you were that he'd gotten dear *Robert's* favor."

"I wasn't jealous!" Selina cried. "I knew he needed help and I was happy Robert could offer it. I'm pleased for Morgan. He loves his wife."

Vale shrugged. "Love is for children. Fools. It makes you weak. And that's what you were becoming: weak. You slowed your schemes, you started spending more family time with Gillingham, and when Roseford came back to Town, with those titled ninnies, I saw you were going to break. You were going too respectable. The entire house of cards was coming down so I had to control it."

"How?" Selina asked, stunned by her words.

"Little trails I left, the ones that led to you."

"The glove," Selina whispered.

"Yes, that damned glove. Meant to make the investigators suspect you. Your family, too. But that was a *last* step. How do you think Huntington and Barber knew you would be hunting at your brother's estate?"

Selina gasped. "You?"

"I gave information. I didn't expect them to be so good at their jobs, though. I figured them for fools and I underestimated you would be so soft as to fall in love with one of them." Vale rolled her eyes. "But I did what we always do. I adjusted my timeline. Decided to finish it now rather than a month from now."

Selina could hardly breathe from the shock that was hitting her in waves. Trust had always been a hard-won thing for her. Her past ensured it. And Vale had been the first person she allowed into that circle closest to her heart. To know it had all been a manipulation, that she had been too blinded to see the truth beneath her nose, it was shattering.

"You look sick," Vale taunted. "Worried. But you needn't be, my dear. I took care of myself."

"Took care of yourself?" Selina repeated. "What do you mean?"

Vale pulled her through a glade and into an open grassy area. The clouds blew away from the moon and the light revealed a tall tower in the middle. It rose ominously, at least twenty feet up.

"*This* was built in remembrance for local boys lost in the Seven Years' War," Vale explained. "When I heard it was here, so close, I thought it was apropos because you and I have known each other..."

"Seven years," Selina whispered, and her heart began to throb. Why hadn't she listened to Derrick's concerns about Vale? Why hadn't she allowed her own a voice? Why had she let the code she held herself up to be one she assumed others followed?

It would be the death of her. She could see that now.

"How did you take care of yourself?" she asked again, hating that her voice broke. Hating that her fear was obvious.

"They used to light the lantern at the top of this tower every year for those who were lost in the war. And then it was just every ten. Now it's crumbling. Everyone forgets those who are sacrificed to be useful. That's why we little people have to take what's ours." Vale smiled as she shoved Selina closer to the tower. "I've gotten quite good at mimicking your handwriting over the past few months. Enough so that your brother's solicitor believed it was *you* who asked for a change to your line of inheritance. You who signed the addendum so I would inherit."

Selina's lips parted as the meaning of that lie sank in. "Vale."

"We're climbing up that tower, love," Vale said. Her hand shook, but she mastered the tremor swiftly. "And I'm going to push you off. The suicide note waiting for your great love back in our room will convince everyone that you couldn't live with it coming out that you were the Faceless Fox. They'll mourn you and cover it up, and I'll get your money and whatever jewels you still have squirreled away."

"Vale, you and I have been *friends* for those seven years," Selina began. "You saved my life. Look at me now and tell me you really want to hurt me."

"We're not friends," Vale said. "If I did for you, it was to help myself, just as I'm doing now. You're irrelevant. Your blind faith in people has always been your weakness. Now let's climb the tower and get this done."

Selina stopped, ignoring the gun Vale pushed harder into her spine. "No."

"Climb the damned tower!" Vale screamed.

"She won't be doing that."

Both women turned, and relief flooded Selina's entire body. Derrick and Barber approached from behind them. They both had weapons drawn.

"Back up," Vale snapped, grabbing Selina and pulling her closer. "I swear I will kill her where she stands if you don't stop where you are."

The men stopped, ten feet away, not close enough to reach her, though certainly close enough to die if Vale decided to turn her gun on them.

"You've only been an accomplice in this so far, Miss Williams," Derrick said softly. "And you haven't killed anyone. If you stop, we can work something out."

"As if you won't sacrifice me for her," Vale said with a dry laugh.

"You've been mooning over her since the first moment you saw her. Even when you knew she used you to protect yourself, you let yourself be convinced it was true love. But Selina has always been able to seduce her way into what she wanted."

Derrick's expression didn't change, it didn't even flutter. He didn't believe Vale. At least there was that. He had faith in Selina. And that meant the world to her.

"Put the gun down, Miss Williams," Barber said this time.

"Or what?" Vale said. "If I put it down, I'm doomed. If I don't put it down, I have a chance. Especially if I put a bullet in one of you. Which one should it be? My friend who destroyed a good thing? The lover who made her waver? Or the man who is so determined to do what's right, he'll die for it?" She moved the gun from Selina's back, shoved her aside and aimed at Barber. "I think destroying a good man might be fun."

Selina screamed as Vale began to press the trigger. She leapt to put herself in the way, but before she could, Robert raced from the bushes and tackled Vale. They struggled, rolling on the grass, the gun wedged between them. When it fired, Selina screamed again, staring down at her brother, at her friend.

Robert rolled away, and it was clear then. Vale had been shot. Her eyes were already glassy. She was dead.

Selina spun toward Derrick and raced to him, into his arms. He held her against him as she realized just what she'd lost that night.

"Selina." Robert's voice was shaky.

She clung to Derrick's hand as she faced her brother, ready to see his censure and his blame. But Robert's face was only bright with relief and love. And he tugged her into his arms.

"I almost lost you," Robert said. "My God, I almost lost you."

"I'm sorry," she sobbed into his shoulder. "I'm so sorry I let you down."

"I don't approve of your methods," Robert said with a shake of his head. "What you've been doing put a great many people, including yourself, in danger." The sternness faded a fraction. "But damn, it's hard not to admire your daring."

Barber cleared his throat and the three faced him. He glanced at the dead woman on the ground and then back toward Selina. She drew in a long breath, let go of the man she loved and the one who was her family, and stepped toward him, arms reaching toward him.

"Mr. Barber, I would like to turn myself in," she said.

Robert and Derrick both gasped behind her, but she ignored that. Ignored her own breaking heart.

Barber stared at her outstretched hands. "We must return to town," he said. "To alert the guard about the altercation and to have the body removed. Let me do that and then let's talk about this other matter. Go with Huntington. Your Grace, perhaps you could assist me?"

"Yes," Robert said, his voice now hollow and shaken. "I assume there will be questions on how this woman was shot."

Derrick turned her away, sweeping her up so she wouldn't have to walk on her cut up feet. But as he took her toward town, she heard Barber say, "Let me do the explaining, Your Grace."

"Will he protect Robert?" she asked, resting her head on Derrick's shoulder as the exhaustion of the night's events washed over her.

"Yes," Derrick said. "I think he will."

"Then I can think nothing but the best of him," she whispered. And then she let herself rest in the arms of the man she loved, knowing it would all be over soon.

CHAPTER 26

D errick fastened the last bandage around Selina's injured feet
and placed them gently on the settee, elevated on a pillow.
She hadn't said much as he tended to her

She hadn't said anything much at all, but it was clear her
thoughts were dark and uncertain.

"I'm sorry about Vale," he said at last.

Her face twitched, pain and sadness and anger mixing there. "I
was a fool not to see the worst in her," she said. "I had been alone for
so long when she came into my life. I suppose I just wanted to
believe the best. Perhaps she's right; that is my greatest failing."

"A failing of hers, not yours," Derrick said, stroking her calf
through her dress.

"Was," Selina whispered.

"Was," he repeated. Then he swallowed. "You were going to take
a bullet for my friend."

She nodded. "Yes. I couldn't let him die to protect me, a criminal.
That wouldn't be right. But my brother saved us all. You saved me.
But now we're here and the end has come, Derrick. We both know
what will happen when Barber and Robert arrive."

"Do you?" Barber said as he opened the door to the chamber and the two men entered. They both looked drawn and worn out from the experience hours before. Robert, especially.

"Please tell me that you're unharmed," Selina said, reaching a hand toward her brother. "Please tell me they won't do anything to you for saving my life and the life of Mr. Barber."

"Shhh," Robert soothed her as he leaned in to kiss her forehead. "I'm fine. Barber took care of it all. You needn't worry about me." He faced Barber. "I appreciate all you've done. But I suppose we all have the same question now. What will you do about Selina?"

Barber shook his head and paced to the window. He stood there for a while, as if gathering his thoughts. Then he turned back.

"Like you, Miss Oliver, my life has always revolved around a code," he said softly. "I come from a family of merchants. There was struggle, but always enormous honor, and that has been important to me. Normally, the right answer is easy to find. Good is very different from evil. But you...you, Miss Oliver, are a conundrum."

"Frustrating, I think Derrick calls it," Selina said, and that elicited a small smile from Barber. Derrick's heart leapt to see it. His friend didn't offer those smiles often, and never just to anyone.

"You are that," Barber agreed. His gaze slipped to Derrick. "You have been my good friend and partner. The best I've ever had. So now what is right? What is good? What is honorable? Do I destroy your life? Do I destroy hers? Do I honor the contract I signed with a bunch of—excuse me, Your Grace—fops?"

"I couldn't tell you what to do," Derrick said softly. "Because I am, as you have told me many times, compromised. By my love for her. By my hopes for the future. I'm compromised."

"Yes," Barber said, almost too low to be heard.

He turned his back to all of them again. And again, time seemed to tick by at half-speed. They were waiting for a guillotine and it was torture.

At least Barber spoke. "Perhaps it turns out Miss Williams was culpable for all this in the end."

"What?" Derrick gasped, at the exact time Selina and Robert said the same.

Barber faced them. "Ah, a chorus, I see. My goal in this was to determine the guilty party. Miss Williams seems to be the guiltiest, what with murder on her mind. My goal was also to return any items I could recover. Miss Oliver, are there items still in your possession?"

She nodded. "Many in my home in London. I'll return them to you upon our arrival. I have no need for them."

"Then I will have fulfilled my second goal."

"But you intended to catch the Faceless Fox," Selina said. "Will you hate yourself for not doing that?"

Barber moved toward her. "The Faceless Fox was never violent. She stole from the worst of Society. And she tried to sacrifice herself to save my life tonight, without hesitation, even knowing that I was sworn to destroy her hopes and dreams." He touched her hand briefly. "And you and my friend are in love. So maybe that matters more than all the rest put together."

"Barber," Derrick breathed.

Barber smiled at him. "I am remanding Miss Oliver to your custody, Huntington. Do try to keep her out of trouble."

Derrick rushed to his friend and tugged him into a hug. It obviously surprised Barber, but he returned the gesture briefly before he stepped away. He cleared his throat. "I must go finish the final matters to do with tonight. I'll see you all later."

He left them, and Selina stared up at Derrick, shock lining her face. "Did he just...did he just let me go?"

"He did," Derrick breathed as a powerful, unstoppable joy tore through his chest. "You're free."

~

T he words echoed in Selina's mind, but they didn't seem real. Free? How could she be free? She had spent the past few days preparing herself for loss and ruin and even death. But this?

She'd never been prepared for this.

Robert cleared his throat. "Do you have something you'd like to discuss with me, Derrick?"

Selina caught her breath as she realized what he meant. And when Derrick's handsome face broke into a grin, she thought she would shatter into a thousand pieces right there.

"Yes," Derrick said, catching her hand. "Your Grace, I would like your permission to ask for your sister's hand."

Robert smiled and then glanced at her. "Do you desire the match?"

"With all my heart," she said swiftly. "But—"

"But?" Robert laughed. "Dear God, this man just rode two days for you, nearly surrendered his honor and probably believed he was going to be shot. What else must he do to prove himself worthy?"

"Nothing," Selina said with a smile for him. "He will never have to prove his worth. But I will. And I can only step into my own future if I believe my family supports me. You say you don't blame me for my past. Will...will Katherine ever forgive me?"

"My dear," Robert chuckled. "Who do you think sent me along on this wild chase in the hopes you would find true love? My wife could never hold a grudge. And when she understands all that happened, I know she'll tell you so and celebrate this marriage with as much joy as she did Morgan's last year."

Selina bent her head. "Then I *am* free. If this gentleman desires my hand, even though he knows all my faults, I could never want anything more in this world than to be his wife."

"Excellent," Robert said, and patted her cheek. He shook Derrick's hand. "Then I'll leave you to the rest of the details. We'll talk again in the morning."

"You don't want to argue and protect my virtue?" Selina called out as he exited the room.

His snort as he closed the door was his only response.

And suddenly she was alone with the man she loved. He came around to sit on the settee beside her, his gaze focused on hers. "Marry me?" Derrick asked.

It was so simple a question. And she didn't need more than that simplicity. After all, they had already endured, said all the rest of the words that needed to be said because they feared the future would part them.

Now that they knew it never could, there was only one word.

"Yes," she whispered as she cupped the back of his head and brought his mouth to hers. "Yes. Yes. Yes. Yes. Yes."

EPILOGUE

One month later

"You have never looked more radiant, and that is saying something," Katherine said as she kissed Selina's cheek, and then positioned her veil more firmly into the beautiful crown of hair the maid had been arranging.

Selina looked at herself in her mirror, and the joy that had been overtaking her all day rose up once more.

"I'm ready," she whispered.

Katherine led her from the chamber and down the long hall. Her heart skipped as they neared the ballroom, where friends and family were gathered for her wedding.

Robert stood at the door, looking devastatingly handsome. Katherine paused to kiss him before she squeezed Selina's hand and slipped into the ballroom. Music lifted behind the door, a signal it was time for them to join the others.

Robert took her hand and tucked it into the crook of his arm. "Ready for your next adventure?" he asked.

She laughed as the door opened. Her brothers were near the front of the room. Morgan with Lizzie, beaming. Nicholas leaning on his cane, his smile a bit more subdued, but certainly filled with support and pride. Barber sat beside him, his expression clear, as if he had no doubts about what they were about to do. She had come to see him as a friend in the past few weeks.

But really her eyes were only for Derrick in that moment. He stood waiting for her, his face bright with joy and love and emotion to see her in the last moments she would be Miss Oliver. Mrs. Huntington would leave that room with him.

"I think my adventuring days are over," she said softly.

Robert guided her up the aisle with a laugh. "Oh no, dear sister. I think you'll soon see they've only just begun."

THE DUKE'S BY-BLOWS

ENJOY AND EXCERPT OF BOOK 3, THE MATTER OF A MARQUESS

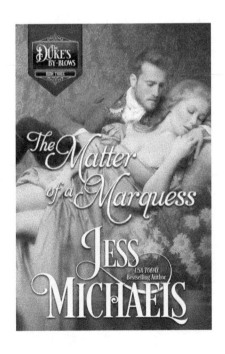

EXCERPT OF THE MATTER OF A MARQUESS

THE DUKE'S BY-BLOWS BOOK 3

Preorder The Matter of a Marquess

Nicholas sat in the parlor at Robert and Katherine's home, a book perched in his fingers, but too distracted to pay attention to the story. Instead, he stared at the crackling fire, his thoughts rolling in circles.

Did he belong here? Here in his brother's home? In the few days since his arrival, he'd found himself looking from place to place, thinking of his late mother and what she must have endured here. Where her place had been. How it had been used against her.

He blinked and pushed those hard thoughts away. They were replaced by others. Because it wasn't just the house that made him question himself. He wasn't sure he belonged in the family Roseford was starting to build with their half-brother Morgan and half-sister Selina and their spouses. They were all so similar. He was so different.

And Roseford had friends here, too. A member of his found family. The Duke of Northfield and his wife. He seemed a good man, honorable and welcoming.

But the discomfort Nicholas felt continued. Because he'd always been lost between two worlds.

"You look very pensive."

He slowly pushed to his feet, a lingering whisper of pain jolting through him as he did so, and forced a smile for his sister as she entered the room. Selina was lovely, as she had always been lovely, with her dark hair and bright blue eyes. But it was different now. She was different. She had married an old friend of Nicholas's from the army, Derrick Huntington, and the new couple's passion for each other was palpable.

"Did I look pensive?" Nicholas asked as she crossed to him and bussed his cheek. "I must have been caught up in my reading."

She arched a brow at him as she went to the sideboard and poured them both tea. She winked before she added a splash of whisky to the cups and then handed it over. He took the brew, shaking his head at her as they sat together. When he sipped it, he coughed and her laughter filled the room.

"Now is the point where I call you a liar," Selina said, drinking her tea without so much as a clearing of her throat. "You weren't reading. You were brooding. It doesn't suit those of our ilk, Nicholas. Roseford sons and daughters do not brood."

He knew she was trying to lighten the mood, but his frown pulled deeper. "I've never been the typical Roseford offspring, though, have I? I *was* brooding, I'll admit it since I know you well enough to recognize you won't let this go until I've given you my heart and soul."

Selina's brow wrinkled. "I hope I can be trusted with your words, if not the rest."

He met her stare. It had come out the previous summer that his sister was a master thief. He'd been horrified as well as impressed, but had watched her rebuild herself ever since, with the help of Derrick.

"You can be, I know that," he said evenly, and she smiled in thanks. "It's not about that… I just…in the day that I've been here, I've already felt outside looking in."

Selina pursed her lips. "Because of the duke connection? All those dukes our brother calls friends? You want to be one of them, don't you? Marquess of Songstrum, and I'll have to my lord you all over town."

He shook his head. "You've never my lorded anyone and I doubt you'll start with me. Yes, I…I want this. I *want* the title, Selina. I know you don't understand, neither does Morgan. But I want the respect that goes along with the title. I want…I want the knowledge that certain things can't be taken from me."

"Taken from you?" Selina repeated. "What do you mean? What was taken from you, Nicholas, that you think you can get back with a title?"

He flinched as his mind flashed to dark blonde hair, warm brown eyes, soft lips brushing his, a honeyed tone saying his name like it was the only thing that mattered.

"Nothing specific," he lied, pushing back to his feet and slowly making his way to the window. "I don't know, I'm just being maudlin, ignore me."

"I won't ignore you, but since the subject seems a painful one I will change it. Do you think some of your feeling out of place is because all these people around you are part of couples? And not just any couples, but in love?"

He faced her, his lips tight. She was watching him closely, one fine eyebrow arched as if she already knew the answer. "Are you matchmaking, sister?"

Her smile was instant, wide and catching. "Can you imagine me as a matchmaker? I'd be rubbish! No, I'm just making the observation that you might be feeling excluded because you haven't found someone to match with." She stepped closer. "Is there anyone in your life who makes your heart beat faster? Have you ever wanted someone and only that someone?"

Before he could find an answer to that troubling question, there was a racket from the hallway. Servants rushing and voices calling out. Nicholas wrinkled his brow. "What's that about?"

Selina shrugged. "I think Katherine invited a friend to join our party. She was saying something about it during our walk yesterday. Lady...Lady something or another. What was it?"

Nicholas laughed. "No one is less interested in the upper-class than you are."

"Probably because not so long ago, I was very interested in them for what my husband says are the wrong reasons." She shook her head.

"Well, why don't we go see who this person is?" Nicholas said. "I won't even mention it if you are taking a quiet inventory of the lady's jewels."

"Old habits," Selina said, and took his arm. They made their way up the hall slowly and were met near the foyer by Selina's husband.

Derrick was tall and held himself like the military man he'd once been. He nodded to Nicholas, his gaze flitting to his leg before he said, "I heard the commotion. This must be our final guest."

Selina slipped from Nicholas's side and took her husband's arm instead. As she stared up at him, Nicholas couldn't help but flinch. He'd tried to ignore his sister's observation that some of his troubles might be because he was alone in a house full of people in love. Now he watched his sister and her husband walk in front of him, her fingers all but vibrating on Derrick's bicep, and the twinge of jealousy ripped through him.

But there was no way to explain that to his family. No way to change it. His life was what it was, and a grand romance like the ones his siblings had lived out, continued to live out, was not in the future for him.

They walked out into the warm summer breeze together, joining Robert and Katherine and their brother Morgan and his wife Lizzie on the top stair. Down below, the carriage door had already been opened, so the crest that might have revealed the identity of their guest was obscured. But it wasn't a moment before the footman reached inside and an elegantly slippered foot appeared from the darkness. The woman stepped out, her head bent as she paid attention to her footing. Her bonnet obscured her face and Selina laughed back at Nicholas. "I swear, it's like a game...who is the mystery woman?"

At that moment, before Nicholas could laugh or Katherine could say the name they'd been waiting to hear, the woman tilted her head back to look up the stairs, and everything in Nicholas's world came to a halt.

"Aurora," he breathed out loud, because he couldn't help it.

Derrick pivoted to face him. "What? *The* Aurora?"

Nicholas couldn't answer. He couldn't acknowledge or respond to his family's questions as they asked him who Aurora was. As Katherine stared at him in shock and dawning horror.

No, all he could do was look down that long set of stairs at the woman who had molded and changed and guided his life since he was hardly more than a boy. The woman who had haunted him every day and every night for almost a decade.

She stared up at him, all the color gone from those cheeks, her full lips parted in just as much as shock as he felt, her hands shaking at her sides. And by God, she was more beautiful than she'd ever been. Tendrils of blonde hair curled from the edge of her bonnet, framing her oval face, drawing attention to those high cheekbones. Her gown was spring green, fresh as the new leaves, and it flowed over her supple curves, hinting at gorgeous breasts and the swell of her hips.

Nicholas she mouthed, silent, and that broke him.

He slowly made his way down the stairs, the pain that usually accompanied that action dulled by the pain of seeing her. The thrill of seeing her.

"What are you doing here?" he asked as he stopped a few feet in front of her. He couldn't go closer. If he went closer, his itching palms might force him to reach for her. If he touched her, all was lost. All had always been lost.

She blinked at him. "Nicholas," she repeated, this time on a shaky voice.

"What is going on?" Roseford called from above, concern plain in his voice.

They were all coming down now to join them. Nicholas felt it rather than saw it, because he couldn't tear his gaze away from this woman. This woman he had almost convinced himself couldn't be real. How could such perfection be real?

She ducked her head, breaking their stare at last, and somehow that broke the spell, too. He was still captivated, yes, but now other emotions made their way to the surface. He hadn't seen this woman since that horrible evening when he realized she'd never planned to marry him, no matter what promises they made in secret. She'd lied to him and sent him on a spiral that had nearly killed him.

Looking at her, the emotion that rose in his chest, long ignored and pretended away, was anger. He was angry that she was still so irresistible. Angry that she was here at his brother's house when she had to know their connection. Angry that she could look away from him, turn away just as she always had, when he couldn't stop staring.

"What's going on is a very good question," he said, still looking at her even though he was answering Robert. "And only Lady *Lovell* can answer it."

"Nicholas?" Katherine whispered, touching his arm and drawing him back to the part of the world that wasn't Aurora. Such a small world now. Such a dull one. "Please, what is going on?"

"Lady Lovell and I knew each other as children, Katherine. Or didn't she share that fact with you?" He noted how Aurora flinched, high color re-entering her cheeks. "Or did we know each other, my lady? Did we ever *actually* know each other?"

Preorder The Matter of a Marquess

The Undercover Duke

The Duke of Hearts

The Duke Who Lied

The Duke of Desire

The Last Duke

Seasons

An Affair in Winter

A Spring Deception

One Summer of Surrender

Adored in Autumn

The Wicked Woodleys

Forbidden

Deceived

Tempted

Ruined

Seduced

Fascinated

The Notorious Flynns

The Other Duke

The Scoundrel's Lover

The Widow Wager

No Gentleman for Georgina

A Marquis for Mary

To see a complete listing of Jess Michaels' titles, please visit:

http://www.authorjessmichaels.com/books

ABOUT THE AUTHOR

USA Today Bestselling author Jess Michaels likes geeky stuff, Vanilla Coke Zero, anything coconut, cheese, fluffy cats, smooth cats, any cats, many dogs and people who care about the welfare of their fellow humans. She is lucky enough to be married to her favorite person in the world and lives in the heart of Dallas, TX where she's trying to eat all the amazing food in the city.

When she's not obsessively checking her steps on Fitbit or trying out new flavors of Greek yogurt, she writes historical romances with smoking hot alpha males and sassy ladies who do anything but wait to get what they want. She has written for numerous publishers and is now fully indie and loving every moment of it (well, almost every moment).

Jess loves to hear from fans! So please feel free to contact her in any of the following ways (or carrier pigeon):

www.AuthorJessMichaels.com
Email: Jess@AuthorJessMichaels.com

Jess Michaels raffles a gift certificate EVERY month to members of her newsletter, so sign up on her website:
http://www.AuthorJessMichaels.com/

facebook.com/JessMichaelsBks
twitter.com/JessMichaelsBks
instagram.com/JessMichaelsBks
bookbub.com/authors/jess-michaels

CPSIA information can be obtained
at www.ICGtesting.com
Printed in the USA
LVHW090119070820
662595LV00003B/710